ARSENIC AND ALIBIS

THE VIRTUAL VIGILANTE

BOOK ONE

EM KAPLAN

FALSTAFF
BOOKS
WWW.FALSTAFFBOOKS.COM

ARSENIC AND ALIBIS

For Mom, who helped me find a home to come back to.

PART I
ONESIES MAKE THE WOMAN

"We are so used to disguising ourselves for others that we become disguised to ourselves, like salad with a gallon of dressing." —Frank de La Roquefort

CHAPTER ONE

A ha! Got you, you little thief."
In a room darkened to minimize the glare on the computer's screen, a solitary figure in a unicorn onesie hunched over her keyboard. Viv—not her real name—pushed back her terry cloth rainbow-horned hood and peered at the screen through her blue light blocker glasses, advancing video feed frame by frame with the click of her finger. She stopped the recording of the CCTV feed she had borrowed from a local store, unbeknownst to them, and tapped left three times.

"And just what are you planning to do with Ida Huber's bulk quantity fiber capsules, young sir?"

Yes, I know it's a lame payoff to rescue an old lady's digestive aids, but that's really not the point. Stealing from an elderly person who's on a fixed income is bad. I imagine she would pay with a mega-pan of cabbage rolls if she had the slightest idea who I was, but I'm not in it for the glory. No one steals from my old lady neighbor. Not off a porch in my neighborhood. Oh, no. Not on my watch.

The store under Viv's surveillance was located just a stone's throw away from the old woman's apartment building, and its parking lot camera had a clear shot Ida's front door, the one with the stone goose that the old woman dressed in a different outfit depending on the season. Viv clicked forward one more time for the best view of the offender's face. She captured the image on the screen with another click and saved it as a local file on her computer.

The photo was a bit grainy, but she had a handy image enhancer program that helped clean up the blurriness just enough to help with facial recognition. Then, she ran the photo through a couple of comparison apps that hit databases of known felons, as well as another one that searched local news outlets. She was no longer surprised at how often people who thought they were sneaky ended up with their faces online or in the news. It was so hard to be a rogue when you were also a narcissist.

Viv pushed back from her chair as the first database scan began chugging and popped the top on her black-label energy drink.

Yeah, yeah. Caffeine dependency is a terrible habit that I'm going to break. Any day now.

However, she was interrupted mid-swig when a hit jumped up on her screen.

"Well, well, well," Viv said with the smug satisfaction. "Nice to make your acquaintance, Mr. Michael M. Thomas of... 33B Walden Way? A recent attendee of Totten Junior College with last place of employment at the Railyard Sandwich Shop. What shall we do with you? Refund Mrs. Huber the price of her fiber capsule from your bank account? Aha, I see your overdraft protection has already failed you not once but twice in the last year. I guess I'll just have to order a shut-off notice for your power the day before the Sox play the first game of the pennant race. I'd offer you condolences because I see you're a big fan based on your Photobook social media page, which isn't even set to private, for the love of Pete. Seriously, you people make it so very easy for me to snoop."

As simple as her arm-chair Robin Hoodery was, this also wasn't her first porch-raider rodeo. Viv had a couple tricks up her fuzzy unicorn-hoofed sleeve. In a previous situation that was similar to this one, the face in the obtained photo had matched with a local high school honor student, Tyler Williams. Part of that annoying brat's education had apparently been a self-taught lesson in supply and demand and the free market —he had a social media page where he had been selling his ill-gotten goods, the stuff he stole off front stoops.

So much for the kid's college scholarship, which she had discovered in an announcement on his high school's website. She'd eighty-sixed his free ride with a little video clip that caught him in some red-handed compromising positions, leaked to a local news outlet. And she didn't feel the slightest bit guilty about it. A kid at the top of his class, already breaking the law in high school, had no doubt been headed for bigger—and more illegal—things.

Nip that felon in the bud. All in a day's work, just like today. Job well done, if I do say so myself. And this is why I would be a terrible parent.

Just as she was about to head to the bathroom for a bio break—getting out of a onesie was no joke and she needed to plan her pee trips with a little buffer time—the laptop on the left side of her desk chimed. Or rather, squawked, thanks to the chicken notification sound she had set. If one of her friends on the gaming forum she frequented tagged her, her computer *bok-bok-bokked.*

Despite the final countdown happening on her bladder situation that, frankly, was about to earn its own hair-band rock anthem, she sat back down and clicked the notification on her screen to open the message board. She logged in and scrolled down to her name, which she had set to appear in bold purple font so she could do a rapid speed-reading scan and find it at a glance. An eye doctor would probably yell at her for not blinking enough, but dang, she liked to get as much information from the computer screen into her brain as quickly as possible.

The truth was, Viv's online reputation as a keyboard warrior of sorts had been spreading, despite her best efforts to stay under the radar. A lot of people were so-called social justice warriors—SJWs—who simply liked to argue fruitlessly on the internet. Viv, however, liked to take bad situations that she found online and make them right. *In real life.* With help from government contacts and programmer friends who were *much, much* smarter than she was, she managed to do a little good.

Lately, she had been working on a script that would trawl a collection of message boards, such as her favorite digital haunts like Gamerson-Gaming.net and TheEndoftheInternet.com for mention of her name and act as an aggregate to combine them all into a feed that she could scroll through and speed read to find the ones that interested her. As it was, she undertook only about 15% of the problems that people sent to her.

There are a lot of people out there with a lot of problems...which may be the understatement of the decade. Maybe of the century.

She couldn't do much about lost dogs and other pets, just because of the overwhelming number of them. Plus, animals didn't tend to leave much of a digital footprint, especially if they didn't have microchips. Hit and run fender benders were almost a lost cause, simply because so many of them happened every week, and if the victims had insurance, she wasn't too worried about helping them. It was the stranded people, the poor, the ones falling through the cracks who needed help. Missing persons and thefts were right in her wheelhouse.

In truth, she belonged to a wide but tightly interwoven online circle of friends who either had access to some mind-boggling data or who knew the right people to get access. Kind of a dark web for sharing information, which she used strictly for benevolent purposes. A light web instead? Like a network for paladins and do-gooders, a modern-day Knights of the digital Templar.

Viv's friends—her pals IRL, *in real life*—had no idea that her side gig as a virtual vigilante was beginning to take precedence over her former semi-successful life as a graphic designer. Her BFFs—Josie, Drew, and Benjy—thought her agoraphobia made her more and more homebound.

She felt guilty that she let them continue to believe she was a freelance graphic designer who produced brochures and book covers for the independent market. True, she had started out that way, but when that gig hadn't been enough to cover her rent, she had gone to her second degree in Chinese language and picked up translation work through her favorite undergraduate professor. It helped that Viv had lived in Shanghai when she was little and her parents were in the Foreign Service. "Promote peace, support prosperity, and protect American citizens while advancing the interests of the U.S. abroad"... and provide an alternate means of income for any washed-out graphic designer children.

Seriously, how do I even have the same DNA as those two people who spawned me? They spent thousands of dollars getting my I.Q. tested when I was little. For genius-level people, it sure took them a long time to come to grips with the fact that they had just an average kid.

Lu Laoshi—her Chinese teacher, Professor Lu—had hooked her up with a translation firm out of D.C. and since then, she had had a steady stream of weird-ass technical documents and instruction manuals to make sure she had all the unicorn onesies her heart desired. Which was more than one and fewer than five, incidentally. Then there were some internships in D.C., which were like glorified—*no, what was the opposite of glorified?*—librarian's assistant positions. Maybe not very intellectually stimulating. Maybe close to mind-numbingly boring. However, she had made a lot of friends during those stints, and her friends had become very valuable as they had each gone on to quite impressive roles.

And if Viv's current, somewhat mundane, remote work coincidentally allowed her to hide her actual agoraphobia, so be it...

She clicked a couple links to read the latest sob story on which she had been tagged. Lost pets, lost people, and people who purposely wanted to stay lost made up the bulk of her electronic requests. She expected this one to be no different...

"Hmmm, what's this then?"

She ignored the mounting pressure in her midsection as the pixelated words in front of her unblinking eyes began to weave a story.

CHAPTER TWO

A couple days earlier and about eight hundred miles south, in a little beach town on the coast of North Carolina, Claire Baldwin had sat on her bed in her totally childish and slightly worn-out mermaid-themed bedroom—but she didn't care, she still loved it—with the water-stained ceiling that made her think she might actually be living under the sea, especially when it rained and the part in the corner drooped. She sat with her finger poised over the Enter key of the laptop that was one of the last gifts from her uncle. Anxiety gnawed at her stomach and made her bite the ragged end of her sandy blond ponytail. She realized she was the living embodiment of the cliché of how every over-dramatic fourteen-year-old girl thought her life sucked, but hers was *legit* terrible.

High-key horrible.

Unlike her, most kids who had just started high school didn't have an uncle who had been found poisoned to death a month ago.

What even is arsenic? *If it's that deadly to people, maybe companies should stop making it? I dunno, just a thought.*

Most kids weren't spending all their waking hours being pissed off at the police detectives who didn't seem like they were doing anything about it, other than make her mother a so-called "person of interest." Most kids weren't about to tell random strangers on the internet all about the injus-

8

tice of her uncle's death. They were worrying about algebra and school musical tryouts or whatever.

"Why would some stranger want to help me? I don't have any money. I'm not famous. I'm just some kid."

"It's human nature for people to want to help someone who needs it."

She shook her head and rolled her eyes, even though he couldn't see her. That was not the case, not in her experience, but whatever.

"Are you sure this is a good idea?" she asked.

From the speaker of her chunky and outdated iPhone with the cracked screen, which was balanced on the ripped knee of her jeans, the voice of her best friend and super nerd, Terrance, said, "Would you just shut up and post your message online already? You and I have already discussed this more than a hundred years' worth of scholars in tweed sweaters have talked about the French Revolution, occultism in Nazi Germany, or how millions of people can trace their ancestry back to that Mongolian man-ho, Genghis Khan."

"Sweaters aren't made out of tweed. That's a suit material."

Still, Claire hesitated. If her mom found out she posted details about Uncle Kip's murder case on the internet, there might be hell to pay. Not just about airing their personal information and secrets, but in emotional damage and other intangible ways. Her mother, Evelyn, was pretty much a wreck since Uncle Kip, her only brother, had died. Like, sleeping pills-and-vodka level of messed up. Like not-showing-up for work kind of bad.

Now that Claire thought about it, she had lost not only one adult role model and the only father figure since her dad had left but *two*. Her mother was basically no longer here. She'd pretty much checked out of reality with the help of drinking, staying out late, partying, and sleeping during the day.

Granted, Claire's already psychologically shaky mother was the one who'd actually discovered Kip dead, which could not have been a pretty sight. Evelyn had stumbled across her brother's deceased body in the alley next to his restaurant. If her mom was a therapy kind of person, the billing hours would really be piling up right now.

Ever since Claire had accidentally discovered in a newspaper article that the cause of her uncle's death was arsenic, and then not-so-acciden-tally searched online for photos, she, too, knew what that kind of poisoning looked like. As it turned out, there was a pretty darned good reason people tried to protect their children from the internet, and now Claire knew first-hand it was, like, a *totally* logical parental instinct. She really wished she hadn't seen some of those disgusting photos now. Hands and feet covered with crusty nodules—that lovely symptom was from arsenic exposure over time. Most of the photos she had seen through the cracks between the fingers she held over her eyes were of people in distant countries whose water supplies had been tainted with the poison.

The good news was Uncle Kip hadn't experienced that. The bad news was he had probably been in a lot of pain. A death like that was not nice. Not nice at all.

He didn't deserve to suffer.

The question was, why did she look online to find out what his death was like? Sure, she was kicking herself now, but if she had the choice of whether or not to Google it, she would still do it. Call it a morbid need to know. Just like how she had made a pact with herself never to stop trying to find out who had killed him, even if the police gave up.

But was asking some *rando* on an internet board her best option?

"I'm not in a good state of mind to post this right now," she told Terrance over the phone, easing her finger away from the keyboard before she made a mistake she might regret.

She herself went to therapy every Wednesday afternoon during study hall, to talk to her school's visiting counselor, Maggie. As long as Claire went to every appointment and willingly participated, she didn't have to go on anti-depressants. She wanted to avoid them because she had seen Terrance turn into a zombie during the six months his super uptight parents had insisted he take them when he had haltingly told them he might not be straight. Not that she thought all people had to avoid them— she just had a bad association with them.

"Li-listen to me," came his voice, a slight stutter sneaking into his speech, which happened when he got emotional about things. "You're in the *very best* state of mind to do this now. I know you don't feel stable, but I swear to you that I, as your best and longest friend, would tell you if you were making a mistake."

"Like that one time, how you swore that dyeing my hair blue wasn't going to turn it green?"

"Theoretically, it should have worked! Your hair is blond. But the green ended up looking bomb-ass, did it not?"

True, but he could probably hear her roll her eyes all the way on his end of the call.

"How about when you swore that Jamie Clarke actually liked me back and I should totally put that note in his locker last year?"

"Okay, so I was grossly mistaken on that one. I had just streamed a rom-com marathon, and anyway Jamie moved away this summer so you didn't even have to face him after that. Plus, I know you're an amazing person, and if he didn't, then it was totally his loss."

Claire stopped to inhale a deep breath, something her counselor had said might help her in moments when she felt like she was drowning. It was weird that a person could be alive for hundreds and hundreds of days and suddenly forget how to breathe.

"Thank you for that. You're a great best friend, but without a doubt, you, Terrance, are a six-foot three-inch tall Black-Asian agent of chaos—"

"Wait, listen to me for a second, Claire, before you go all negative Nancy on me. I know I have made mistakes of judgement in the past. We've known each other since we were six. I have erred now and then, but my track record for telling the truth is still better than any politician out there. I would never lie to you in a malicious way, and I'm telling you right now, if you want to find out what happened to your uncle, you need to *post that message.*"

Maybe he was right. Her finger edged outward and hovered over the keyboard again, but she couldn't make herself press Enter.

"Tell me one more time…who exactly is this Viv person?" she asked.

"From what I've read, she's like a modern-day superhero. Nerdy like us, but almost OP."

Over-powered, like an anime character who didn't have any weaknesses. A normal person doesn't have superhuman strength and an unbreakable rubber skeleton. A normal girl wakes up one day to figure out she's pretty much alone in the world.

He continued, gathering a head of steam and getting breathless the way he did when he either really believed in something or was about to cry. "I mean, she fights for the underdog, the little guy, the downtrodden. People who have been fired from their jobs for whistleblowing. Random kids who have been bullied at school. A cancer guy who was homeless because he was living out of his car and then his car got towed. A guy whose store got vandalized because he's gay. There's a Tumblr page about her. People make memes. She's hard to reach, and she only picks situations that interest her. You just never know when she's going to take up your cause. I don't know if she will help you, but I think she would. I mean, I would. In any case, you never know unless you try, right?"

What would Ariel do?

Did she let a lack of legs prevent her from chasing after a human boy who may or may not have been worthy of her devotion? Okay, maybe a Disney cartoon character was not the best of role models.

What would Darryl Hannah in Splash *do?*

In that movie, Madison had wandered around New York City, unafraid of the world and chasing after her new life. She'd hung off a fricking street sign! That was a better example.

What would the mermaids in the fourth Harry Potter movie do?

Even better! They would swim around the underwater reeds with their scary teeth, pop out when you least expected it, and shriek until they got what they wanted…

Thus fortified, Claire clicked the button.

CHAPTER THREE

On the message board called "The End of the Internet," Viv read the narrative that a young girl named Claire had written. The original post had immediately been quoted and re-posted several times from other social media sites before it had reached Viv. The message was decently spelled out and grammatically correct, like an essay for school, which somehow made the story more poignant to Viv—either the kid had tried her best to write well or she had gotten someone to proof it for her. The effort hit Viv right in the feels.

All the very latest re-blogger had written was "@Viv might b one for u" before reposting it, and the message itself said:

> I'll get right to the point. My name is Claire and my Uncle Kip was murdered three months ago in the small beach town of South Pier, North Carolina. (I know, South in North, right? If that sounds mixed up, just keep reading for more. But I'm telling you, it doesn't get any clearer.) His full name was Kip Baldwin and he was the owner of the Time & Tidewater Grill that is in the same town. You can search for articles about it because it was in the news a lot three months ago, but not very much anymore.

Viv paused and pulled up a map on the web. Even though her parents were frequently out of the country, they owned three small places around the Continental US. One was a condo in Scottsdale. The second was a cabin in South Dakota. The third, however, was a beach house about a half-hour south of this girl's town. Viv had stayed there more than once when she was a teenager, but she hadn't been back in a while, not since a hurricane had rolled through and caused the house to require significant renovations. Hurricane Vicky hadn't been the thing that had kept Viv away—she had just gradually stopped traveling out of state, then out of her suburb, then out of her neighborhood, and eventually she had quit leaving the safety of her apartment all together.

Ugh.

She shook her head, not willing to travel down that well-trodden mental path at the moment. Sometimes a girl was just sick of thinking about herself. Luckily, she had someone else's troubles on which to fixate. One girl's emotional trash was some other troubled person's treasure? At that awkward realization, she quickly read on.

Here's the thing. My uncle was like a dad to me. My bio father ditched us before I was born and my mom raised me by herself. If it weren't for her big brother (Uncle Kip), I honestly don't know what would have happened to us. Not to whine or anything, but we might have ended up on the street or maybe with me as a ward of the state. Mom has had some problems and needs a lot of help, and now that he's gone, she's having a hard time keeping herself together. Especially since she's the one who found him dead. For real.

Anyway to get back to the point, someone poisoned Uncle Kip. This was stated in the report by the doctor who did the medical exam on him. They got it tested in a lab and it was arsenic, which seriously sounds like a Sherlock Holmes remake, not a thing that could happen in real life. Who has arsenic lying around? I don't even know where you would get it, and the super high level of it in his system means that it definitely wasn't an accident.

This happened three months ago and the police don't seem to want to do anything more about it. I don't know why, but other than treating my mom like she's the one who did it, they act like they just want to let it drop, like they are hoping everyone forgets about it. But the thing is, I won't. My mom won't. The people who loved him and his restaurant won't. I don't understand why they aren't investigating anymore. I know I'm just one person in a really small town that nobody thinks about and my mom is just some borderline messed up woman, but if anyone out there can help me... I guess this is the part when I say, "Help me Obi-wan, you're my only hope," like from that old movie. I mean, I know there is a person out there who can do something. I just really need someone to help me.

The photo that had been posted along with the text showed three people, who all bore a family resemblance. The genes ran strong. In front was a small blond teenaged girl with dark eyes, an angular face, and crooked teeth. She was in that awkwardly thin stage of life, all knees and elbows and sharp pointy bits. She definitely shared her uncle's eyes and smile, but her build was a lot like her mother's. Behind her and to the right, the middle-aged woman with a similar frame to the girl could have been anywhere from 28 to 45 with overly processed, fried and bleached hair, slightly sunken cheeks, and a smile that didn't reach her tired eyes. To the left of the girl, her uncle was a big dark-haired, dark-eyed, slightly paunchy man with a belly that signaled he liked beer. Deeply tanned and smiling broadly as if caught just after laughing—he had "dad joke" written all over his expression as if he had just delivered a horrible pun that made everyone groan to his great amusement.

The guy took up a lot of space in the photo, from his big, meaty hands, each of which rested on the shoulders of the two females with him, to his broad shoulders and large, grinning face. Not necessarily the kind of charisma that Viv was drawn to, but she could recognize it and under-stand why others might be. In fact, she tended to shy away from those big and blustery types. In her experience, they were hiding pain or anger, and she didn't trust them not to take it out on her.

It was the girl's face, however, that kept drawing her gaze. A kid that young shouldn't have the rug swept out from under her so abruptly. A kid who was alone in the world and begging for help from strangers, throwing a digital SOS message in a bottle out into the vast and dark ocean with no assurance of a response. Sure, people scammed each other over the internet every minute of every day, and Viv would have to make sure the story was for real, but if it *was* true, who better could help the girl than Viv?

She pushed back from her computer, unable to delay the call of nature any longer. If she was still thinking about the desperate girl with the pointy elbows after she came back from the bathroom, she would take the case. If a person's story stuck with Viv for more than ten or fifteen minutes, chances were it would keep her up at night until she found out more about it—and that was the kind of problem she wanted to solve. Why?

Maybe because she saw a little bit of herself in Claire. The girl looked a lot like Viv did at that age. Thin, fair, and vulnerable—yet just try to mess with her and you'd find the scrappy fighter underneath.

Maybe Viv had felt all alone, growing up the only child of foreign servants abroad. Although her circumstances were different, she still felt the girl's feelings of abandonment clearly. Part of her childhood, Viv had been in boarding school and the rest, she had lived with an elderly aunt in the US. She'd never been the child of a single parent like Claire, but she still empathized.

Maybe it seemed like people had given up on this girl because she seemed unimportant—but Viv knew that seemingly inconsequential children could grow up to be so very important in their own right.

Maybe it was because Viv was uniquely suited to aid this child. She wanted to help and *she was fairly certain she could make a difference.*

CHAPTER FOUR

"H ey, what are you doing right now?" Viv's friend, Josie, asked.
Why do people always call me while I'm in the bathroom?
After washing her hands, she paused in zipping her onesie all the way back up to return to the call. The bigger question was probably why did she answer the phone while she was indisposed, as the old-timey ladies called it? However, if she didn't pick up soon after Josie called, her best friend would get on their personal phone tree and send someone over to check on her, and the last thing Viv would want to do was to open the door to Benjy while she was looking like this: un-showered and in the clutches of her latest bout of insomnia.

Josie had tried to convinced her that Benjy, another of their foursome of best friends, had a serious crush on her and had been afflicted this way since their college days. Josie was totally mistaken about the object of said crush—it was obvious that he loved *Josie* not Viv. However, the length and endurance of his devotion was correct. They'd graduated more than seven years ago. *Wait, was that seven or eight years?* She began to do the math but realized she had gotten the current year wrong... In any case, that was a long time to carry a torch, and Benjy tended to go all white knight on the regular.

"I'm..."

Viv finished zipping up and struggled to come up with an excuse that was not crazy sounding. The truth was always on the tip of her tongue,

17

especially when it came to Josie, her food-critic-turned-sleuth friend who was a pro at sniffing out not only delicious things to eat but also the truth.

I'm trawling the internet looking for downtrodden victims to assist because I'm an underground digital warrior, and by the way, yes, I have a mental illness that makes it hard for me to leave my apartment and also I don't remember the last time I brushed my teeth...

Instead of saying that, she avoided looking at herself in the bathroom mirror and went with, "I'm just analyzing a potential project that I think I might take on."

The vague truth was easier to sell than a flat-out lie. Plus, if someone called her on it later, she wouldn't feel quite so awful about not being forthright with her bestie.

"Hmm," Josie said, as if she could detect that Viv's omissions were much more important than her *admissions*. Then her friend's tone changed. "I'm actually on my way out of town for a job myself."

"Food-related or...other stuff?"

Her friend's side work was as weird as Viv's. Josie did jobs of an investigatory nature for an elderly wealthy woman who resembled a World War II panzer tank more than a Boston blue-blooded matriarch, psychologically not physically. For some reason, Viv's tiny half-Asian friend had a soft spot for the old woman, which was insightful as to what interesting moral machinations went on in Josie's role-model-seeking mind. Maybe it was just as revealing about Viv that she loved Josie more than if they had been biological sisters, but it wasn't surprising. As the sentiment went, friends were family that you chose for yourself. Viv would pick Josie and their other two friends over anyone else on the planet. (She would leave the possibility of life on Mars open for now. Her USS planetary nerd card was still intact, laminated, and on a commemorative convention lanyard in fact.)

"I'm headed to New Hampshire for some R and R," Josie said. Her voice drifted away, but not from any kind of emotion. The volume dropped because Viv had nearly bobbled the phone in shock—her friend never took time off for herself—but then she remembered.

"Doesn't your boss lady live in New Hampshire?"

A telling silence oozed across the airwaves as Viv could feel her friend do a bit of scrambling of her own. None of their tight group of friends liked that Josie did odd errands for the older woman. *No, forget that.* They all felt uneasy about it but knew that it scratched some kind of do-good itch in Josie. Viv could admit to the same about her online gigs with a little pointed self-examination. The only difference between them was that Josie usually ended up in a scrap with resulting injuries. The girl had been racking up the stitches lately.

As expected, Josie deflected like the best of them. "It's just a quick little trip. No big deal. I should even be able to sleep late every morning. But the purpose of me calling is to remind you to get outside at least once a day until I get back. Brush your hair. Change your onesie. Drink more water. Then I'm coming over and we're getting you out of your apartment for lunch, got it? Even if it has to be at that sandwich shop right downstairs from you."

"I'm your best friend the houseplant. Sunshine and water. I'll put them on my to do list," Viv said. Still, she was touched that her friend always checked up on her.

"Uh. Maybe that's not a good idea. I already killed all those supposedly zero-maintenance, air plants you got me for my birthday."

"Good point. Have a good trip. Don't get injured like you usually do. *In New Hampshire. Having some rest and relaxation.* See you when you get back."

Which got Viv thinking about a change of location for herself. She didn't like to leave home, meaning her Boston apartment over the sandwich shop downstairs, which despite the new owners was excellent, and even picky food critic Josie agreed. Viv didn't like the idea of being away from her bed, her desk, and her onesies. But laptops were portable and the internet was everywhere. More importantly, temporarily relocating herself and all the things that made her feel safe to a place that her parents owned might not feel terrible. She'd visited the beach house more than once. It wasn't foreign territory—it was a home away from home.

Contemplating it made her break out into a sweat under her terrycloth unicorn ears, but she needed to push herself. Her therapist had told her to make small, accomplishable goals, but she had always been an overachiever. She couldn't live like this forever, not compared to how she used to command a room, how it had been as natural to be the life of a party as to breathe. She wanted to get better. She could do this.

Maybe.

CHAPTER FIVE

Claire twiddled a lock of hair at the lunch table and stared at her split ends. "How long do I have to wait before someone responds to my message? How do I know if it reached her?" She knew she sounded as whiny as Charlotte, her least liked character on her most favorite show, *The Grovemire Girls*, but she couldn't help it. Claire's life was crumbling to dust around her, and if complaining was the worst way she was reacting, so be it.

Terrance folded back the wrapper of the factory-produced sweet roll he had bought at the counter, took a bite, and made a face. He seemed to consider not eating the rest of it but sighed and carried on. She waited what she thought was pretty patiently for him to finish chewing, swallow, and wash it down with apple juice before she began to bite her chipped mermaid teal polished nail. He would stop whatever he was doing to chastise her because he hated this bad habit. In third grade, their teacher had showed them all the germs that could be transferred from their hands by hanging germy pieces of bread closed in sandwich bags on the whiteboard at the front of the classroom. Every day, they watched the germ-infested bread grow darker and darker. Needless to say, the nail-biting thing really bugged him, even if she did it on purpose.

"Listen," he said, and then silently glared at her fingers until she removed them from between her teeth. "You know how the internet works. We posted your story in all the right places and it has…" He pulled out his phone and clicked a few times. "As of right now, 256 shares. I don't know how that translates to how many people have viewed it—social media companies don't publicize those algorithms—but it's exponential, which means a lot of eyes have been laid on it. Viv has to know your situation by now, and if she wants to respond, she will. I did warn you that there was no guarantee, right?"

Claire fiddled with the empty bag from the corn chips that had been her lunch. "I know and I was trying not to get my hopes up, but I've obviously failed."

"It's okay, kid. Sometimes all we have is hope," he said, his gaze following a beefy football player across the cafeteria.

"Don't call me 'kid.' I'm the same age as you. Actually, I'm three months older than you."

"I think it works because I'm tall. It's an affectation. Part of my new aesthetic. Like Bogart in *Casablanca*. Do you like it?"

"No, not really," she said, however his vampire phase had been a lot more challenging to deal with. Pancake makeup during the North Carolina summer heat was no joke. He'd resembled that scene in the Indiana Jones movie when the Nazis' faces melted like candle wax.

"I was going to use 'sweetheart,' but I think that will either get me slapped by people who think I'm condescending or punched by people who assume I'm sexually threatening them."

"What do you think about doing some research?" she asked, trying to come up with a better strategy than sitting around and waiting for someone to help her.

What would Charlotte on Grovemire Girls? *Sit around and whine—so I should do the opposite of that.*

"Like doing test market research? I guess I could go to the beach with a clipboard and collect some raw data about what kinds of endearments I can call people without offending them."

Claire snorted. She tried to refrain from rolling her eyes because that was *so* middle school. "I'm talking about doing some of our own investigation into my uncle's death. I can't afford to hire a private detective. I've already stooped to begging for help on the internet. Why not just do some legwork on my own?"

"We don't have a car...or driver's licenses, for that matter."

She almost got teary at how quickly he included himself in her plan. He didn't even ask if it would be dangerous or possibly illegal. He was just automatically there. It gave her some serious feels. As broke as she and

21

her mom were, Claire knew that this kind of friendship was more valuable than anything she would want to buy at a store. She wiped her mouth with a napkin to disguise her need to sniffle. Stupid emotions. Probably just PMS anyway.

"We can walk almost everywhere in South Pier for what I'm thinking."

He squinted. "What kind of harebrained, cockamamy slapdash shenanigans do you have in mind?"

Good question. Usually, Claire was a rehash, review, and plan again kind of person, but she was running down the highway of her crazy thoughts without an idea of what might lie in the dark ahead. That made her pause. She didn't want to get into trouble, but she especially didn't want to drag Terrance into anything bad with her.

The fact was, she was in unknown waters. *Adult* territory. There was a reason why kids were supposed to be sheltered and protected from the real world. Things were scary out there. But if the past few months had taught her anything, the truth was, precious little had separated her from harsh reality. Feeling safe was an illusion. Might as well take the risk. No one was really there to catch her if she should fall.

She balled up her empty chip bag and pitched it at the nearest garbage can.

"You missed," Terrance told her.

"Thanks. I hadn't noticed that, Captain Obvious."

"'Here's looking at you, kid.'"

"Ugh."

CHAPTER SIX

Viv debated whether she should do a quick tele-health call with her therapist to see if taking a road trip was a terrible idea. Yes, the sessions were mostly reflective listening to help her ask herself the right questions, but it still helped her sort things out. However, when she picked up her phone, the number her fingers dialed was her parents' lawyer. She left a message, but as was typical for people of their income bracket, he called back within fifteen minutes.

"Hello, Susan," Mr. Horowitz—no relation to Winona Ryder—said. "What can I do for you?"

No one in her family, or anyone that she knew in person for that matter, called her Viv. Her real name made her grit her teeth and bear the weight of her personal history, all the things both good and bad that had happened, and all of the associated burden of playing the role of Susan Whitaker, the one into which she had been born. It all came back to her in that one word, her name, from the way she used to model her elocution, dress, and posture off golden age of Hollywood screen stars like Grace Kelly and Veronica Lake, down to the chignon in her hair. Playing the role of herself had been exhausting and she didn't think she could do it anymore. So much so that she almost hung up at the sound of her real name.

No, I can do this. Just stay on a little longer and see what happens.

She was damp under the arms, but she managed to return the greeting of her family's long-time lawyer. It helped to try to imagine him in a unicorn onesie identical to hers. With his mustache and Mr. Noodle reddish hair, he would probably look pretty adorable.

"Hello, Mr. Horowitz. I hope you're well. Can you please tell me if anyone will be occupying the beach house for the next couple of weeks?"

To offset the cost of insurance and taxes on the property, Horowitz had assisted her parents by occasionally leasing out the place to carefully vetted clientele during the peak summer weeks when they weren't there. However, since it was September now, she suspected the house would be vacant other than for an infrequent but regular cleaning. Viv's mother hated coming back to a stale or stuffy house.

Instead of putting her on hold while he checked his records, he chatted with her amicably about the weather where he was in Florida, asked about her parents' well-being—his guess was as good as hers in that department, but she did her best to keep up appearances that they were a close-knit threesome—and, after just a short delay, assured her that the house was currently empty.

"Your parents mentioned they might use it over the Christmas holidays, but I imagine you already knew that," he said mildly, in a tone no doubt long-practiced not to show any emotion or judgment.

In fact, she was *not* aware whether they planned to come back to the States this year. They never remembered to tell her anything. Currently, they were in Portugal where her father liked to paint when he had free time. They'd supposedly retired from the Foreign Service, but they both consulted on matters of the... Actually, Viv wasn't entirely sure what their areas of expertise were. They each spoke multiple languages and had spent a lot of time in Russia, Turkey, Spain, and now, Portugal.

"Thank you," Viv told their lawyer. "I believe I will stay at the North Carolina house for the next couple of weeks myself." However, even as she said it, a frisson that was a mixture of excitement and fear run down her spine, much like a cat running across piano keys. "Unless something comes up," she added as a vague caveat.

He didn't seem bothered by her wishy-washiness. Perhaps another learned behavior from a career spanning several decades catering to the whims of the medium-ish but unapologetically wealthy. Or maybe he was naturally a super chill person.

"I'll put in a request to have the house freshened up and the pantry stocked for a short visit." He ended the conversation with, "So good to hear from you, Susan. As ever, do not hesitate to contact me if there's any way in which I can assist you in the future."

She'd heard those exact words dozens of times over the years. Today, however, whether from some minute change in emphasis or tone, they had a different ring to them. After she hung up, she frowned at her phone as she tried to replay his voice in her mind.

She shook her head. Maybe it was just her anxiety playing tricks on her. She had never been spectacular at inferring people's implied meaning and hidden thoughts. Probably her own heightened fear about the trip made her imagine things. This was why she liked the internet. She wasn't left trying to decipher expressions or voices. If she didn't understand someone's text or post, she simply asked for clarification with no hard feelings.

Are you being sarcastic? Did you leave off an emoji? Sorry, I'm not sure if you're joking.

She could say all these things online and no one thought anything of it. In real life, however, she was expected to pick up on all that stuff naturally. She was supposed to understand when someone was lying to her when they told her they loved her. She was expected to pick up on hints that she was being tricked into a phony relationship.

With the internet, she was protected from all that, ironically. While other people were being catfished, flirted with by bots, and scammed, her computer screen was the fortress and the power button was the portcullis that kept her safe.

CHAPTER SEVEN

Claire spied Terrance's hulking form as he waited for her on the steps after school for them to walk home together.

"What's the plan, Stan?" he asked with a cocked finger gun and a weird tongue click.

"Please don't tell me you have a fedora."

He ignored her. "I don't have any homework, so I'm free to be your Gal Friday for whatever shenanigans you have in mind."

"I don't know what that means. And why do you never have any homework?" Claire had at least two assignments due in history and art, but she never started it until study hall the next day. Princess of Procrastination, Uncle Kip always called her. This approach to schoolwork was usually good enough for her, but a couple of projects were coming up next week. A person couldn't conjure up trifold presentation board out of thin air, so she would have to make an effort.

She had a mythology-themed mixed-media art project due as well, and she had chosen to construct a chimera out of clay and to add objects that she had found in nature, mostly from the beach. She'd learned about chimeras from a book that her uncle had given her when she was little. Maybe not the best reading material for a tiny child, but she had loved the pictures of mermaids, unicorns, and other legendary beasts. The messed-up chimera had always scared her a little. Part goat, part lion, and part snake had done a number on her dreams back then, but recently she had learned that a chimera could also mean a fantasy or a hope that could never be achieved, like a pie in the sky type of thing that she had never reached. Maybe it was supposed to be a sad, depressing thing, but Claire had come to think of that impossible goal somewhere up in heaven as a place where the scary chimera monster was locked away as well, one waaay out of her grasp and the other, safely so.

The thought actually gave her some comfort.

"I don't have any homework because I do most of it during class. And I'm already done with the mythology art project, so I can be the Robin to your crimefighting Batman. Julie Newmar to your Adam West. Wait, she wasn't Robin. O'Donnell to your Clooney. Tonto to your Lone Ranger. Jacob Batalon to your Tom Holland." At her blank expression, he gave a long-suffering sigh and explained, "I'm your sidekick."

"Oh, right."

Claire had been racking her brain all through the second half of the day to come up with a plan of action. Since they weren't allowed to have their phones out during class, she had scribbled it on her palm in green ballpoint pen. She flipped her hand over to refer to the slightly smudged writing.

1. Revisit the scene of the crime.
2. Interview witnesses.
3. Speak to colleagues and friends.

They could start with number one because she knew where that was, but number two and three was where she was stuck. She didn't want to show Terrance the list because she was pretty sure she had spelled "colleagues" wrong, but he, the brainy human skyscraper, was already peering over her shoulder. If she had forgotten a letter, he was nice enough not to mention it.

"Not bad! Sounds like someone has been doing her research. Have you been watching *Ride Along*?"

Claire gave a noncommittal shrug. Actually, she *had* watched a couple episodes of the reality detective TV show last night on her phone when she couldn't sleep. However, she didn't want to admit it to even her nerdiest, most studious friend who of all people would have understood why. She was in that "fake it until you make it" mindset that her mom used to talk about all the time when Uncle Kip was around. Her mom had scribbled the same words and stuck them to the yellowed front of their

Frigidaire. A sticky note was probably as close as they were going to get to the pillows and shoulder bags with inspirational messages that Terrance's mom screen-printed for craft shows.

"Are you sure you're up for this?" she asked as they hoofed it down the sidewalk. The restaurant was about a mile from the high school, but it was an easy walk in a straight line, and the weather was in the 70s. Pretty typical for early fall in their little seaside town. "I don't want to get you into trouble."

Their guidance counselor had been banging the "everything you do now affects your chances of getting into a good college" drum since Back-to-School night for the ol' South Pier High Sabertooths in August. Claire hadn't given much thought to college. School wasn't her happy place. Terrance had pretty much taught her the only study skills she had, namely, just enough to get her through it. However, there was no way she wanted to be responsible for messing up any of his chances. At the rate he was going, he was on track to be valedictorian someday, and maybe even prom king—or queen, she speculated—because people liked him.

"How could we possibly get into trouble? We're just two innocent kids, and you have a legitimate reason to ask questions. You're directly related to the..." he paused, and she made a gesture for him to continue because she was used to the word now, "victim."

Scratch that.

She was *almost* used to the word, but not quite. Even now, in broad daylight, walking down a busy street alongside her huge hulk of a friend, she still got that "dip in the road" feeling in the pit of her stomach. That rollercoaster free fall feeling that reminded her no one was there to catch her if she lost her grip on the safety bar of life.

But she cleared her throat and pasted on a smile. "You just remember what you said when the college interviewer from Chapel Hill asks you to explain your arrest record from today. Mark my words, Terrance."

They chatted about other things for the rest of the way there, like who of their classmates had been particularly annoying that day—Jordan Prather, hands down—as if talking about their plans too much might jinx whatever the future outcome might be. Before long, however, they stood in front of the Time & Tidewater Grill. Her uncle's restaurant sat on the edge of the intracoastal waterway, which separated the mainland from a small strip of ritzy mansions right on the Atlantic Ocean.

Claire had not been back to her uncle's restaurant since his death. As she stood there with Terrance, it struck her how weird it was that the entire world could change, all hinging like a trap door slamming down, on one day, or on one hour, or one glass of sweet tea. She still thought the building was pretty, if a little too serious and grown up for her. It had *adult* written all over it with its elegant sign, dark colors, angles, and glass windows. She had always felt underdressed in her shorts and sandals.

A week before everything changed, she had come by herself to get something to eat. It was mid-morning before they opened and the lunch crowd came in. Usually, she avoided the place during the summer when all the tourists were in town. She didn't like bothering the staff when they were getting ready for what would no doubt be a super busy shift, and the end of June was peak out-of-towner season.

But on that day, she had been bored, and she knew there were at least three really good-looking boys on the seasonal staff. They all dressed so nicely in black pants and shirts, and even smelled really good when they walked by. One of them was bound to be working at all times, but this day, she was lucky and two of them were there. Uncle Kip always hired the best-looking servers and busboys of both genders. It wasn't an official policy that Claire knew of, but it was one of those known things that everyone was aware of and just accepted. In fact, she was pretty sure if she applied, she wouldn't make the cut. She was just so awkward.

The staff always let her sit at the tiny table at end of the bar, drink a Coke, and munch on some pretzels while she surreptitiously spied on the cute boys, and before long, someone slid a plate with a shrimp po' boy on it in front of her. She hadn't asked for it, but Uncle Kip knew she loved them and he was always telling her she needed to eat better because she was a Skinny Minnie, whatever that meant.

I mean, I knew what it meant. *Duh. I just don't know why he said it. Now, I'll never know why.*

As she and Terrance stood in front of the building now, her stomach reminded her that all she had eaten for lunch was a bag of barbecue Fritos. Her gut gurgled uncomfortably, but the idea of putting anything in her mouth and chewing it up sounded terrible. She couldn't remember when food had last tasted good to her. Maybe that plate she had had sitting at the bar. Now she wished she had eaten the whole thing, but the cute boys had made her self-conscious about chewing for some reason.

The building looked the same. It was all dark wood and leafy palm trees with an elegant sign. Two stories tall, it had a deck that looked out over the water and its own dock in the back. Now that her uncle was gone, it seemed like he had never been here. It should have felt as if the building had absorbed so much of him—energy, loudness, actual sweat—she didn't know what, but she was searching for any trace of him, like his aura should have still been here because he had given so much of his time and energy creating the restaurant. She wanted to think that ghosts were real and he was watching her now, waiting to see if she was going to do something dumb, like snoop around where she didn't belong anymore.

When she snapped out of her reverie, she found Terrance staring at her. "We don't have to do this," he said.

She appreciated his concern, but she told him, "I kind of have to. I *need* to."

CHAPTER EIGHT

efore the deer-in-the-headlights inertia of anxiety—that "tharn" frozen feeling from the doomed bunnies of *Watership Down*— could change her mind, Viv flung open the door of her second bedroom, which she used as a closet. No joke, she needed the space of an entire extra room for all of her clothes and accessories, which was ridiculous for someone who now wore the same onesie almost every day, she realized. But there had been a time before the walls of her apartment came to separate what was safe and controlled from the chaos of the outside world when she had loved to play dress up.

She could measure the significant eras of her life from sections of her costume collection—that's what the clothes amounted to, putting on costumes and playing roles. She had a number of mobile costumer's racks on wheels that she had picked up from a playhouse that had gone under, and she had filled all of them with different collections that represented the personas she herself had played over her short lifetime so far. Dutiful daughter. Obedient child. Socialite college student. Government intern. Closet nerd. Cosplayer. Librarian-like translator. Armchair warrior. Online gamer.

Her college days were mostly high-end designer clothes, elegant and pricy. Many of the luxury accessories had been gifts from the parade of past bad decisions she had called boyfriends. She'd tried to return most of them back to their givers, but without much success. A creamy Prada brushed leather shoulder bag that felt like butter under her fingers. A Gucci belt with their ostentatious logo for a buckle. Versace perfume and sunglasses. Bright pink Oscar de la Renta hand-embroidered sandals. Hermes scarves, more than one, with their trademark traditional patterns. She had quite an embarrassing collection but treasured them more than other people loved photos or ticket stubs.

She'd gone through a spate of expensive-car-driving junior law firm partner types as she had searched for what she thought she wanted: a modern-day Laurence Olivier to her self-styled Princess Grace. Of all the sparkly and beautiful gifts she had received, she had never kept an engagement ring, thank goodness. If she had, her life would have been a lot different and much worse than now, which was saying a lot for a twenty-eight-year-old near-shut in.

That phony Holly Golightly period of her life had concluded when she had met James, whom she had nearly married, but she wasn't ready to rehash her failed relationship with him at the moment. She'd save that for a series of therapy sessions.

Instead, she skimmed through a rack of renaissance faire costumes with velvet skirts, lace-up bustiers, and more brocade than a turkey-leg-wielding bearded man could yell, "huzzah!" at. She'd met a lot of lovely and inclusive free-spirits at her local annual festival. They, in turn, just by their fearless willingness to throw themselves whole-heartedly into another time and another place had reawakened Viv's love of theatre and disguise.

She had wigs and clip-in hair pieces of various lengths and colors. A black Cleopatra shoulder-length blunt cut. A ruby-red glam-bot mop. A white-blond silver screen starlet soft halo. Pink for playing the main character from an obscure 1990s anime. All these, she had acquired when she had gotten active in cosplay and attending conventions. Superheroes, emo anime characters, cult TV show favorites. She'd gotten quite good at pretending to be someone else.

Why can't I play a role now?

She'd been trapped like a hermit crab in her shell. Her sad-sack existence was getting on even her own nerves. Why not exchange her onesie for a new, temporary shell? Why couldn't she pretend to be someone new for a while?

Spurred to action by this thought, she undid the tarnished latches of a battered second-hand suitcase and let it fall like an open mouth in the center of the room. She spun in a slow circle taking inventory of her costuming options. She had a variety of makeup and wigs to choose from. Her body was decently healthy and average enough to be pushed to appear any number of ways. Thinner, chunkier, taller, shorter—all those characteristics could be teased to stand out. Makeup and spray tans could be employed to enhance skin color without being overt. Body language, which she had trouble recognizing in other people, could be faked with a few trademark gestures like nose-wrinkling, gum chewing, or talking with her hands.

Here in her own storage room of treasures, she began to build a new person.

A fiery orange wig, made to suit her face by violet lip color. A makeup foundation a couple shades paler than her natural tone made her look a bit Irish, as did added freckles to her nose, which would be real after a few days in the sun. A shiny gold hoop clipped on for a nose ring meant that people would focus more on it than her actual features. She tossed a pack of pale green contact lenses into her vintage suitcase.

This girl—the name Olivia popped into her mind—favored spandex leggings, the brighter the better. She had a sweet tooth and always kept a Blow Pop or two in her shoulder bag so she might suck on a lollipop whenever she felt the urge, which made her look like a smoker trying to quit even though she wasn't. Maybe she had lived in Southern California or maybe she was from Utah trying to seem like she was edgier than she actually was. Or maybe she was from Nashville, but she had never had an accent and didn't care much for country music.

Shoes made the woman. Olivia wore cheap flip-flops, knock-off Italian flats, or colorful combat boots when she was hitting the pavement in search of work. Her other accessories were large shoulder bags in which she kept everything under the sun, from stale chewing gum to tampons to an extra pair of panties. Sunglasses were a must, especially in a beach town. She also definitely needed a vintage pinup swimsuit, but only if she also had a maxi-dress beach wrap, a sun hat, and 70 SPF sunscreen.

As Viv assembled a collection of clothes that would fit the idea, the personality of this Olivia woman, and tossed the whole armful of them into the suitcase, she told herself this trip was totally doable.

She dragged her suitcase over to the door and grabbed a light coat. All she needed to do was gas up her hybrid car and go. She got as far as putting her hand on the doorknob and gripping it, but she couldn't bring herself to open it. A mirror above the table next to the door caught her eye. She was still in a unicorn onesie. Her hair was a ratty, bed-head-looking mess.

What am I thinking? I can't do this.

Ten minutes later, she was still arguing with herself with one hand on the metal knob, which had gotten a little sweaty while she struggled with herself. The only thing that changed was now she couldn't look at her reflection in the mirror. She realized that having a mental WWE grudge match with herself for that long was weird and possibly a problem, but while she couldn't get up the courage to go outside, neither was she willing to give up the fight. A little girl needed her help, and this was Viv's chance to force herself out of her comfort zone and possibly make a breakthrough at the same time.

She pushed down the wave of anxiety that was making her both hot and cold at the same time in alternating waves. If she made it through this, she was going to need a long shower and a stick of maximum-strength deodorant.

Is it possible for one person to have both a fight and flight reaction at the same time?

Whatever reaction was winning, it made her feel woozy.

She blew out a shaky breath and focused on turning the knob.

Turn the knob. You can do it. Just turn the knob—

In her palm, the handle turned of its own accord and the door swung inward. Benjy stood with a confused frown on his normally placid face. Ripped jeans on a thin frame, two hoodies, the inner one zipped up, and hand-knitted mittens made up his familiar look, and a sense of relief filled Viv just seeing him on her doormat. His sweeping gaze took in her bed head, her undoubtedly pallid and sweaty face, her rumpled onesie, and her packed suitcase.

"Going somewhere?" he asked.

CHAPTER NINE

Claire stood with Terrance in the alley to the side of the Time &
Tidewater Grill near the rusty metal dumpsters which honestly
did not smell pleasant. Combined with days of full, hot sun, the
sickly-sweet waste from bar fruit and outright *stank* of seafood shells…
yeah, this wasn't a wonderfully smellerific locale to hang out unless you
were a starving alley cat. The odor was downright sick, and her stomach
wasn't doing that well from anxiety to begin with—also, the lack of food
all day wasn't a good foundation for this kind of work, which her high
school guidance counselor would have told her.

"Is this the place?" Terrance asked, eyeing the ground around their
feet. She could tell he wasn't trying to be pushy, he was just supremely
uncomfortable. Come to think of it, she wondered if he believed in
ghosts.

She pointed to the pavement by the side entrance, just to the left of the
garbage containers. "It was right there, I guess. Mom said she found him
lying outside by the door. He was supposed to come over for dinner that
night, and when he didn't show up, she came to look for him."

Actually, he had told them he was bringing them dinner. When he
hadn't shown up, Claire had ended up making herself a pack of ramen
noodles.

Thank goodness there wasn't any sign of what had happened there.
The asphalt was uneven with big cracks like a broken cookie, maybe from

the weekly weight of the garbage trucks coming in for pickup, or delivery trucks with the fresh catch of the day or local produce. Uncle Kip used to get up early to order food and supplies. He used to promise, or maybe that was threaten, to come wake up Claire at the crack of dawn one day so he could show her what he did.

She blinked as the ground blurred.

"I think we should leave," Terrance said and put a big but gentle hand on her shoulder. He'd clearly noticed her mental state, and maybe had seen her tears.

She kind of wanted a hug, but she would never in a million years ask him for one, cause that would be super embarrassing.

"In a minute," she promised him, and then gave herself a mental pep talk. She appreciated her big bear of a best friend, but they had come all this way. She wasn't going to waste the trip. She would be as stalwart as the Little Mermaid Statue looking out to sea...wherever that was. Sweden? Denmark? Norway? Whatever icy Scandinavian country with socialized healthcare Hans Christian Anderson was from, where they probably had Viking DNA and were immune to the powerful scents of deceased creatures of the sea. She'd seen YouTube videos of people gagging over the fermented canned fish from one of those countries.

What would that whiny loser Charlotte from Grovemire Girls *do? She would go home, so I'll do the opposite.*

Her mother said she had driven to the restaurant to check on her brother when he didn't answer her phone calls. Evelyn didn't come very often. In fact, not unless she had a specific reason, like a paper she needed him to sign or if she was short on rent money. Claire's mother was a waitress, not at her brother's restaurant but at a bowling alley. He said he had been happy to support her, but he made it a policy never to hire family. Claire wasn't dumb though. There were a lot of reasons why her uncle might not have wanted her mother there. For one thing, all of his servers were super young and attractive, and Evelyn looked like she had been around the block a few times, as she had heard her uncle once say. Also, Evelyn tended to show up for work whenever she felt like it and often slept through her alarm. Claire wasn't stupid about that either. She saw all the wine bottles that went into their recycle bin. Her mother hadn't been an easy person to get along with even before any of this happened.

"Okay, I'm ready to do this," she said, pushing her hair behind her ears, and took them a few steps closer.

When Claire and Terrance were just a few feet away from what must have been the spot where her uncle had died, the side door swung open violently and banged backward against the building.

Arletta Malone, Uncle Kip's business partner, said to someone behind her, "Tell them I'm not paying for rotten pineapples. I'm trying to run this business the best way I know how, which includes not letting those dishonest bastards cheat us. I'm not giving them another damn cent. They can sue us for all I care!" She stomped out but lurched to a halt when she saw Claire and Terrance standing there with shocked faces. She held an unlit cigarette between two fingers and a lighter pressed against them with her thumb.

"What are you doing here?"

CHAPTER TEN

Arletta's eyes, which were distorted behind thick glasses, narrowed. She was a tiny woman, shorter than Claire, but she managed to intimidate the life out of her with just a glare.

Claire's gut instinct was to make a run for it, but she stayed still. Did Ariel the mermaid cower in fear and flee in the face of strange humans and a weird new world? No, she did not. Then again, she had also been incredibly naive about a lot of things, so maybe that particular cartoon character wasn't the best example, but still, she had been brave. She went after what she wanted, and she did well in the end. What about Ursula? She was a big bad meanie, and no one ever scared her away from her goals.

Arletta had gray hair and thin lips and wore clothes that made her look like someone who probably took arthritis medicine. Her short-sleeved button-down tropical shirt tucked into high-waisted pleated pants gave her a grandmother vibe—but not the type of nana who baked you cookies and told you she loved you just for being you. More like the type of strident woman who smoked Camels with her arms crossed and judged you for your dirty shoes while you were on the sidewalk, before you even reached her clean kitchen floor. Not that Claire had ever met her mom's mother. She only knew what grandparents were supposed to be like from movies and TV.

Kip's business partner didn't seem to recognize Claire even though they had met more than a dozen times before, including two staff holiday parties. To be fair, Claire had grown up over the years and her appearance had changed a little—that temporary greenish mermaid hair when she was ten could have confused anyone. Then again, how many skinny freckle-faced girls could Arletta mistake her for in this tiny little beach town? Granted, there was a large temporary tourist population that swept in and out every year, but *what the what?* Claire was her long-time partner's niece.

Before Arletta could tell them to scram, Claire channeled her inner sea witch and spoke up. "I'm Kip's niece. I'm not sure if you remember me."

Arletta's expression changed as quick as someone hitting *Next* to skip a bad song on a playlist. The woman flinched for a half of a second as if she had a stitch in her side, like the kind Claire always got in P.E. that Ms. Peters thought she was faking but wasn't, and then the woman grimaced. "Of course I know who you are, sweetie. I'm so sorry I didn't recognize you at first. You're a lot taller than I remember."

They had also both been at Uncle Kip's memorial service a couple months ago, but maybe Arletta didn't recall that either. The woman either had a serious short-term memory issue or else Claire wasn't all that memorable. A lot of people didn't notice you when you were a kid, and they lied to pretend they did. Sometimes Claire didn't know if she wasn't memorable, or if all grownups were self-absorbed.

She, on the other hand, remembered a lot about her uncle's business partner. Arletta had joined Uncle Kip about ten years ago when he had been having trouble running the place. Claire had seen how stressed out he was, how he used to come over late at night after closing and hang out at their place chatting with her mom. They'd drink a lot in the kitchen long after Claire was in bed, and sometimes in the morning when she woke up, he'd be snoring on the couch, sleeping off a hangover, no doubt. When he and her mom got together, the wine bottles could really fill up the bin the next day.

During one of those late nights, they had come up with the idea of him taking on a business partner. Right after that, Uncle Kip had found Arletta and brought her on as an investor. Arletta supposedly knew a lot about running a business, but she didn't talk much. When she did, it was generally to complain about something or someone: the kitchen was messy and they had an inspection coming up, a waiter was always late, the parking lot needed new lines painted, and other stuff like that. Maybe they were legit things that needed to be fixed, but Claire always thought the lady could have been nicer about it, especially since she didn't seem to know anything about actual food or drinks. Even Claire knew if you wanted to be able to taste things, you had to stop smoking. She didn't need a DARE anti-drug program at school to teach her that.

"I was actually going to come talk to you," she fudged, "about applying for a job."

Yeah, I'm applying for a job in a stinking alley where my uncle died. Nice cover, dumb-butt.

Coming here now felt like a terrible idea. She wasn't going to discover, like Sam and Dean from *Supernatural*, a stray remnant of the past crime lying right there, undiscovered this whole time.

"Well," Arletta said, hesitating. "Times are tough, you know? Business drops off after the summer season ends. I mean, we still do good the rest of the year, but... How old are you again?"

"I'll be fifteen in a month."

"You can't learn to be a server until you're at least sixteen, but—what am I saying? *Of course* you can work here. It's what he would have wanted."

Claire thought she might be imagining things, but were those tears in the woman's eyes?

"Tell you what, hon. In the spring, you come back and see me, and we'll find something for you to do. It might be clearing tables, if that's not too crummy for you. We take busboys who are fifteen, so I'm sure I could find a place for you. I mean, of course we will. You're Kip's niece after all, and that means you can always come here. Don't you worry about it. We'll get you in here and making some money right quick." Arletta seemed to warm up to the idea the more she spoke about it.

The restaurant's side door burst open again, and Arletta's husband, Brad, strode out.

The heavyset man wore all khaki, and his shirt pocket had a patch with his name stitched on it, like the kind Claire had seen on car mechanics or plumbers. Where his wife was shrewd and just a little bit mean, he seemed like a nice man, and Claire had never gotten a creeper vibe from him even though he looked like their school janitor.

"Oh, hey, Claire," he said, clearly recognizing her. "I didn't know you were here. You should have come around to the front side. Did you stop by to get something to eat?"

As if mooching off a restaurant that she wasn't connected to anymore wouldn't be totally inappropriate and humiliating. She would *never* do that. He was a decent person, but kind of clueless.

"She's asking for a job," Arletta said, pausing to light her cigarette. "I told her to come back after her birthday."

"Oh, yeah. And if you want to wait until the spring, April should be a great month for hiring clearers," Brad said. "Gearing up for the summer season."

He had gray hair, too, like his wife, but he managed to look a lot younger than she did by about ten years. Maybe a bad attitude aged a person a whole lot faster. They had a weird vibe between them that Claire couldn't figure out. Probably because they'd just been caught arguing by some dumb kids in the alley.

"Thanks, I appreciate it," Claire said, totally embarrassed that her lie had worked so well. "It's only my mom and me, and I want to help out if I can." She was rambling now, but she didn't know how to say goodbye casually without it seeming like Arletta had scared them away, which she kind of had.

"Yeah, sure."

"What about you, son?" Brad asked Terrance. "Do you need a job, too?"

"Oh, no, thank you, sir," he said. "I already have a job lined up, but thanks for asking. It keeps me super busy, so much so that my mom's worried it might affect my grades. In fact, it's time for me to be getting to work now, so we should be on our way."

Maybe it was her glasses, but a weird look crossed the woman's face. However, Arletta didn't seem to mind their hasty exit and waved her cigarette at them as they said goodbye. She was complaining to her husband about rotten fruit again when they walked away.

Claire waited until they were out of earshot and then added a half-block more for good measure. "Is it just me or was she defensive about me being there?"

"Well, we *were* hanging out in a disgusting alley acting suspicious."

She smacked him lightly on the arm, and he pretended it hurt.

"I don't trust her. I mean, she didn't even know who I was."

"Have you ever had a real conversation with her that she would actually remember?" he asked.

Claire thought back. "Not exactly. It was more saying hi with a few waves, I guess. Maybe she asked me what grade I was in a couple years ago."

"Then, what did you expect?"

"Fine. You're right. And you have a job? You didn't tell me that," Claire asked him accusingly. "What is it, tutoring after school?"

"Nope," he said. "Hanging out with you is a full-time job."

CHAPTER ELEVEN

To his credit, Benjy didn't comment on Viv's attire—he completely ignored the onesie in the room, so to speak. He did, however, invite himself in and go straight into the kitchen where he stood in front of her fridge with the door open. She thought about asking him to leave, but it wasn't like she was going anywhere soon, so she took the glass of pink lemonade he offered her one in her favorite Hamburglar collectible glass from McDonald's. He used Ronald himself, and she didn't even mind that she would have to hand wash them later because the dishwasher would scrub off the decoration.

"So," he said and sat on her blue velvet couch, which she had gotten at an antique shop and reupholstered by herself. "Tell me, what's going on in your world?"

Usually, Benjy looked pretty footloose and fancy free. His tousled blond curly hair was on the longish side right now—it had grown the last couple of months since she had seen him—and the top threatened to hang in his blue-green eyes. He swept it back with one hand, but it didn't stay in place as he looked at her with unmitigated concern.

She said, "Did you know that reportedly, Winston Churchill invented the precursor to what we now know today as the onesie? During World War Two, he designed a one-piece coverall called a siren suit that he could pull over his actual clothes when an air raid occurred. Apparently,

though, the only wear and tear his suits received was when he accidentally burned them with the end of his cigars."

Benjy raised a single eyebrow. "Why are you deflecting the question?"

"What do you mean?"

"You always bring up weird trivia when you're nervous."

Actually, she fully understood what he had asked—why she hadn't
been hanging out with them at O'Malley's, their favorite bar. In fact, she
hadn't left her apartment except to walk to the deli directly downstairs
once or twice. And oh, also that she had been stuck in the doorway
talking to herself and probably looked like she had been kicked out of
unicorn city for poor hygiene practices.

*The first known mention of unicorns in literature was by a Greek physician
and historian in about 400 B.C. In addition to a horn, it had a white body, purple
head, and blue eyes.*

He took a silent, deliberate sip out of the Ronald cup.

She recognized this interrogation tactic from a couple of training
courses she had taken, and she wouldn't crumble. He intended for his
silence to pressure her into speaking. The longer he waited and the longer
the quiet dragged on, the greater the urge she had feel to—

"*Fine.* I was trying to make myself go on a little trip south. My parents
have a beach house in North Carolina, and I thought I'd drive down there
and stay for a week or two, to see what a change of venue would feel like.
I didn't mention it because I'm not sure how long I'm staying. If it doesn't
feel good, I'll turn around and come home. You probably already know I
haven't gotten out in a few days, but—"

"Twenty-three days," he said.

"What?"

"That's how long it's been since you last came out with us."

She was more gobsmacked that he had kept track of her than how
many days it had been. She began to argue that she had been out of the
house for groceries, but that wasn't true, thanks to a delivery service app
she used. She had a tele-health appointments with her therapist, not in-
person sessions. She paid her bills electronically, the same way she
received her paychecks. Thanks to email and text chat programs, she
wasn't sure if she had used her vocal cords every one of those days.

*Maybe I need a cat. I could at least talk to it. Or a plant...a plastic ficus I
can't kill.*

After her initial denial, she felt defensive. She stamped into the
kitchen, which was somewhat less effective when one wore slippers, and

examined the Subversive Cross Stitch calendar pinned to the wall. This month's design said, "Spark joy or get the eff out." She jabbed at the squares and counted backward to the last time she had met her three friends for dinner.

"…Twenty, twenty-one—aha! It's only twenty-two."

"Today is Friday, not Thursday."

"Well, shoot." He was right. "How do you even know this anyway?"

"I pay attention. That's what friends do."

Friends. She cringed at the word.

Mayday. Mayday. That's a definite friend-zoning.

Josie kept trying to tell Viv that Benjy had more-than-just-friends feelings for her, but she knew the truth. He'd once confessed to Viv his deep and abiding love for *Josie*, who was now dating Drew. All they needed was for Viv to fall in love with Drew and the corners would be drawn to complete the perfect love-square. Fortunately, she was not. Things were complicated enough.

"I appreciate your concern," she began, smoothing a hand down the front of her onesie.

"What if it's more than simple concern?"

She frowned. "Does that mean you're…*super* concerned?"

"Something like that," he said.

She was still confused, and why did he look so amused? "Is this an intervention?"

Maybe he was coming to physically drag her out of her apartment. Was he planning to force her on a daily jaunt like an overweight lapdog that needed walkies?

A term, incidentally, coined by famous dog trainer and author, Barbara Woodhouse, who believed there was no such thing as a bad dog, only an inexperienced owner.

Viv imaged Benjy arriving at her door every day at the same time with a big smile and a leash in hand. And then her mind fixated on the leash and went to a very strange and possibly kinky place that made her face feel as hot as a furnace.

He caught her expression and chuckled. "I'm not here for an intervention—it looked like you were intervening with yourself plenty in the doorway when I got here. What was that all about?"

Was she was starved for human interaction? Maybe it was because he was so easy to talk to. She'd known him for so long and trusted him with some of her deepest, darkest secrets. Whatever it was that set her at ease, she began to tell him about her struggle to get out the door. She even opened her suitcase and introduced him to Olivia, the persona she had created to help trick herself into going on her road trip. She showed him the bright orange wig, the makeup, the crazy clothes and tight leggings.

When she finished speaking, he sat with a perplexed expression. His brow creased and she started to squirm under the weight of the silence. She wondered if he was judging her and if he would come to the conclusion that she was totally crazy. When he sat up and thunked his empty lemonade glass on the coffee table, she was full of dread at what he might say.

He thinks I'm nuts and he's going to try to get out of here as fast as possible.

"I think I know what's wrong," he said, not allaying her fears in the least. Then he said, "Hear me out for a minute. The reason why you want to be Olivia is because you don't want to be yourself at the moment for whatever reason." She started to interrupt, but he put up a finger, so she held her tongue. "I'm just putting forth a theory. You feel like there's something wrong with you, and even though I don't accept that, it's none of my business. You have to work that out with yourself in your own head, but here's the thing that might help you right now…"

He put his warm hands on her onesie-clad shoulders and guided her to the door—correction, not to the door but so she stood in front of the mirror by the door.

"You're having trouble getting out the door because you can't leave safety of your apartment *as yourself.* Do you understand what I'm saying? You have *to be Olivia* to leave here without being stopped by fear."

In the mirror, her face scrunched up in confusion.

"Stay with me," he said sternly, meeting her gaze in the reflection. With gentle fingers, he tweaked the limp unicorn horn on the top of her head. "What you need to do is go change your clothes. Put on Olivia's clothes and her…eyelashes or whatever. Put on all of that stuff that turns you into her. You have to *become her* before you go out that door. Normal Unicorn You may not be able to walk out the door, but I'm one hundred percent sure *she can.*"

CHAPTER TWELVE

When the two teens got to Claire's house after school, they made microwave popcorn and sat at the kitchen table.

"Claire, I have an idea," Terrance said, shoving a handful of popcorn in his mouth. He loved the stuff, but his mom refused to buy it. "I think we should start a Help Us website page and collect money to hire a private detective."

Although it was a good idea—no, a *fantastic* idea—Claire's heart did the proverbial sink to the pit of her stomach thing. Even Terrance, her most faithful and gung-ho friend, had realized she wasn't going to be able to accomplish anything on her own. He'd witnessed her screwing around and messing up hugely at the Time & Tidewater and knew that she needed the help of someone who knew what they were doing. Or, at least, an adult.

She was desperate enough to dig her life's savings out of her mirrored Barbie Mermaid jewelry box—cracked but still cute because she bought it from the dollar store when she was six—to eat dinner at the junky tourist trap restaurant that Frank and Linda Kahoe owned across from her Uncle Kip's place. Their restaurant was called It Smells Fishy in Here, which was the *worst* name for a fried seafood shack that Claire could have come up with. Those two had always had a gripe with her uncle, so Claire considered them high on the list of suspects who'd want to do him harm.

"Are you giving up on me?" she asked.

"No! It's the total opposite. I'm *investing* more in you."

He stuck his giant hand in the popcorn bowl and crammed another fistful in his mouth, a surefire sign that he was nervous or excited, or both.

"What do you mean?"

"You know how I made some money this summer? I was going to give it to you."

She was honestly stunned. Terrance had done all kinds of weird jobs between school years, from pet sitting an iguana to dressing as a clown and singing to kids at the local exotic animal park, which incidentally, he had been really amazing at. His clown name was Bim Bam the Bashful, and kids seemed to love him despite his large stature—or maybe because of it. Who knew? Kids were weird, and most of them didn't seem to have any sense of self-preservation.

"You can't do that! That's for your trip to Japan someday."

He shrugged. "This is more important."

She wanted to throw her arms around him and give him a great big hug, if she could even reach all the way around him. However, they weren't *that kind* of friends. It was mostly her fault. She wasn't a natural hugger—her mom wasn't one either—and Claire didn't know how to start hugging people now. Maybe she had missed that boat.

All the same, she didn't want to sit around and do nothing but beg for money on the internet. Setting up a fund was a good idea, but it would take precious time. Meanwhile, her uncle's killer was still out there.

"You're kind of the best," she told him. "In fact, let's talk more about this at dinner. I'm going to take you to get fish and chips."

Screw the microwave popcorn. I might as well get a real supper out of this.

And, yes, she did kind of love her gay best friend, but she was taking them to It Smells Fishy in Here tonight. Her need to spy on the Kahoe family was far greater than her self-control and her ability to be passive about something so important. Yes, she was just an annoying kid, but she knew she was going to be an adult one day and the promises she made to herself now would reverberate through the rest of her life. Everything mattered.

Which is how they ended up stuffing their faces with a basket of hush puppies and fried flounder, staring through a salt-scummed window at the boats on the intracoastal waterway about an hour later.

"Even more delicious than popcorn," Terrance moaned after a large gulp of sweet tea before he dug into his fried flounder sandwich.

You kind of really have to like to eat fish when you live in this town. I wonder what it's like to live elsewhere, maybe in a place where a girl just like me is sick of eating thick juicy steaks and double cheeseburgers.

She was glad she had taken the entire seventy-five dollars of her meager life's savings out of her jewelry box. She was going to need all of it at these prices. Is that how this place did so much better than her uncle's? Huge mark-up on food and—she looked around at all the moms and dads guzzling fruity drinks out of cups with bright red bar cherries and umbrellas in them—alcohol. She knew from listening to her uncle that adult drinks were where all the money was made. She also suspected that was where all the extra funds from her mom's paycheck from the bowling alley went.

"Maybe I should have used one of these dolls for my art project," Terrance said, staring up at the ceiling. "But they kind of look desperate, like they gave up on life and hung themselves. Then it would have turned my piece into an environmental statement about plastic and the ocean, and that's not really capturing the mystique and scrappiness of mermaids, which was more where I wanted to go with it."

Yes, it was totally tacky in here. Surfboards with fake bite marks hanging from the ceiling, the mermaid Barbies with matted hair, and plastic starfish tangled in fishing nets dangling from the rafters, and every inch of the place covered with yellowed and dusty photos of famous boats and people who'd grown up in the area. On top of that, everything was so old, it was covered with sticky fryer grease and clumps of dust.

Why do people keep coming here? What's so great about this place?

Claire took another bite of a seasoned fry. Luckily, any accidental sounds of pleasure that came out of her were drowned out by a shout of laughter from the table next to them.

Okay, that fry was really amazing, but can't they at least clean the place better?

It hurt her deep in her soul that this restaurant did so much better than her uncle's classy, elegant, adult place, and now that he was gone, the Time & Tidewater's parking lot always seemed empty, even during the dinner hours. It wasn't fair.

She swallowed hard and tried to say in as casual a tone as possible, "Anyway, I wonder what Arletta Malone was so upset about when she came out into the alley. Something about paying bills. I wonder if she's in financial trouble with my uncle's restaurant. That would be a shame if she did something shady to get full ownership and then accidentally made it go bankrupt, don't you think? I mean, she doesn't have experience in running the food side, only the business aspect of it. Definitely not a people person like Uncle Kip, you know."

"No idea," Terrance said, scanning the laminated dessert card, which was no doubt sticky like everything else in this place. He wasn't through his meal and he was already assessing their dessert options.

Go big or go home? That's another thing Uncle Kip used to say, which sounds like a sports motto and probably is.

Their server came back, and Terrance ordered something called a Chocolate Volcano. Claire got a brownie hot fudge sundae. She had to admit that the desserts here were more her style. The mango cannoli that her uncle had created was delicious, but nothing beat ice cream with a bunch of hot gooey chocolate all over it.

Sorry, Uncle Kip, she mentally offered up when it arrived and she dug in with gusto, sighing at the total chocolatey, fudgey deliciousness. *Mmm, whipped cream and a cherry, too.*

At a table in the middle of the room, a waiter burst out singing a funny birthday song. Another person brought out gigantic slab of cake with a sparkler embedded in it. The birthday "girl" was someone's grandma who looked about 180 years old—several someones, actually. A whole table of friends and family had brought her. Lots of smiling faces and infectious laughter seemed to spread joy to the tables nearby. It struck Claire that this was the kind of place where people brought their families to celebrate. Was this the element that was missing from her uncle's restaurant?

While she had been gazing with unabashed envy at the birthday party, Terrance had paid their bill looking like a gosh darn, full-blown grown up as he slid his debit card out of his wallet. Claire didn't even have a bank account.

"What are you doing?" she protested. "I want to pay it."

"Seriously. Did you see how much I ordered?"

"At least let me chip in for my half." She was totally mortified. This extravagant meal had been her idea and now he was forking over the cash for it. "Don't make me wrestle you for it. You're much bigger than me and you'll beat me. Then, I'll have to cry in public and we'll both be humiliated."

She shoved some money across the table at him and told him she needed to use the restroom. She left him playing a game on his phone, so she knew he would be fine for a bit if she took her time. The truth was, she didn't need to pee at the moment, but she did want to see if she could find one of the owners.

At any given time, Frank or Linda Kahoe was likely to be in the kitchen or in the back office, which they kept open, even during meal hours. More than once, Claire had heard her uncle bitch about how unprofessional he thought this was. He always said, "Cooks should be left alone to cook, and the business office door should be kept closed because people didn't need to see the clutter." He kept a neat desk and strict imaginary boxes around the different parts of his business, but now, it was working out in Claire's favor since she was trying to spy on his rivals.

As luck would have it, the restrooms were right down the hall from the business office, exactly as she remembered. She cruised right past the two doors that had a sailor and a mermaid on them, a dumb and cutesy way of calling out genders that was exclusionary and totally North Carolina, and stopped directly outside the open door of the office, which was unoccupied.

Before she could let her nerves get the best of her, she stepped inside the office.

CHAPTER THIRTEEN

C laire had hung out in her uncle's office a million times. He'd kept it really tidy. Everything had been neatly filed away. The top of his glossy wood desk was always free of clutter and clean, not even dusty. He'd had a framed picture of the three of them on the table by the window, and a few sparkling reviews of the Time & Tidewater that he had been extremely proud of hung framed on the walls. His office had been more like a study or a library.

In contrast, this office seemed like a teachers' break room, messy and slightly desperate. Paper cups half-filled with cold coffee—some of them with lipstick stains—littered the desktop and even the windowsill. Papers, some of which looked like invoices, magazines, envelopes, and used napkins even, were stacked everywhere, including on the floor in the corner of the room and under the desk, as if they had fallen there and no one cared to pick them up. The desk was a metal one, like an old teacher's desk. Chairs has been wedged around it, filling the small office so she could barely walk in.

So much chaos.

She didn't even know where to start looking. No doubt, if someone here was an arsenic poisoner, they wouldn't just toss the receipt for it down on the floor among—she bent down and tilted her head to read what she had found—a cancelled check made out to the Kahoes from Arletta Malone, her uncle's business partner?

What? This can't be right? Why is she giving them money? Isn't she almost broke?

Claire picked up the check and held it closer to her face as if that would help make everything clear. Claire didn't have a checkbook, but she certainly understood how checks worked. The name of the person paying was at the top: Arletta Malone, followed by the restaurant name, street address, and phone number. The name of the person receiving the money was on the line: Frank or Linda Kahoe. In this case, their names had been typed out and printed by a computer. The signature at the bottom was Arletta Malone's in tiny, pinched lettering. Thank goodness it wasn't cursive, which Claire couldn't read because they didn't teach the slanted sloping handwriting style in schools anymore. The amount was also typed out both in words and numbers: $35,000.00.

Whoa.

This was more money than Claire had ever seen in her life, even if it was only a canceled check and not actual paper money. This had to be a significant clue, and she had no idea what to do about it. The only responsible, dependable person she knew was Terrance, and he was just a kid like her, although he might know the right person to give it to.

However, the check in her hand was only one random piece of evidence that might not possibly prove much, she wasn't sure. Maybe she needed more checks, more evidence to prove that something fishy was actually going on, no pun intended. She edged over to the desk between the closely arranged chairs and moved some papers aside, careful not to knock over any of the gross coffee cups. The desk had one of those metal spikes that should have had kitchen orders stuck on it, but this one was empty, all the papers scattered in a mess around it. Yes, Claire could be a horribly sloppy person herself, but this was out of control, even by her standards.

A hand landed on her shoulder and a man said, "Hey. What are you doing? You shouldn't be in here."

In her lifetime, Claire had felt panic at forgetting her key and being locked out of the house when her mom wasn't due home for hours. She'd experienced the anxiety of forgetting to study and not knowing how to figure out a single answer on a math test at school. She knew what the stomach-sinking despair was like to hear that her uncle, the only person in the world who knew how to keep her mom sober, was dead. However, none of that compared to the sharp spike of sheer terror at this moment of being caught red-handed snooping around.

And thanks to her terrible improv skills, she froze up and was unable to wiggle out of this. If she were Terrance, she could smile and charm her way out. Instead, she was just skinny, pale Claire who had suddenly lost her ability to speak. Claire who had absolutely *no business* being in this office. Claire who had only a minute ago jammed a crumpled-up—yes, cancelled but still stolen—check in her pocket.

Frank Kahoe frowned at her. His dark eyebrows scrunched down on his shiny forehead, which was weather-beaten and speckled with sunspots. The seventy-something year old sounded like he was from New York. Maybe he knew a bunch of mob-connected bad guys who would take her out on a boat, toss her to the Great White shark that was known to be in this area, and make her disappear.

Although she had never met Mr. Kahoe, she knew who he was. Her uncle had talked about him frequently and bitterly, saying things like, "Those Kahoes are running a crap establishment and making hundreds of thousands of dollars duping tourists into paying top dollar for the privilege of eating frozen fish. They aren't even from around here. This is their retirement plan, not their lifelong dream like me. Why do they have all the luck? I work my fingers to the bone over here. I put my blood, sweat, and tears into this place and what do I have to show for it? A mountain of debt and empty tables that should have a thirty-minute wait."

Claire squirmed under Frank's stern gaze. "I'm sorry," was all she managed to get out.

"Do I know you?" he asked. "I feel like I should know you. You look so familiar."

Her heart, if possible, raced even harder. She definitely did not want him to recognize her, especially since he had caught her looking around in their private office.

If he did, would he summon the police? Would they call her mother? Would Claire be expelled from school and sent to juvie? Maybe one of those scared straight boarding school programs where the tough girls beat up skinny girls like her until she had to start doing chin ups so she could defend herself?

Behind him, his wife Linda entered the already crowded office. She had a deep tan like her husband and had as thick of a New England accent as his. To be honest, they looked like they would be pretty awesome grandparents...if they weren't currently scowling at her.

"Hey, Linda," he said. "I caught this one digging around on the desk. Probably looking for money."

"Too bad," she said. "We ain't got any."

They laughed uproariously, but Claire couldn't even fake a smile.

*I am sooo dead. I'm deader than dead. I'm so dead, I'm un*dead.

"Should we check her pockets for dust bunnies?" Linda joked.

"Nah, we got enough of those to spare a few."

"Listen, honey," the older woman said, sitting in a chair, which made Claire feel less crowded in the cramped space. "We don't keep anything valuable in here. It's more like a place we hang out and relax. I don't know what you were looking for. Are you in trouble? Maybe she was looking for a phone, Frank. Does she need to make a call? Did you already ask her that?"

"No, not yet." He turned to Claire. "Are you hungry, sweetheart?"

She could have been offended, but she wasn't at all—she knew she was super thin, but it was partly a genetics thing, not just a terrible diet. She could eat like crazy and still looked like a toothpick. Theoretically, that was, if she actually tried to eat like crazy consistently instead of having popcorn for dinner. She was in awe of their concern for her well-being, unless it was all an act.

What if they already called the police and are just stalling and treating me nicely so I won't run away before the cops arrive?

She felt herself get a little sweaty with nerves all over again.

"I'm really sorry." She finally found her voice. "I shouldn't have come in here. I know it's private. The door was open, and I was curious, I guess."

And now, to dash out of here like Roadrunner being chased by Coyote and never, ever set foot in this place again. Which was sad because she had kind of loved her dinner.

"Not so fast," Frank said. "We only want to know what you need. Are you looking for someone?"

He blocked the door with his wiry grandpa body, which didn't seem all that hefty except for a well-developed beer belly. She might be able to run by him, but maybe not. He looked like he spent weekends drinking Bud from a cooler out on his boat. Which he was *definitely* going to use to dispose of her body, she felt certain.

What would happen if I screamed my head off right now?

She didn't think she could actually push a scream out of her throat. Barfing from terror was more likely, and maybe even just as effective. She was still considering it when another voice came from the doorway behind the old guy.

"Hey! *There* you are! You walked right by the bathroom door. It's back that way, silly. The one with the mermaid on it? We were waiting for you in the car while you were lost. I know you love this place, but it's time for us to go home!"

She couldn't see the person who said the wonderful words that were magic to her ears. Her savior should have been Terrance. He was the only person who knew she was here and who could have come to her rescue. But it wasn't him—the voice was loud and brassy and that of a woman.

Frank turned around, and in doing so, re-angled his beer belly, which gave Claire a glimpse of the newcomer.

Bright red hair, freckles, makeup worthy of an Instagram tutorial that somehow made fuchsia lip color look amazing, a blue lollipop in one hand, and an empty souvenir piña colada glass in the other—none of this crazy clash of colors helped Claire's confusion. Above hot pink yoga pants and a "cold shoulder" top with the cut-out sleeves in eye-searing tropical colors, bright green eyes met hers. One eye winked fleetingly, leaving her to wonder if she had imagined it.

"Uh, sorry!" Claire finally found her voice and had the wherewithal to say something.

She scooted past Frank and his large midsection as fast as her wobbly legs could carry her and joined the strange woman, who put her bright blue piece of candy back into her mouth. With her now-free, well-mani-cured hand, she clasped Claire, who went willingly, in a close hug. The woman smelled like cotton candy and some flowers. Claire wanted to guess lilies. She was warm, as if she had just power-walked a mile.

The woman moved her sucker into one cheek and said to the Kahoes in a cheery voice, "Thank you for finding her!" She didn't allow them time to respond before she gave them a wave and guided Claire out of the office. The woman escorted her through the crowded dining room of noisy celebrants and crying kids, all the way out of the restaurant and into the parking lot where Terrance waited. Claire breathed a sigh of relief when she saw him, and the fresh evening air touched her over-heated face.

"Oh my gawd! I almost got caught! I feel like vomiting." She looked at the woman who had saved her. "Who are you? Thank you so much."

She could see the white teeth of Terrance's broad smile even though the sunlight had faded and the parking lot lights had yet to come on.

"Claire, this is Olivia," he said, and gestured to her rescuer. He confused her further by handing her the money she had left on the table to help pay for dinner. She accepted it before she could figure out that she should object to him spending his money, but she had to know what was going on. She'd been trapped in the enemies' evil lair. How had she escaped utter and certain doom?

"Sorry, who are you?"

Claire had not recognized the woman, and knowing her name now wasn't helping either. The woman stuck her hand out. Numerous plastic bracelets clacked on her wrist. Claire had to quickly shove the money back into her pocket so she could shake the woman's hand while she tried to figure out what was going on. She still didn't know how she had escaped being taken to juvie or wherever they took bad kids who snooped in places they shouldn't.

"You can call me Olivia. *Or Viv*, if you want."

PART II
NOTHING IS FACE VALUE

"Don't believe everything you read on the interwebs." —Abraham Lincoln

CHAPTER FOURTEEN

After arriving in South Pier, Viv didn't have any trouble finding Claire.

Thanks to the girl's wide-open social media accounts, particularly the one on which she liked to perform endearingly awkward dances, it had been easy-peasy to figure out who her bestie was. Many of the videos had featured Terrance prominently, and he was hands-down better than Claire with the complicated moves. From an objective outsider's point of view, the boy had a true Elvis-like swivel to his hips. The best Viv herself could ever manage on a dance floor was the Single Girl Shuffle, a stiff side-to-side tap step while she held an adult beverage...also aided by said drink.

Leapfrogging from Claire's account, Viv had been able to trace Terrance to his, where she had discovered his name and general location. He'd looked like he might be older than a high schooler, thanks to his size, but some of his photos had been taken within the halls of their school, even in some of the same classes as her. His last name was simple to find after that—Master Terrance Bonaventure had quite a long resumé of local theatre plays and musicals in which he had acted. His theatrical experience explained his impressive dance skills.

Armed with his name, birthday, and street address from a local directory, she had used a friend's credentials to delve into some security-clearance-only servers to track the latest transactions on his bank card, which is how she had found the two of them. But seriously, though, this crazy seafood restaurant with the mermaid dolls hanging from the ceiling was like a creepy beach-bum and voodoo nightmare mashup.

As tall as Terrance was, he was a snap for Viv to pick out in a crowd, but Claire wasn't with him. However, it had been the work of a couple minutes for Viv to introduce herself to him, help him get over his initial shock, and then locate the little mermaid's room where the girl had told him she needed to visit.

The grimy, multi-stall restroom, which was long past needing an overhaul and deep clean, was empty other than a sole woman changing her toddler's diaper on a drop-down plastic counter.

Incidentally, the first baby changing station was invented in the mid-1980s by a bunch of Minnesota businessmen, which later morphed into the Koala Corporation. Now the fold-out counters are ubiquitous in airports and restaurants, including both men's and women's restrooms.

Personally, Viv would not have trusted this particularly ancient-looking ledge with her oldest handbag, but the woman probably didn't have another option, based on the odor and the apologetic grimace she shot Viv. Otherwise, the garishly painted room with the rip-off hand-painted Disney mural—*yeah, there is something wrong with Ariel's eyes...they are going in different directions*—was empty and absent a certain knock-kneed teen. On determining Claire wasn't there, she had backed out quickly but then found the girl in the office down the hall.

Voila. Target acquired.

It seemed that the girl had also gotten herself into a bit of a mess. The Kahoe couple had surrounded the kid in their business office like two gray-haired lions closing in on a baby wildebeest on the Serengeti. Viv had done some cursory research about them the night before when she had begun to read about Kip Baldwin. They were two people who might have wanted him to meet with an untimely demise, and right now they didn't look as if they were going to let Claire go anytime soon.

To be fair, Viv didn't know if they intended to grill Claire about why she was there or whether they wanted to smother her with affection. Their peculiar and aggressive brand of grandparental attention seemed to be the type where overly elbow-greased face-washing might actually knock out a child's loose tooth. Six of one, half dozen of the other—the end result was pretty much the same: a girl who was caught red-handed and scared stiff.

Hansel and Gretel, the rather frightening children's story, is ostensibly about two kids who wander into the woods and discover a gingerbread house covered with sweets. Underneath, however, it's a cautionary tale about stranger danger and how kids should listen to their parents. Or you could be eaten up by a cannibalistic old lady who is definitely not your grandma.

Viv—or actually, *Olivia*—had hustled right in and extracted Claire out of the increasingly uncomfortable situation. Standing in the parking lot after her hasty exodus, the kid's euphoria at having escaped the clutches of Ma and Paw Fish-wich was evident on her flushed face as she thanked Viv.

Viv brushed it off with a casual "No problem."

And busting into on the Kahoes' office truly hadn't been much of a struggle *because she was dressed as Olivia.* Sure, she had felt quakes of nerves, but nothing to the extent that had kept her at home, fearful to go out.

"Also, I should give you this. I took it and now I don't know how to give it back." The girl handed Viv a crumpled-up piece of paper, which turned out to be a check for a shockingly large amount for a teen to be carrying around. Because it was a cancelled transaction that had already been deposited, Viv wasn't too concerned about taking it back inside and causing further problems with the Kahoes. The names and amount, however, were very intriguing, so she put it in her bag to look into more later.

As far as Viv was concerned, the girl's elation at having escaped was one hundred percent *not* a good thing. It was exactly the opposite. The adrenaline rush could encourage her to do something risky again in the future, and that was the *last* thing Viv wanted.

Aaaaaagggghhh.

However, as much as she had disliked her own childhood and teen years, she remembered enough about herself to realize that commanding Claire to stay home and do nothing would stand up about as well as hairspray in humidity.

In the short time Viv had known the girl, her lack of self-preservation was worthy of concern, including posting the details of her uncle's murder on the internet—Viv was well-aware of the irony. But if she had busted into McFishville back there, barking orders, she might as well have given up and gone home.

McDonald's introduced the Filet-o-Fish sandwich in the early 1960s to tempt Roman Catholic patrons who didn't eat meat on Fridays.

"Here's what I need you to do," Viv told her. She glanced at the boy, implicitly demanding his cooperation. "You see, I have access to a lot of tools that you don't—" She saw Claire was about to interrupt, maybe to quiz her on what she knew, but Viv went ahead. "But you have much better inside information that I'm not privy to. For example, are you still able to get into your uncle's house?"

Viv already knew that he lived in a townhouse about ten minutes inland and south of the restaurant in a nearby town, in the upscale Windfall area, and as of two days ago before she had gotten into her car to drive south, the home had not been listed for sale.

"I have a key," Claire said, and then confirmed Viv's theory. "My mom wants to move into his place, but she's not sure if she can afford the payment. It's so much better than the apartment where we live right now, but it would also mean that I'd have to change schools." She glanced at her friend, whose eyebrows shot up in surprise and concern.

"No way!" he said. "You never mentioned you might move."

"I didn't want to bring it up. It's not going to happen," she said. "The monthly amount just to live there is really high. The mortgage payment or whatever, plus the neighborhood fees. My mom needs to face the fact that the only way she'll get some money is if she sells it. I mean, it's in a really good area." Claire's thin face scrunched up with longing for a second before she told Viv, "I can definitely get you in there if you want to see it. Not only do I have a key, I know the passcode for the front gate."

"Whoa. It's one of *those* places," Terrance said.

"Right on a golf course. My mom doesn't even golf. I'm guessing she had rather meet someone who lives there, if you know what I mean. Not to slam my mom or anything, but…"

"No worries," Viv said. "People do what they have to do to survive. I'm not here to judge anyone." Not yet, at least. She hadn't even met Claire's mom. Viv would save her opinions until after she talked to the woman.

In a previous incarnation, Viv had dated plenty of guys who had money and so-called social status, so she was not one to pass a sentence on another woman. Pretty gifts and a ticket to social events had gone a long way in covering up a significant moral or emotional deficiency. But even Viv had her limit.

"What time do you get out of school tomorrow?" Viv asked them. "Maybe I can pick you up and you can show me the place. Just make sure you tell your parents where you're going. I don't want to get anyone in trouble. You can tell them…"

Viv's mind stuttered to a halt as she searched for an acceptable reason why she might shuttle two underaged kids around after school. Unbidden, Hansel and Gretel popped into her mind again.

"You got a dollar?" she asked Claire.

"I have seventy-five," the girl said, digging a wad of bills out of her pocket. "I was going to buy dinner before Mr. Big Spender here paid for it —thanks, by the way. I forgot to say that earlier before I almost got caught and thrown into the Big House for trespassing in their office."

"Don't do that again, by the way," he told her. "I don't have enough money on my debit card to bail you out."

"I only need one dollar," Viv said, and when Claire peeled one off the stack and handed it to her, she said, "Okay, you've hired me. We've entered a verbal contract, and I've accepted payment in full. I'm your private investigator."

Many famous people have refused a salary and worked for only a token dollar, all the way back to the Teddy Roosevelt days, and even earlier. They're actually called "dollar-a-year-men," which is a tad sexist, but women weren't often paid for anything back then. One of the most recent people to refuse a salary was Arnold Schwarzenegger when he served as the Governor of California.

Viv, in fact, had an unused private investigator's sales tax license from the state of South Dakota where her parents owned a cabin. South Dakota didn't require any further licensing to be a private investigator. Viv wasn't sure if it would carry any weight in North Carolina—*probably not, but hey, might as well make a minimal effort to be legal in case I get into trouble.*

And to further emphasize that she wasn't a bad guy, she told them, "Before I come and get you after school, make sure you don't have any homework. Or if you do, get it all done before it's time to go. I will not be a party to the downfall of today's youth."

Claire rolled her eyes, but the bright red flush on her fair cheeks seemed to indicate her gratefulness. Maybe she wasn't used to an adult having her back—that thought made Viv a tad uneasy. She was hardly the type of person to set a good example for a wayward kid.

"Count me in, too," Terrance said. "Your uncle was a cool guy and all, but I bet he had some things he wasn't telling you. What if he has a box of money in a secret safe behind a painting? I wouldn't be shocked if he did, and I want to see it when you find it—no offense."

Claire shrugged. "I'm not offended. We have a half-day tomorrow. We're done at noon. Meet you outside the front?"

"I'll be there," Viv said.

CHAPTER FIFTEEN

Viv spent the rest of the night decompressing from having "peopled" more in the last day than in the past entire month, and settling herself into her parents' place down the road south a bit. The house was a two-stories perched on top of its own garage, which was typical of the area, just one short block away from the vast salty waves of the Atlantic. The exterior siding was a lovely pale green that contributed to making the strip of houses on this street resemble a row of pastel-colored Easter eggs all neatly nestled in a carton. Her mother had redone the interior of the house in pale blues and yellows, and its five bedrooms and three baths were perfect for vacationing families who wanted to wake up in the morning, toss open the balcony doors, and drink their coffee with the ocean breeze on their faces.

"Kind of excessive to have a three-quarter-million-dollar place as your third home," Viv had said to her mother.

"Don't be ridiculous, darling. In this market, it's not even over seven hundred thousand," she had been told in response.

No small potatoes for a house with a nine-out-of-ten flood risk. Viv suspected it would be pulled into the ocean by a hurricane any year now. It was only a matter of time before some Caribbean-fueled storm with a mundane-sounding moniker wreaked havoc on this small but pretty strip of coast that people flocked to from January to September.

But now that it was the off-season, the neighborhood was quite peaceful without any touristy foot traffic or kids shouting. Viv still shut all the doors and drew the cottage-chic drapes as tightly closed as she could. She pulled off the red wig of the Olivia persona, took a warm shower to wash off the thick layer of makeup, and crawled into a fresh onesie, of which she had brought a few.

Despite the gorgeous view and proximity to the beach, Viv's parents had not scrimped on the internet connection, thank her unseen electronic overlords. On the rare occasion that her *pater familias* was able to visit the beach, he always brought consulting work with him, and that required a secure and stable connection to his spy servers or whatever it was that he did. After all these years, he still refused to tell either Viv or her mother. For that matter, her mother brushed off her own work as being secondary and clerical in nature, but Viv was suspicious of her downplaying it.

Good internet was also a hit with the vacationers with teenagers who brought their gaming systems with them. At the moment, as Viv booted up her collection of laptops and extended screens, she was feeling pretty appreciative of it as well. In the darkened room sitting in her onesie, she felt like she was safe and in familiar territory. Just as she had hoped, she felt like she was in a home away from home.

Except...what is that smell? She sniffed at the woven seagrass basket of shells and potpourri that sat on the dining table beside her. It smelled like lemons, mint, and...briny like dried seaweed. *Ew. Well, almost like home.*

Viv had started researching Kip Baldwin earlier, and now that she had a minute to herself, she began revisiting some of the bookmarks she had saved. The first article she opened was from a local news website in South Pier:

The body of Willard "Kip" Baldwin, 41, was found deceased in the alley next to his restaurant, the Time & Tidewater Bar and Grill, an up-and-coming spot for elegant dining and classy beverages. The charismatic businessman was discovered by his sister, Evelyn, on Saturday morning after he failed to show up for a family dinner the night before.

The cause of death has not yet been released by the Medical Examiner's Office, but an autopsy is being performed. A witness who was interviewed after the body was found stated that Baldwin was "in real bad shape and looked like he had been upchucking from food poisoning. He also had some froth around his mouth." Foul play has not been ruled out at this time.

Friends of the restauranteur say that the bar, which was his second foray into the South Pier eatery scene, was his pride and joy. His first restaurant was in the location of the current popular family eatery, It Smells Fishy in Here. The previous restaurant was a fish and chips stand that he named Thank Cod It's Friday. Baldwin sold this restaurant when he and his now-ex-wife moved briefly to Asheville.

At the time of his death, Baldwin was single and had no children from the earlier short and failed marriage.

Viv grimaced. *Oof. That's a little bit graphic, and also, judgey much about that divorce? Methinks someone at the newspaper knew him.*

She made a note of the byline of the article, "contributed by Sandy Sommers," and planned to do a little research on her...or him, she amended, since the name "Sandy" could be a nickname. No point in jumping to conclusions, other than the fact that the author sniped at the dead man for his failed marriage.

Viv found it interesting that Kip's first restaurant's location had done really well after the Kahoe family had taken it over. That had to have frustrated him when he returned to South Pier, opened the Time & Tidewater Grill, and struggled so badly. Only a saint wouldn't have hard feelings. He could literally see his old location from his new bar's parking lot, and on busy nights when the cars streamed out of his rival's place, she imagined he was probably ready to tear his hair out.

Location, location, location, after all...

Another noteworthy point was the eyewitness who'd described Kip's condition after Evelyn had discovered his body. It sounded like the person had gotten an eyeful of his not-too-pretty state. Viv wondered just how much else they had seen.

Viv had so much to start with from that one bit of local gossip that passed for news in this small town.

"Fire up the Google machine, Jeeves," she said aloud, clicking open her browser.

The first thing she searched for was Thank Cod It's Friday, Kip's original restaurant. She wasn't sure what information she would find since the place had not operated under that name in many years, at least a decade, but two articles popped up.

The first was a critique of the food, only one paragraph out of a longer article about cheap local eats. The reviewer had given it four stars out of five, with high marks for the friendliness of the staff and the price. The food itself hadn't excited the writer beyond a middling "decent, hot, and fresh, not frozen." Around these seaside parts, that wasn't exactly a glowing recommendation.

The second write-up was to announce the sale of the place to the Kahoe family, who had moved down the coast all the way from Atlantic City, New Jersey. In the article, the Kahoes stated that they had both been card dealers at a casino, but now they wanted a calmer lifestyle in their retirement days. Viv wasn't sure how much easier running a busy seafood restaurant in a tourist town could be, but at least the weather wasn't going to dump ice and snow on them. Just a hurricane now and then.

When they had relocated, the Kahoes had brought two adult children, Christopher and Jessica, and their families with them, which included a few grandkids. *Interesting.* They'd transplanted their entire clan. Either they were a very close-knit family, or they had had a specific reason to leave New Jersey. Like, of the waste management monopoly, casinos, and organized crime type of reason.

Thanks, Hollywood. Like I didn't have enough dumb biases of my own without your help.

She made a mental sticky note to look into the news reporter later and prepared herself to begin digging into the Kahoes' background. They were setting off some alarm bells in her mind and she needed to figure out if her gut was right or if she was pinning suspicions on an innocent family.

After all, I am a woman who spent the last few months in a unicorn onesie. Am I the right person to be making these kinds of judgement calls?

CHAPTER SIXTEEN

F rank and Linda Kahoe, according to New Jersey property records, had lived in a $120,000 house. In some areas of the country, that amount of money could buy a decent living arrangement. However, in urban New Jersey, it meant a rundown three bedrooms, one bathroom, and a chain link fence around the front yard.

Current satellite street-level photos showed the house was up for sale again although the most recent owner had done nothing to increase its curb appeal. The single scruffy shrub by the side of the door failed to soften the grimy faded yellow siding. An air conditioning unit hung onto a windowsill by what looked like its last screw. The roof looked newish, but telephone and electrical wires trailed down from nearby poles and snaked across the shingles into the house. Not much you could do about older wiring, Viv knew, but it added to the aged feel of the place.

Pretty much what she had expected from a depressed area of a city that had last thrived in about 1930. Anxiety spiked through Viv just looking at the photos, not only from its run-down state but from its obvious lack of love. She couldn't imagine trying to raise two kids or spending supposedly golden years in a decrepit home in a gray and cold city.

Christopher and Jessica were two of the most popular children's names in the mid-1980s.

Viv had an itch in the center of her back, but she ignored it. Instead, she dug a little deeper into New Jersey public records around the time the Kahoe kids had been growing up. She didn't find much on either of them until later. No news articles during their school days and nothing after their births. Either they had been good if unremarkable kids or they had stayed under the radar.

Christopher had a drug possession charge for oxycontin back in 2004. The record said as a first-time offender, he had been offered the alternative sentence of a drug treatment program, after successful completion of which the charges would be dropped. However, he had failed to show up for all of the sessions, which must have pissed off the judge, because he had subsequently been sentenced to a small fine, a couple weeks in jail, and sixty hours of community service.

On the other hand, a current charge in that state of Simple Possession of unauthorized prescription drugs was a third-degree indictable offense, which meant up to five years in prison and big fines. So, maybe he had gotten off easy. Viv wasn't entirely sure. All she knew was, according to North Carolina public record, it seemed like he had been able to stay clean since they had arrived in South Pier.

A blog post on "40 Under 40" eligible bachelors from a few years ago had featured him. Viv zoomed into the photo that accompanied the article. *Not too bad looking.* Dark hair, dark eyes, and a deep tan like both of his parents had. He had a wide smile with very straight, white teeth that didn't even hint at his delinquent past. Then again, good dental work wasn't an assurance that he wasn't a psychopath.

Some sources have said that one of Ted Bundy's friends whom he met when he was a Republican activist, once said, "He was the kind of guy you'd want your sister to marry."

The article that mentioned Christopher Kahoe also stated that he was the general manager at It Smells Fishy in Here. Maybe it was worth putting on the red wig tomorrow morning to go speak with him. In public. With a lot of witnesses. Viv took a big breath as her pulse spiked again with anxiety. The itch in the back of her onesie was still bothering her. She gave it a short scratch and shook her head.

Olivia can do it. She's brassy. Not much intimidates her.

Viv switched gears because Christopher had clearly unnerved her. Instead, she dug around for information about the Kahoes' daughter, Jessica. No articles or blogs came up, but the woman's social media page painted Viv a pretty clear picture of who Jessica wanted the world to think she was: a put-together involved mom with a politically conservative, Christian world view. Her posts were full of memes about nutrition-ally balanced lunches for her kids, reminders about PTA meetings—she seemed to be an incumbent officer in that association—inspirational sayings about her savior in flowing cursive, and recipes for gingerbread cookies even though Christmas was still a few months away.

Whew. Viv was exhausted just reading through her posts. It was like doomscrolling through bad news posts, except all about being a Stepford wife. The more Viv read, the worse she felt until she was nearly as creeped out about Jessica as her brother.

Probably, they are both completely normal people and I am overreacting in my usual socially anxious way when confronted with people in general. I am not good with peopling at this moment, but my phobia is not me. Just like the meme says...oh no, what if I have developed a phobia of becoming a meme?

The itch in her back brought Viv's focus out of her head. She pulled the seam of her onesie away from her neck and discovered the end of a plastic sales tag had been scratching her neck. While she removed the tiny irritating tag, she blinked at the circuitous nature of her own ridiculous thoughts. The bottom line of her evening's research was that the Kahoe offspring were worth checking out. Hopefully, she would get the oppor-tunity to observe them in person.

Her stomach growled, which made her wonder what the house main-tenance service had stocked in the kitchen. To be honest, she felt a little too warm in her onesie, too. It was one thing to swaddle yourself entirely in terrycloth this time of year in Boston, but late September in coastal North Carolina was still pretty darned balmy. She wrestled with herself for minute and then pulled back the curtains to open the balcony doors.

Ahhhh. Instant cool ocean breeze.

The curtains billowed, which hit some of her anxiety bells, but she tied the flowing fabric back and instantly felt better. This seemed like a decent compromise—cooler air, even though it was from outside, but she was able to keep her onesie on.

Is this a baby step toward recovering my former self or just another coping mechanism?

She wasn't sure, but her counselor told her to try not to overthink everything, and she felt like this was probably of those times.

Now that she wasn't about to erupt into sweaty flames, she retreated into the kitchen to forage for snacks. She'd skipped dinner in favor of catching up with the kids at It Smells Fishy in Here, but she didn't have high hopes of finding an actual meal. Usually, buried beneath the painted nautical decor, a visitor would find cups of instant noodles, a few cans of mixed nuts, and some juice for kids. However, Mr. Horowitz must have alerted the service that she was the one who was visiting this time.

In the cupboard next to the stove, she found Cap'n Crunch cereal (the original flavor, not anything fancy with berries or peanut butter), two large bags of trail mix with M&M candies, three large pouches of teriyaki beef jerky (which must have cost a fortune because that stuff was more expensive than gold bullion), and some pistachios in the shell. In other words, he had had the place stocked with all of her favorite snack foods from when she was a kid...and who was she kidding? Also still favorites now.

Yes, he was paid well to do his job and to hire underlings who also did their jobs well, but it still caught Viv right in the feels that someone had cared enough about her to make the effort. Salary or not, and even if he only remembered her favorite things because he had read notes from a file. Her parents couldn't have guessed what kind of junk food she liked.

A burst of laughter came through the window from the street below. Viv peered through the curtains at two women who passing on the street. They were chatting and giggling over some shared joke. They moved within fifty feet of where Viv stood, and she had the sudden realization that she could easily be them, moving freely down an empty street, even in the dark of night. The moon hung bright in the sky, and the sound of the ocean reached her even where she stood hiding behind the curtains that her mom had hung.

She thought, *I can go out, too.*

CHAPTER SEVENTEEN

V iv got dressed up in brightly colored Olivia armor again, although she didn't spend as much time in front of the mirror applying makeup because it was dark outside, but mostly because she was lazy. This time, she didn't stand at the doorway as she had at home but plowed right through it before she could think about it.

Don't overthink. Don't overthink it.

Her plan had been to drive thirty minutes back up the coast to the restaurants in South Pier, but when she got into her car and realized by the dashboard clock that it was already past ten, the wind got sucked out of her sails and she lost her motivation. Not entirely, but enough to make her hesitate for a second. She shook her head and attempted to block the anxiety out of her mind.

She slid her tropical-pattern-clad backside out of her car and peered from her parents' house up the darkened street from where the two giggling ladies had come. The faint thump of drums caught her attention, not for its loudness, but the fact that it wasn't the boom of bass or anything electronic. The music beckoned her and her feet tripped along the pavement until a neon sign came into view.

Sassy Ann's Redux was part steampunk musical hall, part crazy cat lady house—she had seen at least two felines, a tabby and a calico, outside on the porch—and one hundred percent hopping for a Thursday night. Viv wasn't sure how the cozy pale yellow Victorian home with dark green trim could be an original structure after all the hurricanes that had rolled through here over the years, but maybe the building had a magic spell over it. It looked a little witchy, to be honest.

Hurricane season for the Atlantic Ocean generally runs from June to November every year. Globally, May has the fewest hurricanes while September has the most. One of the worst hurricanes to hit this area was Hurricane Hazel in 1954, which had a storm surge of up to 18 feet in some places.

She pushed her way through the double front doors and blinked her eyes as she adjusted to the chaos. The winter holidays had come early, or maybe they had never left, because strings of multicolored lights swooped down from the exposed wood beams among tacked up street signs and wooden saloon placards. The tattooed bartender wore a peach-colored, spaghetti-strapped tank top over light-brown skin that looked velvety smooth. Her hair was pulled back on her half-shaved head so the multiple piercings on her ears, nose, and brows glinted like ornaments on a punk rock Christmas tree.

A band, the members of which couldn't have been alive very far back into the previous century, played a bluesy rockabilly song with a seasoned if not fittingly jaded stage presence. Viv brushed back an errant bright orange strand of her Olivia wig and sat at the bar.

"What's your poison?" the bartender asked and pointed to the chalkboard on the wall behind her. "Full array in bottles and plenty on tap. Or if you're feeling fancy, we have a Sassy Sloe Gin Fizz tonight."

Regular gin is usually made from juniper berries. Sloe gin has added sugar and sloe berries, which gives it a red tint.

"Can I get an Angry Orchard? And a menu if the kitchen is still open?"

"Sure." She slid a single-sided menu across the bar toward Viv, who glanced at it and then ordered some hot wings.

"You're going to have funky-ass dreams eating those spicy things so late, but you won't regret it. They're slap-your-mama delicious. Coming right up."

The woman grinned in conspiratorial encouragement. She left to put in the order and came back with an opened bottle. They had some minor chitchat during which Viv's anxiety relaxed its hold on her and she admitted to being an off-season visitor.

"So what brings you down here from Boston?" the bartender, whose name was Annabelle, asked, leaning a mocha-colored arm on the scarred but shiny wood of the bar top—it was a well-used surface but must have been resealed again and again over the years.

Annabelle is the name of a 2014 horror movie about a possessed doll who terrorizes a family. Despite pretty terrible reviews, the film went on to have a sequel and even a prequel.

Viv decided to play it utterly straight—maybe because she was at the end of a very long day or because she had already downed half her beer on an empty stomach. "You know that restaurant owner in South Pier who was killed a couple months ago? As a favor to one of his family members, I'm poking around to see what I can find out about his death."

Annabelle's eyebrows shot up, and the silver hoop in her right one jiggled. "No kidding? You mean Kip Baldwin, right? Billie Kennedy used to date him."

At Viv's blank expression, the bartender clarified, "Sorry. I know you're not from around here. Billie is the singer of the band up on stage right now. She went out with him for a few months. You should hang around until their set is done. They take a break in about a half hour."

With rollicking, up-tempo tunes to entertain her and spicy wings that were hot enough to make her forehead sweat, the time passed quickly for Viv. Before long, she sat at a table sipping from a fresh bottle with the band's pinup-styled singer, whose wig styling was even better than Viv's. Billie's hairdo was a swept-up jet black pompadour that reminded Viv of Veronica from the *Archie's* comics.

"Just a club soda for me," Billie said, peering into a vintage silver compact to fix her deep red lipstick after Viv offered to buy her a drink. When it arrived, she extracted a bamboo straw from her handbag and plunked it into her glass. "Save the sea turtles," she said by way of a toast before she took a long drink.

A man named Leo Baekeland invented the first plastic, Bakelite, in 1907. It was an entirely manmade substance. None of its molecules occur naturally in the world. It's ironic that plastic pollution has reached some of the most remote places in nature now.

After Billie swallowed, she said, "I hear you want to know what dating Kip Baldwin was like. We dated for a couple months about two years ago."

Viv had a sudden moment of panic—well, a different type than her normal kind.

"I'm sorry to have to ask, but…do you know he passed away?"

Billie waved a manicured hand in front of her face. Her nails matched her lipstick more perfectly than a Revlon ad. "Yeah, I know about that. It was all over the news for weeks when it happened. More details than I wanted to know, to be honest. They went on and on about the upchuck and the blood. Not exactly how you want to remember someone you were hoping might be The One—you know, your happily-ever-after guy?"

"Oh, wow. Sounds like the two of you were serious."

Billie snorted. "You know how it is. I can tell by the way you put yourself together, we're alike, you and me. We like to make an effort. We want the fairy tale that we've been fed since we were little girls. The unreasonable beauty expectations are supposed to pay off when you put the work into looking good and acting correctly."

Viv wanted to protest, but that was her whole Princess Grace, Holly Golightly phase in a nutshell. She knew firsthand how playing a role might get you stuck in that same claustrophobic niche for the rest of your life. Instead, she nodded in sympathy at Billie.

"So, yes, I was serious about him, but that's how I approach every date with a guy. I'm always evaluating them and hoping they might be the one to put an end to all the dating and hunting, the blind dates and the one-and-dones. I mean, I'm twenty-eight, and frankly, I've done a lot of searching, if you know what I mean. I've been around the so-called block and my feet are a little sore."

Viv was also twenty-eight. However, she was nowhere near as mission-oriented as this woman. It was probably pretty obvious to all Viv's friends that she had shut down her social side completely and had no plans to re-enter the dating pool anytime soon.

"Kip fell short of your expectations?" she prompted the woman.

"He was a nice enough guy. Super cheerful, outgoing, and great at a party, which I loved. Always the center of attention with the eyes of the crowd on him. I would have been totally happy with a man like that. He was good looking, too. He had a bit of a beach-bum, dad-bod look to him, you know? Not my usual type, but I would have gone there if the chemistry had been right."

"Interesting. So there was no spark?"

"That's the thing that was so weird. For the first three dates, it was wining and dining. Lots of romance and having fun getting to know each other. I hate to admit it, but yes, I did get hopeful. But then after that, all of a sudden, he didn't seem interested anymore and I couldn't figure out why. Our intimacy level was fine and advancing in the right direction. I was ready to take the next step and—bam!—he turned into this distant and kind of cold automaton. It was truly bizarre. I started doubting myself, questioning what might have gone wrong. I even wondered if he had met someone else or if he was two-timing me, you know? It was that level of disengagement—just a harsh disconnect. He basically ghosted me in an emotional way."

"Do you think it was fear of commitment?"

"I don't think so. He seemed like such family guy material. I saw him with his niece all the time. He was so sweet and caring with her, but not a push-over or anything. I know he was involved in her life since her dad split when she was a baby. I thought he would make a great dad with his own kids. Maybe it was me?" She shrugged and then scowled, her full dark lips bunching up in a pin-up pout. "No! *It wasn't me.* There I go again self-doubting even a year later. It's annoying that one guy can affect me so much."

Don't I know it, sister!

Viv had put all her bets on one guy, too. She'd been engaged and had flown to San Francisco to be with her so-called Happily Ever After person, but James had turned out to be not at all who Viv thought he was. He was partly the reason why she had trouble leaving her apartment.

She shivered and nearly lost her train of thought.

But I'm Olivia now. Be the character. How would she feel? How would she act? She can get through anything, she reminded herself when she felt a shiver of panic at how far away from her safe apartment she had ventured. *All the same, thank the nice lady for speaking with us. It's time for Cinderella to hurry home and crawl back into her unicorn onesie.*

CHAPTER EIGHTEEN

Viv initially chose a bedroom on the floor directly above the garage, but after tossing and turning sleeplessly in bed for several hours, she moved upstairs to the highest bedroom where she opened the balcony door and let the ocean breeze rustle through the room. She finally fell asleep toward morning and dreamt she was in a hotel next to a busy freeway, in her sleep state mistaking the real sound of the ocean right outside for traffic.

The next morning, a shower in the upstairs sand dollar-themed bathroom did very little to refresh her, but for some reason putting on her Olivia costume of the day—a bright pink tank top under a sheer white button-down shirt, another pair of bright leggings, sandals, and a swept-up style for her bright orange wig—made her wide-awake. Maybe it was the adrenaline rush. Her anxiety was still through the roof but at a much more functional level than it had been in the last six months.

Just keep swimming. I'm like Dory from the movie, Finding Nemo, *mashed up with Alex Trebek, the king of trivia games. That's what you get when your absent parents send you memory puzzles and Mensa practice tests your entire childhood.*

Her first plan of action was to track down the reporter for the *South Pier Gazette* who'd written the initial article about Kip's death. After some basic internet digging, Viv discovered that the *Gazette* offices had closed down except for a small business office not too far from Claire's school.

Sandy Sommers, as it turned out, was Alexandra Sommers, aged 53, of 1131 Ocean Avenue, a long-time resident of South Pier who was originally from Winnetka.

Winnetka, Illinois, is where the real house from movie set of Home Alone *is located. In the movie while his entire family takes a trip to Paris, eight-year-old Kevin McCallister is accidentally left home alone over Christmas. Slapstick antics ensue.*

The reporter was easy enough to find, but Viv was racked with indecision about the best way to approach the woman without freaking her out. An email might take days to get a response. However, calling someone on their unlisted number might mean zero response and possibly some cursing.

As Viv paced back and forth in her parents' beach house trying to figure out what to do, she caught a glimpse of herself in the mirror with the intricate shell frame by the front door, right by the hand-written chalkboard sign that proclaimed, "Life's a beach!"

Cute, Mom.

Maybe so, but Viv needed more courage than a goofy vacation motto at the moment. Her reflection, however, reminded her that she wasn't Viv. She wasn't Susan. *She was Olivia*, the gutsy feisty champion of a young girl named Claire who needed an ally on her side.

Viv picked up her phone and called Sandy Sommers.

"Hi, Ms. Sommers. I'm sorry to bother you. I'm a student of journalism. I'm in the area and I'm very interested in the Kip Baldwin case," she began. Technically, none of it was a lie. Would it stand up in a court of law if she were under oath or being charged with fraud? Of course not. None of her shenanigans were probably legal, not even in South Dakota.

Fortunately, Sandy Sommers was a peach, a very chatty peach, and Viv didn't have to spar with her to get her to engage.

Barbara Walters, famous for getting her interviewees to spill their guts, once said, "A conversation isn't a competition."

"Hi, hon. I bet you're one of those UNC-W students they keep sending me. Y'all are absolutely welcome to call me anytime you want, no need to apologize. I'm happy to share any trade secrets I know, which is a lot of knowledge after a quarter-century in this business. The only thing keeping the government from being taken over by politicians and Big Pharma is fair and unbiased media. We gotta create new up-and-coming journalists, and a lot of 'em."

"I really appreciate it!" Viv tried to sound as gung-ho and Olivia-like as possible.

"That's what I like to hear, unbridled enthusiasm! I remember what it was like getting started, and let me tell you, I was the only woman in the office for years. I can't tell you how thrilled I am every time I see another young woman entering the field. Girl power, Pantsuit Nation, and all. You say you're interested in that Kip Baldwin case? Really sad story. I don't know what he could have done to make someone mad enough at him to kill him in such a horrible way. Arsenic, you know. Not a nice way to go. Poor man must have been scared out of his mind at the end. It wasn't a crime of passion like a strangulation or a stabbing, but it was right up there with someone wanting him to suffer. I didn't much like his restaurant—it was too fancy for this area, I always thought—but an overpriced entree is not enough reason to kill someone. The police still haven't solved it, but there are a lot of suspects, just let me tell ya."

"I'm hoping you can tell me about all of them," Viv said.

"Oh, you bet. I could give you an earful. All the stuff that wasn't fit to print, too."

Sandy chatted on and on for close to an hour more. By the time Viv could extract herself from the conversation and hang up, she felt like a whirlwind had swept over her, enough so that she patted her hair to see if her wig was still in place. Also, she had agreed to meet Sandy in a local coffee shop for an in-person second pass of it.

The world's top producer of coffee beans is Brazil, almost double that of Vietnam, which is the second largest producer. Most coffee tastes like dirt to me, but the smell is divine.

"What do you look like, hon? So I sit down with the right person this time," Sandy had said with a chuckle before they hung up. "I was at the wrong person's table more than once, but that's also how I met my husband, so I can't really complain. Don't knock it, till you try it, my mama used to say."

"I have bright orange hair," Viv told her.

"Love it," Sandy said.

When Viv arrived at the Beachin' Beans Café to meet Sandy, she noted with amusement that the older woman's pixie cut was a fiery shade not that far off from her Olivia wig. In a Rite Aid, it would have been about two boxes of dye down from hers, and probably super affordable with a coupon. Viv hoped she had at least forty percent of Sandy's pizzazz in twenty years. Although they were solidly into autumn, Sandy wore a tank top with her jeans, and her brown arms were thin but wiry, probably not from exercise but from constant motion. Her bright blue eyes sparkled out from a deeply tanned, weathered face that looked like she had seen a lot of…stuff over the years, to put it mildly.

"Sit down, hon," Sandy said, smacking the bench seat next to her that had been made from an old wooden surfboard. "Let me fill your ears with some riveting gossip about our most famous local crime."

CHAPTER NINETEEN

"K ip's murder story was picked up by some of the biggest national news outlets. My little article was read far and wide," Sandy said. "It was the 'Little Byline That Could.'"

The Little Engine That Could is a children's book based on an American folk tradition tale whose lesson is that hard work and gumption can power you through some of the most crappy situations.

Viv couldn't fault her for being proud of the fame, which she understood was part of the appeal of being a journalist—not just getting the information out, but a bit of notoriety as well. However, she couldn't help feeling like the people outside of the immediate bubble of South Pier were probably reading it for the gruesome details.

Viv said as she unwrapped a lollipop, "Before you dive in, can you tell me who the witness was in your article? You wrote that someone had seen the body and I don't mean to get too graphic, but they said that Kip had gotten very sick just before he died, which was fairly descriptive. The person must have been at the scene when they discovered him, but you didn't identify who it was."

"Good for you, girl! Don't be afraid to ask the hard questions first. That's what captures your readers' attention, so ask away and don't ever feel shy with me. Poor Kip was a mess. I didn't print the worst of it because he had actually upchucked red stuff, if you know what I mean. All kinds of bodily fluids. He was looking really bad. I don't like to get *too graphic* in the details that we disseminate to the public. We have a lot of elderly readers who are from a more sensitive time and place. None of this live broadcasting real-time crimes on the internet and so forth. However, it is always important for you, as the journalist, to have a clear and full picture of the facts."

It was true that Viv had seen a lot of terrible incidents and actual deaths online in full color and live, from people offing themselves or others both accidentally and on purpose, to teens out hiking and geocaching who found a body. She was, after all, a regular lurker in some of the darkest corners of the web. However, she was fairly sure that previous generations were no strangers to violence and were unquestionably aware of how awful humans could be to each other.

I mean, the Civil Rights Movement wasn't that long ago, and this is North Carolina, after all. There was the Wilmington massacre of 1898 before that where a group of white supremacists overthrew the local government. This place has violence in its very DNA.

"So did this person witness the actual death or only discover the horrible aftermath? Do you think the person would be willing to speak with me?"

Sandy gave a short chuckle. "Oh, they absolutely would, and I know this because *it was me.*"

Viv wasn't sure about the ethics of presenting oneself as an anonymous third-party witness and as a source in their own article.

Self-citation is a well-known practice in scholarly journals. However, if the knowledge is not common and easily acquired, you must cite it as you would any other source, otherwise it may be considered plagiarism...even of yourself.

All the same, it seemed a bit shady to Viv, even for a tiny news site in a small beach town. She wasn't sure if Sandy was the right person to be regularly sharing her insider tips of the trade with newbies fresh out of journalism classes. Then again, maybe students were the perfect people to spy something morally questionable.

Or, *then again times two,* maybe Viv shouldn't be the one to decide these types of things, since she was snooping around under suspicious pretenses.

"Wow. I definitely found the right person to ask then," was all Viv said before Sandy began to spill what she knew.

"I was doing an exposé on local businesses and recycling, which is why I was hanging around the alley outside of the Time & Tidewater. I don't normally hang around dumpsters, and if I wanted to interview dumpster divers, I'd go out back behind the Target store. So, I get to the restaurant and I see what looks like a mannequin on the ground outside the back door. I didn't know what I was thinking, really. What would a dummy be doing in the alley next to a bar? But as I got closer, I realized what it was, and then *who* it was."

Sandy rubbed her forehead as if to wipe the details from her mind. So far, it was her only tell during the entire conversation that she had found the events disturbing. Viv realized she had been anxiously picking at her own cuticles. She clasped her hands together to prevent a bloody mess.

"Did you know he had been poisoned right away?"

"Well, no. I'm not familiar with that sort of thing other than the Tylenol bottle tampering case in the 1980s that got the whole country crazy for all the safety seals on every little thing you buy. Do you know how much extra waste that makes for our landfills? Safety seals, child-proof bottles that you need a damn hammer to open, paper beauty queen sashes on your hotel toilets. The world went nuts."

The Tylenol tampering murders occurred in Chicago in the early 1980s. Seven people were killed, including children. Plus, others were later determined to have been killed by a copycat. Not only did drug companies beef up their safety measures, but they stopped producing medicine capsules that could be taken apart and put back together without detection, like those half-white, half-red water-soluble ovals.

Sandy went on, "The only other poisonings I know about are e.coli in Romaine lettuce and whatever residue they were dumping in the Cape Fear River. Believe me, that's a whole 'nother discussion. So, when I saw Kip, I honestly thought it might be rabies or something. He had some bubbles around his mouth and the other stuff, but I knew he was done from his poor color and not breathing. I didn't touch him though. I called the police right then and backed away. Didn't want to mess up any poten-tial evidence. I've been around long enough to know that at least. Heck, you could learn that from a TV show."

"Okay, so you found Kip dead. Hopefully you didn't have nightmares after that. You learned later that he was poisoned—with arsenic, we learned later—but do you have a theory about who might have killed him? And have the police made any progress on an arrest?"

Arsenic is a metallic chemical element, on the periodic table as As, with an atomic number of 33. As a poison, it doesn't have a smell or taste. It can be white, yellow, or metallic, and it's very deadly to humans. There's no treatment for arsenic poisoning other than to administer fluids and electrolytes. And to pray, if that's your thing.

"Right. So, the tests came back from the lab as arsenic, but they aren't sure where it came from. But that, at least, settled down the public's mind that the food at the restaurant didn't have bacteria, that there wasn't some spoiled oysters or what have you, that could have ruined the whole tourist season. As for who might have killed him, there were plenty who had reason to want him dead."

CHAPTER TWENTY

S andy pulled out a miniature spiral notebook from her shoulder bag and flipped back some of the pages. "Are you ready for this? The first person of interest was his partner, Arletta Malone. I'll talk slow if you want to take your own notes. You sure you can remember all this?"

Viv pulled her phone out of her own shoulder bag and set it on the table. She opened up the dictation app and set it to record. "Ready."

Sandy was impressed but skeptical at the same time. "Those things are really cool, but I don't know if I fully trust them. What if it doesn't actually record? Or worse, what if someone gets ahold of the recording who shouldn't? Like the government." She grimaced at Viv and paused, as if she expected her to put her phone away. Viv merely shrugged, not willing to give in to the unfounded fears of a technophobe, and eventually, Sandy proceeded.

"So anyway, let's talk about Arletta Malone first. She's his business partner. Doesn't know a lick about restauranting—she's a trained CPA, an accountant—but he brought her on as an investor maybe a year ago when he was spiraling into debt and she actually wanted to take a hands-on role in the partnership and learn more about how to run the place. She's 37, married to a groundskeeper fix-it kinda guy, no kids, and not much of a motive for wanting Kip dead. Her finances will go down the toilet with the restaurant when it eventually fails."

"Is the Time & Tidewater that much in trouble?" Viv asked, as she paused to speak between moving her lollipop from one cheek to the other.

"You bet. Circling the drain as we speak—and faster now that she's trying to run it with no experience or know-how whatsoever. It's a shame. She's a smart lady, so she should have been savvy enough to hire experts, restaurant people who know the business. Maybe they didn't have enough funds for that and she's trying to do it all herself. If I were anyone on the staff, from the cook to the carpet cleaner, I'd be putting my resume out there and jumping ship as soon as possible."

"What about the family who owns the Fishy place?" Viv couldn't get the older couple off her mind, especially after she had seen them descend on Claire like overly neighborly vultures. Maybe Sandy could spill the tea about them and their suspicious kids. Viv had a bad feeling about reformed thug Chris Kahoe.

However, Sandy merely shrugged. "They seem like hardworking, decent people for the most part. They give to charity. They sponsor a community softball team. Their place is a family restaurant that people like. I haven't dug up much about them other than their son used to have drug issues, but he's kept his nose clean for a long time now. Can't really hold a bad past against a person these days. We're not the 'I never inhaled' society we used to be."

Viv nodded. Something still felt off about that family, but she had no problem doing some more digging on her own. She had a few contacts in high places who might look into things for her in exchange for past favors.

"Okay, who else then?"

"Kip had an ex-wife named Felicia. She still lives in town. She's a big-name real estate agent with her face all over the billboards. She calls herself and her employees the Extreme Dream Team. No kids there, but that marriage was a bit of a tragedy. They had everything going for them as a couple. They were high school sweethearts who broke up. He went and started that little fish and chips counter with the cute name that was going gangbusters. They rekindled their flame and got married, but she wanted to move to Asheville because it's an artist community there and she was doing jewelry. Big chunky pieces with natural stone. I bought a malachite necklace of hers that I still wear. It's supposed to open my heart and my chakras or some nonsense like that. She talked him into selling his place and giving her jewelry-making a go, but that ended up sinking them. They got a divorce maybe fourteen, fifteen years ago. Rumor was, he had a mistress here in town that he didn't want to leave."

"He cheated on her?"

Sandy shrugged. "Accusations flew. She even took out an ad in the personals to rant at him. She's a feisty woman, that Felicia. No one ever admitted to the adultery, not him nor the alleged other woman, but the gossip alone was enough to break up the marriage. I guess we'll never know the truth about that one. After he came back, he started this new bar on his own, but it never really took off—and the ironic part was Felicia ended up coming back to live here in South Pier, and then her real estate business took off."

"That's quite a story." Viv wasn't sure if Sandy's opinions on it were one hundred percent unbiased. Even her article had had an accusatory tone when mentioning the couple's split.

"Oh, I'm not done yet. Something appeared in the mail to my newspaper inbox just this morning. Not email but actual paper and ink. I can't give you the original—I have to take that to the police—but I made you a copy so I could show you."

The older woman dug in her shoulder bag again and shoved a piece of paper across the table. Viv's eyebrows shot up as she realized it was an anonymous tip. The sender had printed in block letters that clearly disguised their handwriting:

TO WHOM IT MAY CONCERN
I KNOW WHO KILLED KIP BALDWIN.
FIND A MAN CALLED DELROY BENNETT. CHECK THE DNA.

"What DNA?" Viv asked over the top of the piece of paper. "Did someone leave trace evidence behind?" And where had the DNA sample been left, on Kip himself?

"That's what I want to know!" Sandy burst out. "I didn't hear about any DNA from anything. I put a call into the Medical Examiner's office to my source. I'll let you know what she says. I don't personally know who did the autopsy, incidentally. The M.E.'s Office here is a little bit different from other places. It's a network of doctors who perform all the exams for all these little coastal towns that don't have their own M.E. We could get one from Raleigh, Wilmington, or even as far out as Charlotte. I suspect it's a little like being called in for jury duty for these doctors. But if I don't get anything out of my friend over there, I have a connection over at the police department. One way or another, I'll get us some details —you better believe I will!"

Viv wanted to get back to the note. "But do you know who this Delroy Bennett is? I haven't heard him mentioned in your article."

Or anywhere for that matter. He was an entirely new suspect. This was a new piece of information to chase down as soon as she got back from meeting Claire and her friend, which, incidentally, Viv needed to do soon. Her phone battery was probably dying from recording this conversation. She made a show of looking at her watch as a hint to the other woman to speed things up, but Sandy didn't notice.

"I don't have the faintest idea who this fellow is. Of course as soon as I opened the note this morning, I checked the local white pages. Incidentally, do you know how difficult it is to find an actual white pages these days?"

"It's all online," Viv said. "Actually, it's much easier to keep directories up-to-date online. As soon as you print those big books, they get outdated." And much more environmentally conscious, she wanted to add, but it felt a bit like picking a fight that would have no winners.

"If you say so," Sandy snorted. "I still use my trusty book directories. I like to have them right by my desk. So quick and easy to look something up."

Viv didn't know how to answer that. Maybe it was a generational difference, but they would just have to agree to disagree. Silently, and one-sided on Viv's part because she wasn't going to press the point. Instead, she again returned to the note.

"Now, we have a bunch more questions. Who is Delroy Bennett? Where is he and what's his connection to these people? Why would he want to kill Kip, and who wrote this note?" Viv said, ticking off each of the questions by tapping a finger on the tabletop.

She didn't ask Sandy for the copy of the note, but she did surreptitiously stop her recording of their conversation to take a photo of the handwritten message with her phone. She had four percent battery, so she quickly snapped the photo.

"That's right," Sandy said. "A whole lot of leads and no clear suspect that sticks out more than the others. If you had to choose someone right now, who would you look at?"

"Without looking at the facts and just going with my gut reaction, I'm interested in knowing more about the rival restaurant owners, the

Kahoes. Did they have something to do with why Kip's restaurant was failing?"

Sandy shrugged. "Sometimes it's just bad luck. I don't know anything that points to them in particular except that they're outsiders. They aren't from around here and that makes people suspicious."

"Well then, what's your gut feeling about who did it?" Viv asked.

"Well, let me put it this way. People tend to kill for either love or money. I think there's a money trail somewhere in all this, and if we follow that money trail, we may find some answers. However, Kip was also tangled up with a woman or two. It could go that way as well. In fact, I think we should track down that unknown mistress. That's where we'll find out a thing or two. Now, mind you, I've been a journalist for many decades, but I've also been married four times, so I do know my cheaters and hustlers perhaps a little better than some people do."

"Goodness," Viv said and tried to keep a neutral expression.

But she wasn't entirely sure whether that experience only proved that Sandy just had poor judgment and a few blind spots herself.

CHAPTER TWENTY-ONE

V iv's mind swirled with the additional suspects that Sandy had presented to her, and she wanted to get back to the beach house to start digging up dirt about them as soon as possible. However, she was a minute or two late to pick up the kids and got stuck at the end of the carpool lane.

What fresh hell is this?

She didn't have any experience with parenthood, but this whole scene seriously blew chunks. She'd never wanted to be a mom, but another yuck factor thrown into the mix that she had never considered was having to deal with other parents. She'd been sitting at the back of the line breathing SUV exhaust for twenty minutes after school had let out. Kids clustered on the sidewalk outside the front doors waiting for their rides, but the line hadn't moved once since Viv had arrived. She had the urge to lay on her horn, but she refrained. She didn't want to seem like *that kind* of mom.

A latchkey kid is a child who comes home from school to an empty house, to no child minder or after-school supervision. Many people who fall into the Generation X category were latchkey kids, which may or may not have affected their social skills and general outlook on life. Offspring of Gen Xers have had almost every moment of the day planned out and occupied, perhaps as a reactionary result. Now, in a handful of states, it's illegal to leave a child under a certain age home alone.

"Come on, Little Billy. For crying out loud, say goodbye to your friends and get in the car. You'll see them tomorrow! …What am I talking about? You'll see them in ten minutes online in *World of Warcraft*."

She glanced down at her phone, thinking she might send Claire a text that she had arrived. However, recording the conversation with Sandy had killed the battery, and it died the second Viv tried to wake it up. Someone as plugged in to technology as Viv was should have kept a charger in her car. The fact was, she hadn't been in her car very much in the last six months. She was lucky it had made the drive down from Boston without any trouble after being neglected for so long.

Thankfully, Claire was watching for her, and even though they didn't know what kind of car she drove, they saw her—thanks to her Olivia wig —and walked down the line of cars, thereby saving her from the Eternal Pickup Lane of Doom.

"Oof. Sorry I was late," she said and maneuvered them out of the line.

"No biggie. My mom doesn't remember to come get me. The walk home isn't terrible unless there's a hurricane or something."

Viv checked the kid's face, but she wasn't joking. Claire seemed pensive but not upset. She sat in the back and peered between the seats through the front window. Terrance had crammed his long legs into the passenger seat beside Viv. In contrast to the girl, he looked ready to explode from excitement.

"We're doing actual gumshoe things. This rocks. I love this. This is my best day ever! I want to be in *The Maltese Falcon*. We're doing a stage adaptation next spring." He bounced up and down like a Clydesdale-sized toddler.

"Wow. That seems *intense* for a high school production."

"No more than *The Crucible*. We hung witches in that one. Or *Our Town*. We were pretty much all dead for that."

"I think you should do *Heathers*," Claire said from the back. She was still withdrawn.

"Doesn't a bomb explode at the end of the musical like the movie?" Viv asked. She recalled a very strong anti-establishment, anti-authority vibe to the whole thing. Plus bullying, suicide, and sexual assault. *Yikes*.

"Pretty much. Take a left at the next intersection."

"So, you're saying life is a dark comedy."

"Again, pretty much. Minus the comedy part."

Viv could hardly argue with the kid. Claire had been through a lot in the past few months, and she wasn't old enough to have weathered many other major setbacks. She didn't realize that things could get better because all she knew was the bleak stuff—single mom with a probable substance abuse problem, bio dad out of the picture, and her own father figure taken away in a terrible and dramatic fashion: murder. Still, it gave Viv good insight into the girl's mind...but also made her more concerned what would happen if they were unable to discover who had killed Kip.

How badly would it affect her?

Talk about bleak.

Images poured through Viv's mind of Claire dropping out of school and turning to drugs, meth lesions marring her currently clear pale skin. Without a father figure, she might spend the rest of her life dealing with daddy issues and become a stripper or other type of sex worker. Viv gritted her teeth. Failure to find out what happened to Claire's uncle was not an option.

"Is this it?" she asked, pulling into the gated driveway where the girl had directed her.

Her question was partly rhetorical, partly disbelief as she punched in the code that Claire dictated, and the wrought iron gate rolled open. White stucco gazebos dotted the gently sloping lawns. Live oak and boxwoods stood up among pristinely landscaped beds of roses and, of course, North Carolina's famous azaleas. They passed an Italianate mansion with a third story balcony, lovely country club buildings with circular drive, and a resort-sized pool with cabanas and a lifeguard station.

After a few twists and turns, they arrived at a cluster of townhouses that seemed bigger than the rest of South Pier. Viv parked, got out of her tiny hybrid car, and stood staring at the pristine greenery that surrounded the area—a golf hole and a water reservoir. It was so clean and tidy here, she felt like they were on a movie set, a little like she was in the *Twilight Zone*.

"Wow," Terrance said with the same dumbstruck expression Viv was sure she wore. "Being inside these walls feels so insulated. It's so unreal. Like, in here racism doesn't exist."

"Well, *poverty* definitely doesn't," Claire said with a snort. "Everyone is wealthy in this neighborhood."

She dug her keys out of her bag and led them to Kip's front door, which was oversized and made of solid wood with a wrought-iron decorative grate over the beveled glass cut-out in the center. The door alone probably cost more than Viv's monthly rent payment, which in Boston

ARSENIC AND ALIBIS

was not insignificant. She glanced around one more time before they went inside.

It's like living in Disneyland for grownups.

The interior of Kip's townhouse was predictably as luxurious and well-kept as the outside. The only difference was that it had a decidedly bachelor pad feel with its sports memorabilia, dark leather furniture, and massive TV that dominated one wall of the living room. On the opposite wall, Kip had built-in bookshelves with souvenirs from participating in sports—pennants, trophies, and collectibles like a signed Michael Jordan UNC Chapel Hill jersey—and various well-read cookbooks. Viv didn't know much about cooking or the restaurant business, but she took out her phone intending to snap a photo in case she needed to ask her food blogger BFF, Josie, about it. But duh, dead phone.

"I mean, I'm not a sports-ball person or anything, but this place is really cool," Terrance said. "Now, whenever I picture myself as an adult, it's going to be in a house just like this."

Me, too, Viv thought, still planning to start acting like a real adult one of these days.

The kitchen was equally ritzy and spacious for a two-bedroom, three-bathroom place. A full set of copper pots hung from one of those fancy racks above the island, which had a quartz countertop and stood clean and clear of clutter. She touched the shiny surface with a finger and came away free of dust like an old Pledge spray commercial. She peeked into the kitchen garbage can but found only a new, empty plastic liner bag. Someone had been in the house recently. It didn't smell stale at all.

"Were the police ever here to look for clues?" Viv asked.

Claire shrugged. "They said they were, but it doesn't look like it. Isn't there supposed to be, I dunno, fingerprint powder or something?"

"I don't think this was the crime scene," Terrance reminded her.

The place *was* unusually spick-and-span though.

"Did your uncle have a cleaning service?" Viv asked.

"Yeah, there was a woman who comes every other week. I think her name is Laura. She also does the neighbor's house on the same day." Claire indicated over her shoulder at the wall Kip's townhome shared with the home next door.

Viv hadn't heard a single sound from that direction. A townhome this well-made and this pricy was bound to have extra soundproofing between units. She wondered if anyone next door was home and would be willing to talk with her, but as she caught a glimpse of her bright orange hair in the reflection in front of Kip's microwave, she remembered she was dressed crazily and clownish as Olivia.

Probably not the best way to be well-received in a neighborhood like this. Just guessing.

In fact, she wouldn't be surprised if some of the other residents weren't already peeping through the windows at her. Then again, maybe they were out golfing in their backyards even though it was a weekday afternoon. People here might not be slaves to the nine-to-five.

CHAPTER TWENTY-TWO

W hy are you looking in the fridge? What's in there?" Claire asked, coming up behind Viv and peeking at the bright white and barren shelves over her shoulder.

"It's been cleaned out as well, just like the garbage. Do you think your mom already decided to sell this place and is getting ready for a real estate agent to start showing it to prospective buyers?" Viv cracked open the dishwasher and found one glass with a lipstick print on the rim resting in the top shelf.

That's odd. Maybe a real estate agent's? Although there's no lockbox on the door...

"Uh... Getting this place ready for sale sounds like a well-organized and well-thought-out plan," the girl said, leaning an elbow on the counter behind Viv. "And definitely not at all like something my mom would do. She can't make up her mind about anything. I swear she doesn't decide she's actually going to work each day until she gets into her car, drives, and actually arrives at the bowling alley. Planning is not a familiar concept to her."

Ouch. Poor kid.

Terrance called to them from one of the bedrooms, "Hey, check this out!"

They followed the sound of his voice.

"That's just an empty guest room. He uses it as an office—" Claire started to say, but she stuttered to a halt and froze in the doorway like a deer caught in the headlights.

The spare room, which was spacious just as everything else was in the townhouse, was fully decorated with a white four-poster bed with a canopy, Art Deco mirrored armoire, teal velvet chaise lounge, and a thick area rug that looked like someone had modeled its color and texture after their poodle. In short, the room was decked out to the nines, but not bachelor-style whatsoever. In fact, if Viv had to guess, she had to say it was set up for a teenaged girl—one in particular.

"When was the last time you were here?" she asked Claire, who had gone a little red-cheeked. It seemed she had the curse of the pale-skinned and freckled—all of her emotions, whether good or bad, played out across her face. Without her current caked-on layer of facial armor by Maybelline, Viv was the same.

"I dunno. A couple weeks before he…you know."

"And I take it the room wasn't like this?" Viv already knew the answer to her question based on the stunned expression on the girl's face, but her thought that the room had been fixed up without Claire's knowledge was confirmed when she shook her head no.

"Do you think he was dating someone who had a daughter, someone I didn't know about?" Claire asked in a small, halting voice that made Viv's heart break just a little.

Based on her previous night's trawling through Kip's spending habits with his personal credit card accounts and his cell phone records, Viv could say with some certainty that he had not been dating anyone at the time of his death. She hadn't found any patterns that indicated routine expenses around travel, hotels, flowers, jewelry, dining out—none of the signs of an active social life. In fact, what she had seen was a lonely guy pattern of a cheap monthly subscription payment to an adult website, premium TV channels, and frequent pizza charges. Not exactly the money trail of a player.

The fact that Claire would see a delightful room that someone had created for her—a teenager's dream room, minus the new clothes and accessories that would be a *must have*, at least in Viv's mind—and automatically assume that it was for someone else broke Viv's heart some more. It made Viv want to gather her up and make sure no one hurt the girl ever again.

She'd probably get an eye roll in return. Plus, she didn't know Claire that well.

Even Terrance had been clued in quickly. He dug out his phone, typed something, and then held the screen up for them to see.

"Hold on a minute. Just you wait a gosh darned minute. Claire, this is your mood board on Canva." They all stepped closer to examine the small screen in his hand as he showed them the digital collage of images she had set up and obviously shared with him. He pointed out the matching elements, comparing her on-screen scrapbook with the room in front of them. "Look here. Mirrored dresser. Poster bed with the fluttery curtain thingies. Fluffy Pomeranian looking rug. Fuzzy fainting couch in a greenish blue color. Claire, that is a *mermaid* color. That's your aesthetic. Everyone knows that's your thing. Tell me it's not the same darned room. Did you share this link with him?"

"I guess he asked to see it once when I was working on it. I mean, I thought it was for fun and that he was just being nice."

Viv took a couple seconds looking back and forth before she arrived at the same conclusion. Combined with what she knew about Kip's expenses, the only reasonable explanation for a girl's room at his house was that he had set it up for her.

But why?

Claire entered the room a step at a time, looking as if she was afraid it might all go away before she got a chance to see everything, as if she were walking in a dream. While the girl was occupied, Viv wanted to make sure she didn't miss anything else in the house. If the guest room had formerly been an office, Kip had to have moved his papers elsewhere, and Viv wanted to find them and rifle through them *like nobody's business*.

She left Claire and Terrance to have a private moment in the room and continued down the hallway to Kip's bedroom. Because someone had cleaned the place, Viv wasn't worried about stumbling across any dirty socks or underwear on his bedroom floor. She pushed open the door —*solid wood with an iron press-down handle, which was appropriately manly, understated, yet expensive*—and walked right in.

A massive king-sized bed dominated one wall, and oddly, the covers had been turned down on one side, and the sheets were rumpled. Someone had slept there since the cleaning woman had last visited.

What the actual heck? Who is sleeping here...Goldilocks?

It wasn't Claire because she would have noticed the other bedroom first. Could it have been Claire's mother? Or perhaps a girlfriend Viv didn't know about? Or maybe Kip's ex-wife, Felicia, trying to stake a claim on the place? Even though it made her more uncertain than anything else, Viv filed the oddity away in her mind for later. She had more exploring to do at the moment.

Despite the large bed, the room was big enough that it didn't seem the least bit crowded. In fact, there was a fireplace and seating area on the opposite wall, and a heavy wood desk in the corner—presumably his new office space since redoing the other bedroom.

A laptop sat on the desk, and Viv's fingers practically itched to get into it. She wondered if Claire would let her take it overnight to see what was in it. The rest of the desk was clutter-free and dust-free like the other parts of the house, so Viv turned her attention to the drawers. There were two deep filing drawers on the right-hand side of the desk, and nothing else, so she slid open the first drawer and discovered a motherlode of messy papers.

Thank goodness.

She'd been wondering if whoever had cleaned the place had taken all of his mail, notes, and generally life-affirming bric-a-brac that always seemed to collect in people's lives, even for Viv, who strove to do every-thing online and thereby avoid "peopling" as much as possible. She scooped the entire pile of paper out of the drawer and pulled up the desk chair so she could flip through it without dropping anything.

In the stack, she found receipts for the furniture, which made sense. Most of them dated to roughly three months before he had died, which also made sense if he had had to order it and pay at the time of ordering. He'd special ordered most of it from a local shop called McAllister's Fine Quality Home Furnishings, which again, gave Viv a case of the feels. She imagined him working with a salesperson to select each piece with Claire, unbeknownst to her, and her online mood board in mind.

Did he plan to surprise her? Was he going to ask her to live with him? The furniture receipts had a phone number listed, and on a whim, Viv picked up the landline phone that sat on Kip's desk to check to see if it still worked. To her surprise, it was still connected. Even though she dreaded making calls with the hate of a thousand burning-hot suns—or introverts—she decided to do it to satisfy her burning curiosity, and for Claire.

The phone rang only twice before the store picked up.

Claire said, "Hello, this is—" But that was all she could get out before the woman on the other line cut in.

"Is this Mrs. Baldwin? I saw your caller ID. This is Jenny. You spoke with me just the other day when you called to start arranging for the refund of the furniture. Did you settle on a date and time for the pick-up to begin? And again, let me express how terribly sorry we all are about what happened to Kip. He was so enthusiastic about his niece coming to live with you both."

Even in the best of times, Viv was not good at improvisation. With blood rushing into her ears, nearly blocking out her ability to hear, she could hardly think how she should respond.

"I...uh..."

"If you haven't decided on the date and time yet, please don't stress yourself out about it. We will definitely work with you whenever is best for you."

Viv struggled to grasp what was going on. If the salesperson recognized a female voice calling from this landline, did that mean Evelyn had been sleeping here and trying to arrange for a cash exchange for the furniture Kip had bought Claire?

But then the furniture saleswoman said, "You've always been an outstanding customer for us, recommending us to all of your new home-owner clients. We will, of course, do everything we can to accommodate you in this difficult time."

"I appreciate that," Viv managed to say, her voice no doubt distorted with her confusion. She could barely get the words out, which may have made her sounded overcome with grief and easily mistaken for...Kip's real estate mogul ex-wife? "Please let me call you back when I have more information."

"Of course. Don't worry about it, Mrs. Baldwin," the woman said before hanging up.

Viv hung up quickly and sat staring at the phone as if it were a cobra about to strike her lying self. If Kip's ex-wife had been staying here and planning to return Claire's bedroom furniture... Had she and Kip reconciled before his death?

Waitaminute.

Viv glanced around, drawing the layout of the townhouse in her mind as a thought occurred to her. The house had only two bedrooms. Where was Claire's mom supposed to live?

From everything the girl had told her about Evelyn Baldwin—the substance abuse, the lack of food in the house, and forgetting to pick Claire up from school—could Kip Baldwin have been preparing to fight for custody or guardianship of Claire? If so, her life would have changed drastically if he had not abruptly been cut out of the picture, which meant Evelyn had a large motive for wanting him dead.

Add her to the growing list of suspects.

CHAPTER TWENTY-THREE

Viv sorted through the rest of the papers and didn't find much of interest. No smoking gun, so to speak, just a property tax bill and some other utilities that had been paid and were up-to-date. Incidentally, the property tax rate in this area was about a tenth of the insane rate in Boston, Viv noticed. She made a personal mental note about that, on the off chance she was ever in the market for a house. Josie, Benjy, and their fourth friend, Drew, would kill her if she moved away from Beantown, but this was kind of a big incentive. Plus, there was the whole appeal of living near a beautiful beach, even if she had been here a full day and had yet to go see the ocean.

She moved to the bottom desk drawer and pulled it open to find another big pile of papers which she pulled out and plunked on the desk alongside the laptop. She pushed back the numerous, clacking plastic bracelets on her wrist and began to flip through the stack. Empty check register booklets and unused deposit envelopes. An organizer and calendar for the previous year with nothing written in it on any of the pages, which she carefully checked. A Victoria's Secret catalog from four years ago, which she gingerly put aside using two fingers, touching only the very corner of the pages, just in case he had used it for...personal reasons.

Next, she opened the first of two manilla envelopes, which revealed his passport with a few pages stamped with destinations to the Bahamas and Mexico, his birth certificate that said he was born in Atlanta to Wendy and Matthew Baldwin, and his Social Security Card. These pieces of identification gave Viv pause and caused a slight shiver to go down her spine. A person couldn't go anywhere without these bits of identification, and now his were here, not needed anymore. The finality of it made her feel a little sick. In a sad sense, Kip had expired before his passport, which was still good for two more years.

We're all so fragile, and life is short. Am I doing enough to savor each day of my existence? Should I make a travel bucket list? Croatia is supposed to be gorgeous and safe for travelers. In a recent poll, over eighty percent of Croatians speak English. Maybe I should go there. How can we not wonder what's important when I think about Kip, whose life was abruptly cut short?

She shivered again, thinking about young Claire and her friend. Then, Viv thought about her own friends, and her parents who were so far away. She'd spent the last few months holed up in her home. What if those were wasted moments she could have been spending with them? How would she feel if something happened to any of them?

Okay. Another sweat is breaking out on my forehead. Moving on. Focus on Kip and Claire.

She paused to unwrap a lollipop and shove it in her mouth like the sucrose-laden raspberry-flavored pacifier it was.

The only way to bring some peace to this situation and to allow Claire to heal and move on was to try to find some answers for her. Dumping out the rest of the contents of the envelope, Viv discovered a bunch of loose photos, including instant Polaroids, some of them old enough to have turned a sepia tone. There was nothing sordid or seedy in the pile, about a dozen baby photos, which she took to be of Kip himself and his parents, no Evelyn in any of the photos. A handful of the images showed his growth through Little League baseball, playing in the waves at the beach, and—she tilted her head to read the frosted writing on a birthday cake—a ninth birthday party with a lot of other kids in attendance. The final photo in the stack, when he was maybe a year older, showed him holding a fair-haired baby.

The timing matched up. Viv assumed the child was his sister, Evelyn, Claire's mom, but it was the last photo in this envelope and it didn't have any notes on the back side, so she couldn't confirm it. However, there was a second envelope, about as equally puffy as the first.

Aha. More photos of the blond baby girl.

Viv took them out one by one and looked at each. Some were upside down or flipped over, so she sorted through them. Baby Evelyn was a precious little thing with chubby cheeks and rolls on her thighs. However, when Viv got midway through the stack, her mind stuttered to a halt so abruptly, she wouldn't have been surprised by an audible screeching sound.

In the photo she had just turned over, the same baby girl that had been in the previous photos sat in a man's lap, but the *man* was Kip Baldwin—not young ten-year-old Kip, but the fully grown adult man.

Viv reached for the previous envelope and dug out the photo of young Kip with the baby in his lap. She held the two photos side by side and compared the two little blond baby girls. Other than a slight difference in the set of their eyes, they looked almost identical. One was definitely Claire—because there was that little freckle under her eye that she still had—while the other was her mother, Evelyn. However, they were nearly spitting images of each other. They could have been twins. No, not twins —genetic clones, like how people sometimes cloned their favorite pets years after the original's death.

Okay, that is weird, but it totally makes sense. Kip was there for Claire when her own dad wasn't. The bio father ran off before she was born. He was out of the picture, so big-hearted Kip must have stepped into the role of dad.

Viv got over her moment of confusion and continued through the photos until she reached the end of the stack. The images showed Claire aging through the years—elementary school portraits from picture day with missing teeth and hair bows askew, some of them with her name written on the back along with the year in what looked like her own wobbly kid's handwriting. Viv could imagine her presenting her uncle with a photo each year, describing how she had carefully selected her outfit for the day or how she had wanted to do her hair but had to attempt to fix it again after coming in from recess.

Viv finished going through the stack and sighed, feeling the weight of emotion. Kip had been a guy who was proud of his niece. She, in turn, was down the hall standing in a room that he had thoughtfully set up for her, a room that she might never live in if her mom sold the place.

Ah, kid. I don't know how to make this turn out okay for you, but I'll try.

She thought the second envelope was empty now, but just as she began to stuff the photos back into it, she felt a hard lump in the bottom corner, so she upended the envelope on the desk. With a clink, two small keys slid out. Identical and attached together by a plastic fastener string, they looked shiny and new.

Huh. These look like keys to a safe.

Kip's bedroom had a couple of large framed pictures on the wall, as well as a mirror over the fireplace. She eyed them, wondering how silly she would feel pushing each one aside to look for a hidden safe.

Pretty fricking goofy.

She was still going to do it, of course. However, she was saved from having to look like Miss Marple all by herself when the two kids joined her.

"What are you doing?" Claire asked.

"Can we help?" Terrance immediately added.

Viv held up the set of keys she had found. "People, we're on a mission. I think these open a safe. I just don't know where the safe is, but if it's here, we're going to find it. I need you to check carefully behind all of the pictures in here."

They ran off with a glee and alacrity that made Viv re-question her whole stance against personally procreating. Maybe having kids wasn't just for people other than her. Within a couple minutes, they had checked not only the frames in Kip's bedroom, but all the other ones in the townhouse.

"Nothing," Claire said, somewhat breathlessly when they returned.

Oh, to be that enthusiastic about anything.

Nevertheless, Viv was still somewhat charmed by them. She became even more so when she sent them off to look in every closet and soon heard a cry from the back of Kip's large walk-in, which adjoined his en suite bathroom.

"Found one!" Terrance shouted. "It's not that big! Do you want me to bring it out—oh, never mind. It's too heavy to lift."

Viv followed the sound of his voice through the luxurious expanse of tumbled marble, past a spa tub with bubble jets and a multi-person shower—she could probably drive her hybrid through it—to an equally large closet that smelled like a Christian Dior scent, if she had to take a guess. Claire followed behind as they found Terrance kneeling beside a beige colored box that didn't look as if it weighed as much as it probably did. To be honest, it looked plastic, but the exterior was a powder-coated metal, so it blended in well with the rest of the closet.

"All right. Let me give this a try," she said, and Terrance scooted out of the way to make room for her.

The key fit right in the lock, and she started to lift the heavy lid of the safe with some trepidation. After all, she had the man's niece right next to her. If they found anything illegal or damning in anyway, Viv wasn't sure how well the girl would take it.

She paused. "Do you want me to check first to make sure there's nothing bad?"

Claire shook her head. "I want to see. Nothing will bother me."

Viv knew for a fact—based on the flush in the girl's face—that wasn't true. *Everything* probably affected her, and she was just trying to hide it, to be strong for herself because no one else was. Yet, she let the girl's declaration stand uncontested and proceeded with lifting the top of the safe.

"What if there's a million dollars inside it?" Terrance speculated.

"Then he wouldn't have let the restaurant struggle so much," Claire said. Although Viv wondered if she meant herself, not his business.

"What if it's gold coins from a sunken ship that he found on one of his trips to the Caribbean?"

"What if it's drugs and weapons?" Claire asked Viv. "Will we have to call the police?"

"Probably," Viv said. "But we'll deal with that if it happens."

She pushed the lid the rest of the way open and propped it up to make sure it wouldn't slam down and concuss her, or worse—the thing was heavy enough to dent an armored truck.

At the bottom of the safe was a flat file folder.

"Oh," Claire said, her voice sounding deflated as she peered into it. "I don't see any money or jewels. It's just more boring papers. I guess I'm going to go back to the other room."

The kids might have lost interest as soon as they saw it wasn't cash or jewels. To Viv, it looked like abundant treasure in the form of documentation. It was a fertile and valuable research trove, which was as close to treasure as she could have imagined. the papers practically made her salivate and she wanted to dive into them as soon as the kids left the room.

"Don't you want to know what it is?" Terrance asked, following Claire back out. Viv watched the back of her narrow shoulders shrug as she disappeared from sight.

"You'll tell us if it's anything important, right?"

"Of course," Viv assured them. After all, that's why she was here—to do the boring adult legwork for Claire and to get access to things that the girl wouldn't be able to on her own.

She scooped up the folder and flipped it open. The first thing on top was a gift shop receipt. She turned it around because it was upside down. Someone had spent $15.95 at the New Hanover Regional Medical center on a stuffed animal, a pink teddy bear to be exact. Under the receipt were a couple of photos of Kip in a hospital room holding a newborn baby.

Newborn babies...not very attractive. Humans in larval form, pretty much.

Viv flipped through the photos to the file's last sheet of paper, which was upside down again. She must have opened the folder backwards. She tilted her head to see better as she turned it over and was surprised to find it was an official government document with a border around the edge.

It was a birth certificate.

Claire's birth certificate, to be exact.

The date was fourteen years ago in May.

The place was City of Wilmington, New Hanover County, North Carolina.

The mother was Evelyn Michelle Baldwin.

The father was...Willard Kennett Baldwin.

What the ever-loving...? Kip was Claire's father?

PART III
SEPARATE THE LIES FROM
THE TRUTH

"I'm always disappointed when a liar's pantaloons don't actually catch on fire."
— *Joan D'arc*

CHAPTER TWENTY-FOUR

Viv drove the kids home in a stunned silence that they didn't notice as they chattered away to each other. She honestly didn't know what to say to Claire, so like any other awkward moment with teenagers in a car, she turned on the radio, and they listened to a pop station on the short drive back to Claire's house.

She certainly didn't want to confuse the kid before she could research this new and disturbing discovery, so she had told Claire that the papers she had found in the safe were mortgage documents for the townhouse. Viv didn't like lying, but informing the girl her uncle was actually her father seemed much, much worse.

The possible explanations for this bizarre situation were far more unsettling than she wanted to admit. She mentally scrambled for options other than the most horrible one, incest. What if Kip wasn't Claire's biological father, but her had allowed his name to be put on the birth certificate to assume responsibility for her? Viv would have to check out the legality of that in North Carolina. And if that was the case, why did he let Claire live alone with Evelyn, a questionable guardian from what Viv had gathered, while he carried on with his bachelor lifestyle? What about Kip's ex-wife? Did Felicia know about the birth certificate? Right now, Claire was fourteen years old, which put her birth around the same time as the divorce. Viv would have to look into the timing.

Ahhhh. So many more questions than I arrived with this morning.

What she needed to do as soon as humanly possible was track down Claire's mother and ask her what in the ever-loving heck the story behind who the girl's father was. In short, Evelyn had some 'splaining to do. Claire had told Viv where to find her mother, who was waitressing the dinner shift at a bowling alley and pub in nearby Wilmington, so that was next on Viv's to-do list.

She pulled up to the curb in front of Claire's tiny house. "Don't forget to…uh…do your homework and stuff. And I'll text you later as soon as I'm done looking at Kip's laptop." She patted the Dell, which sat next to her on the passenger seat where Terrance had placed it after sliding his oversized body out of the door.

"Sure," Claire had said before closing the car door, clearly noncommittal about the whole learning gig—and possibly even less optimistic about Viv finding out any new information about Kip.

Viv had a whole speech on the tip of her tongue about getting through the boring stuff to get a diploma, to get into college, to get into debt, to get a low-paying monotonous job… Thankfully, her mouth was slow to catch up to her brain and none of what would be the opposite of a pep talk came out. Instead, she gave an awkward little half-wave and drove off, intending to text the girl later. Hopefully, she would find out some bit of news both encouraging and not horrific with which she could update Claire.

Sigh. Things are not looking great on that front.

Left with a few hours until the end of Evelyn's bowling alley shift and with an empty stomach, Viv decided to grab some dinner and ended up, not so coincidentally, at the Time & Tidewater. Just inside the entrance, a cute server with dark skin and a halo of naturally curly hair in black pants and a white dress shirt told Viv to seat herself anywhere she wanted. She had her pick of the place other than one or two occupied tables. Not a great sign for the restaurant's future, along with the lack of a hostess, which suggested that they were already paring down their staff.

"Hi. I'm Lindsay. I'll be taking care of you tonight. Can I start you off with a drink?"

Viv looked up to discover the same person who'd told her to take a seat was also now her waitress. Also, she hadn't brought Viv a menu or a drink list. She pointed out her lack of menu to the girl, who apologized and said, "There are so many things on the menu that we're out of right now. I don't really like to show it to people. Actually, it's probably easier for me to tell you what we *do* have."

After a shockingly short recitation of drinks and dishes, the girl took Viv's order for a Corona and a chicken sandwich, which she suspected she could have gotten for a lot cheaper at a fast-food drive-thru window. Hopefully much better here, but she had begun to get worried. With the lack of customers, the kitchen staff would have a hard time using supplies before they went bad unless they relied on frozen and other preserved foods.

Maybe I should revert to my childhood habit and say a prayer before I eat. Maybe I need last rites.

When her meal arrived just a short while later, it was serviceable, not fancy. Lindsay had given her extra pickles and chips on the side, although many of them were crumbled and looked as if they had come from the bottom of a bag.

"Let me know if there's anything else I can get you," the girl said but then added, "and I'll sure try." As if she wasn't certain she would be successful filling any special requests.

"I do have one question," Viv said. "I don't mean to be rude, but do you have another job lined up? Because I don't think this one is going to last much longer, just based on what I can see."

The girl gave a short, rueful laugh. "Yeah, I know, I've worked here for three years, but it's okay. This is my second job. I show up for my shifts expecting the doors to be locked any day now. We're down to the bare bones staff, and as you noticed, we're low on everything with no re-orders. I don't even know why we're staying open. Just running the electricity probably costs more than they're making."

She shrugged and leaned a hip against Viv's table.

"I heard what happened the owner, Kip, even though I'm from out of town," Viv said.

"He was a nice guy. Super friendly but fair as a boss. No head games, so you always knew what to expect—except what happened to him. We were all shocked. Our new boss, Arletta, most of all. She was really unprepared to run this place." Lindsay leaned in to whisper, "And it shows because it's going down like a sinking ship."

"How is she taking it?"

"She seemed like a zombie at first, walking around like she was in shock like the rest of us. For the first couple weeks, she had this blank look on her face all the time, even with her husband here helping. She barely spoke to anyone, even him. Then total denial that she needed help.

I think panic hit when she realized she couldn't keep it all going by herself. Now, it's more like depression."

It sounded like stages of grief to Viv. She recognized the phases from the many failed relationships she had gone through. Her personal array of terrible boyfriends was almost like a 64-color giant box of crayons, both vibrant and dark in their individual variations. The question was...was Arletta mourning the loss of her business partner or the business itself? If she had killed Kip for the financial gain, she wasn't doing a good job of staying afloat.

"Anyway," Lindsay said. "I've chatted your ear off enough. Enjoy your meal and if there's anything—"

A crash of dishes came from the kitchen and Lindsay froze, her dark eyebrows shooting upward. Almost directly after the shatter, a man's angry shouts rang out, amplified when the kitchen door swung open and a small gray-haired lady stormed out.

"Speak of the devil," Lindsay said. "That's my boss."

A man—the source of the vocal ruckus—followed closely at her heels through the door, still shouting, oblivious or simply uncaring of the handful of customers who had gone still in mid-chew as the drama unfolded.

"Dinner *and a show*," Viv murmured under her breath.

CHAPTER TWENTY-FIVE

I t took Viv a second or two to recognize Christopher Kahoe, but she remembered his photo from the blog article about the forty bachelors under forty years old. Plus, he looked a lot angrier now, and rage tended to distort a person's face. Didn't he realize that any one of her fellow diners could post a new and more accurate image of him online using a cell phone?

Confronted with such a violent emotion in such an unexpected place, Viv, along with the handful of other people in the restaurant, froze, caught between wanting to see what would happen or wanting to hide in case there was some kind of terrible fallout. Viv had a spike of anxiety that blurred her vision and sent blood pounding into her ears. She glanced down at her cell phone, not to take a photo, but in case she had to make an emergency call. Too bad her battery had already died.

Every day in the United States, over one hundred people die from shootings. How many of those are from heat-of-the-moment outbursts of anger?

Christopher shouted, "Where's our money, Arletta? You're already three months late! We've been more than patient. We've given you plenty of time to come up with the repayment funds. We're not going to wait forever without taking action! We're going to get our money back one way or another, and if you don't pay it back willingly, you might not like the other way!"

Christopher towered over Arletta by at least a foot, and when he threatened her and jabbed a finger in her face, the smaller woman had a slight backward bend to her spine just to look him in the eye. To her credit, however, she stood her ground and didn't budge even when the spittle flew.

Ew. Say it, don't spray it, Mister Eligible Bachelor.

"Good luck getting your money back!" Arletta said, and Viv could see the clench of her jaw below her owlish glasses from all the way over where she was sitting. "I don't have any and I don't know what Kip did with it. You can search under the tables and in the booth cushions for loose change, for all I care. If you come up with any, that's more than I've been able to do. I can't squeeze any profit out of this place. Maybe you can do a better job than me!"

He looked like he was going to say something more. In fact, his fists were clenched even though he kept them down at his sides, and Viv felt another jab of fear and quelled the urge to dive for cover under her table. Just as Christopher opened his mouth, however, the kitchen door banged open and an older man stepped out. He wasn't as tall or as muscular as Christopher, but he had a bit of girth to him and knew how to use it, especially when he stood beside Arletta and placed a large hand on her shoulder.

"I believe it's time for you to leave," the older man told him.

Christopher seemed to swallow the words he had been about to say and changed tactics. He lowered his voice just slightly. "You have until the first of the month to give us the payment, or you'll be hearing from us again. We tried to be nice about it, but we're done with that!"

Then he brushed past her, ignoring the shocked customers, and left through the front door. The restaurant door slammed behind him with a bang, which seemed to snap people out of their stupor. Chairs scraped along the floor as diners stood up to leave as quickly as possible.

Viv's appetite was gone, not that the mediocre chicken sandwich had done much for it. Her friend, Josie, had a theory that she could tell when food was made with love. Even Viv could feel the dearth, the absolute absence of it here. Combined with the loud argument, the food seemed about as appetizing as the frozen packaging it probably came in.

"Uh, yeah. Let me get your check," Lindsay said and scurried off without another word.

At least there hadn't been any violence, Viv thought, her pulse still racing with leftover adrenaline. She liked watching the occasional shoot-em-up TV show or old movie, but her nerves were just too jangly for anything that resembled reality, including the raw, visceral punch of an angry and explosive person. She felt queasy. Viewing it through a screen from the comfort of your couch was a whole lot better than this.

Christopher had done nothing to change her first impression of him from the internet. She still thought he was a thinly disguised thug masquerading as a suburban single dude looking for his soulmate. Unless he had an evil twin, he was just a not-nice person wearing a nice person's mask. He was good looking, true, but he set off a lot of Viv's red alert alarms based on just the way he had menaced Arletta with his posture.

Viv fished in her bag for her wallet so she could pay and get out as quickly as possible. She came out with a handful of junk, including several empty gum wrappers, receipts, and the crumpled canceled check that Claire had stolen from the Kahoe back office last night. It seemed like the large amount was part of Arletta's repayment. If so...how much more than thirty-five thousand dollars did Kip borrow from them? And how badly had he needed money if he had gone to his rivals for a loan? Based on his pricy townhouse and lavishly decorated room for Claire, he had money and credit before everything had gone down the drain.

When Lindsay came back with the bill, Viv asked, "Is your boss okay back there?" If Arletta was truly in danger, she needed to report the confrontation to the police, especially if this wasn't an isolated incident. Based on what Viv had just witnessed, she would definitely file a report about the incident.

"She seems okay. Not too rattled or anything, but she's a pretty cool customer. Other than being stressed out all the time."

"Does she have a lawyer or something?"

Or maybe a restraining order?

Lindsay leaned in again and lowered her voice. "I honestly don't know how above-the-board their deal is—you know, if it's formal. I haven't seen or heard anything about a lawyer, so take it with a grain of salt because I'm not here as much as I used to be when they gave me more hours—when we had more customers—but Arletta's husband, Brad, helps with a lot of stuff around here, too. He's the nicest man, one of those shirt-off-his-back types of people. He volunteers at the local blood bank. He helps register voters. Works in the community center garden one day a week. He was in the local news for taking a homeless guy out to dinner one night. I think he's a plumber or an HVAC guy or something. I've seen him up on the roof fixing stuff, so she's not totally alone in all of this, good thing."

117

Viv debated with herself for a minute or two whether she wanted to try to speak with Arletta, but her social anxiety got the better of her. She'd just witnessed an explosive situation and she was more than happy to give into her desire to get the heck out of the Time & Tidewater, whose time, it seemed, was almost up.

As a compromise, a kind of bargain with herself, to push her own boundaries and not entirely throw in the towel for the evening, she resolved to allow herself to leave Arletta alone for the time being, but to still track down Claire's mom since it was just getting toward the end of her shift at the bowling alley.

She settled up her evening's bill with Lindsay, abandoned her half-eaten chicken sandwich, and left the restaurant feeling unsettled and a little bit depressed, not only for the remaining employees, but for Kip, whose hopes and dreams for the place had ended on the cold, hard ground in the alley beside it.

CHAPTER TWENTY-SIX

Terrance had invited Claire over to his house for dinner, but she turned him down, even though his mom had invited her as well. For a tiny Asian woman, Mrs. Bonaventure could be pretty forceful and she was a fantastic cook, especially with the *lumpia* egg roll things she made. Those were Claire's favorite, and if she weren't so embarrassed about it, she would eat there every night if she could. Instead, she tried to limit herself to saying yes only once every couple months. Whiny Charlotte from *Grovemire Girls*, whose aesthetic on the show was unicorns and the color pink, definitely would have made herself a regular at the Bonaventures' dinner table, but Claire didn't want anyone to think she was mooching off them.

Because she unexpectedly still had her seventy-five dollars of savings —correction, seventy-four after giving Viv one dollar—she thought she might treat herself to something special. Sitting in her kitchen alone after Terrance went home, she ran through the possibilities in her mind of everything within walking distance. In one direction lay McDonald's, and she loved their addictive fries, but she had to walk through a shady apartment parking lot to get there. In the other direction was a Shop Now grocery store. She wasn't the best cook, but the freezer section held a lot of options, so she put on her shoes and headed that way.

Since she had gotten home from her uncle's house, she had avoided thinking too hard about what she had seen there, but for some reason, it was all she could think about on her way to the store. Maybe because it was the first time she had been alone all day since Terrance had left. He'd done an excellent job keeping her mind off things. Maybe that was why she liked him. Not only was he physically large, like a gentle Godzilla, but his personality took up a lot of space and helped her not think about herself too much.

Usually, her mind ran over the "what ifs" in a relentless way, like a toddler asking the same question over and over. What if Uncle Kip had invited her to live at his house? What if he hadn't died? Would she be there right now, maybe watching TV with him when he got home from work? He liked to watch sports and old sitcoms like *Full House* and *Friends*. He'd made her watch a bunch of those with him. Maybe he would cook hamburgers, and because she didn't really like beef, he would grill a turkey burger or one of those fancy vegetable patties for her.

Her mean, mean brain took her down the path of what it might be like to go into that pretty room to do her homework with the laptop he had already given her. She could ask him for help if she got stuck instead of texting Terrance like she usually did. Then, after her assignments were finished, she could have a snack if she wanted, although she had would probably still be full from that big dinner, so she would brush her teeth in her own bathroom at a sink that looked shiny and always clean. She could wash her face and pat it dry with a fluffy towel, just like a commercial. Then, she would crawl into that big, beautiful bed with the canopy and fall asleep like a mermaid in her underwater cave, cozy and safe, all the way until morning.

A car honked and abruptly pulled her back to reality just as an ambulance with its siren shrieking zoomed past her. She could feel sad and sorry for herself, but the truth was, she wasn't any worse off than she had been yesterday. Nothing had changed. She was totally fine—in fact, she was better off than she had been the day before. Now, she had someone on her side—she had Viv.

At the store, Claire pushed one of those mini shopping carts that single people and old ladies liked to use. She went up and down the aisles looking at boxes and cans carefully but was so overwhelmed by the choices that she gave up and went to the fresh foods, where she selected two green apples—one for with dinner and one for tomorrow's breakfast. She picked some orange juice because she remembered a song about scurvy from a cartoon. She honestly couldn't remember the last time she had had some vitamin C, but she was careful to choose the generic store brand because it was a dollar less than the kind in the commercials. After that, she ended up in the frozen food row, just curious if they had egg rolls—which they did. She picked out a box of those, and then saw a two-for-one deal on family-sized chicken pot pies, which looked delicious, like someone's grandma would cook while wearing a frilly apron. They were normally eleven dollars each, but she could eat one of them for like three days, so it was worth it.

Before she wheeled her cart to the cashier at the front of the store, she patted her pocket to make sure she still had the comforting wad of bills folded up in her pocket. She did not want to get all the way up there and have to put everything back for whatever reason, like she wasn't able to buy it or she was trying to scam someone, like an imposter from that *Among Us* game on her phone.

The cashier hardly looked at her while he ran her items across the scanner. "Did you bring your own bags?" he asked.

He had bad skin and looked like he might go to her high school, but she wasn't sure.

"No, I don't have any bags."

"They cost ten cents each for plastic or you can buy a reusable one for ninety-nine cents."

She really didn't want to spend more money than she had to, but it was for the earth, for goodness sake, so she said yes to the woven bag with the store's logo on it.

After he rang up the two pot pies, he paused, staring at his screen between them.

"These are two for one if you have a Bucks Card. Do you have one of those?"

She shook her head. "No."

"But they're two for one if you do," he said, if that would change her answer.

"I don't have one. I don't know what it is."

"It's a store discount card, but you have to be eighteen to get one. What about your mom or dad? You could just put your home phone number in the keypad and see."

Claire could have bet the rest of her money that her mom did not have a Bucks store discount card. Her mom only remembered to carry her driver's license because it was attached directly to her car keys. Yet, she dutifully punched in the phone number into the machine.

"It didn't work. Do you still want both of them?" He held up the second box, and she stared at the picture of the steaming chicken pie with silky gravy.

"Yes, I want it," she said quietly, because first, she was embarrassed, and second, she was almost drooling thinking about sinking a spoon into it and chomping it down for dinner.

The cashier at the next register left her lane and came over. She was a thin woman with muscular arms, as if she had lifted a lot of groceries in her day. She had lines around her mouth because she was probably a smoker, but when she smiled at Claire as she pulled a card out of her pocket, she looked pretty. "Use this card," she told the guy cashier, who shrugged and swiped it without really caring.

"Thank you," Claire said fervently, careful to clear her throat first so her voice didn't do that weird cracking thing that happened when she felt emotional.

"No big deal. We do it for everyone who forgets their card," the woman said to Claire, who didn't know whether to believe her or not, but she nodded anyway, feeling relieved and lucky.

Claire was going to go on the internet as soon as she got home to see how old she needed to be to start working at a job like this. Maybe Mrs. June, her school counselor, would write her a letter of recommendation to get a job. While having money was a nice thought, she also kind of wanted to be just like the cashier woman who had wielded the power to make someone's day.

CHAPTER TWENTY-SEVEN

About twenty minutes away from the Time & Tidewater, Viv pulled up to Pete's Pins, the bowling alley where Claire's mom, Evelyn, was just finishing her shift.

Some of the first bowling alleys in America were in New York City and opened in the mid-1800s, but supposedly, archeologists have found much earlier ones in Egypt that date back to thousands of years, B.C., which makes you wonder what kind of shoes they used back then.

Thursday night must have been league night, Viv surmised, based on the clusters of people in matching shirts. The shouts and the clash of falling pins caused her to press her back against the nearest wall and threatened to undermine the whole Olivia ruse she had created to trick herself into being okay. She dug around in her shoulder bag but couldn't find a lollipop.

A large group of people is called a No Thanks.

When she realized her breathing had grown choppy and she had begun to hyperventilate, she had a little internal Come to Jesus meeting.

If she gave up and went back to the beach house now without confronting Evelyn, she was absolutely failing Claire, and it was plain as the nose on Viv's face—or the strands of bright orange hair hanging in her eyes—that the poor girl had no one else who was looking out for her. If Viv threw in the towel now, she was letting her own shortcomings interfere with a greater purpose. Even worse, she had gotten involved in the case now. It would be like holding out a piece of bacon to a starving stray dog who was just looking for a handout, a few scraps of food—and then snatching it back.

Focus on the task at hand. Let's do this.

Here in the bowling alley, some of these people were serious about their group bowling experience. They carried their own shoes and balls in monogrammed bags. Viv had thought a social experience like this was a remnant of a bygone era, along with Brylcreem and soaking your fingertips in Palmolive dish soap for a manicure, but clearly it wasn't—and she was intrigued.

Yes, I've spent the last six months living in a cave, but have I gone back in time?

"Hey, y'all! Group selfie so I can put it on our Instagram account!" someone shouted. And then, someone else said, "Y'all better put some filters on that photo before you post it. Make me look like a movie star or I'm unfriending you!"

Nope, definitely not transported back in time.

Viv bought herself a Cheerwine soda and made a sweeping circuit of the place to search for Evelyn. She overlooked Claire's mom twice before she realized the woman had changed her hair to jet black since the photo that Claire had posted online.

New hair, new you.

Viv in her red Olivia wig certainly was in no position to judge another person for a drastic change in her appearance. However, what she did totally understand was that the upheaval in Evelyn's life had caused her to make a severe outward change to herself. She was broadcasting her inner turmoil to those around her like a warning sign.

It reminded Viv of how a poison dart frog could hop around a rainforest in full bright colored skin, unmolested. Other species had evolved to learn its bright color was a warning that it could easily kill them. Kind of the same as a bright blue drink special that was served in a fishbowl, like the one that had just been placed in front of Evelyn near lane number one. That thing was definitely a killer drink.

Viv may never have been a parent nor wanted to be one, but she had just enough instincts to know that if she had a fourteen-year-old girl who'd been home alone all day since noon, she'd want to go right home to check on her after work and not drink a toxic-waste-looking cheap drink special with some of her regular customers right after her shift.

A portly red-faced guy with "Frank" stitched to his shirt pocket put his arm around Evelyn's thin shoulders. She didn't shrug him off, but neither did she smile at or directly acknowledge him. Viv couldn't hear everything they said because someone had cranked up the Garth Brooks, but Frank had a voice like an umpire's for a softball league of stage-mom Teamsters that cut through even the roll of the bowling balls and crash of pins, so Viv heard him order another pitcher of beer.

Lady, what are you doing? Go home to your poor kid.

Even worse, Viv would bet dollars to donuts that Evelyn wasn't planning on getting a ride home after drinking that whole fishbowl. If she thought she would drive herself after imbibing all that post-work alcohol, she would endanger not only herself and other people on the streets, but her child's entire future. Any DUIs Evelyn racked up could mean Claire might end up in the foster system.

With the rhythmic crash of pins around her, Viv struggled to figure out how to approach Evelyn and what to say if she did.

Stupid social anxiety. Stupid agoraphobia.

Isaac Marks, a British psychiatrist originally from South Africa, was supposedly the first person to classify social anxiety as a phobia distinct from all the others. The term came into use in the 1960s and has been on my mind constantly the past six months.

Reminding herself that she was Olivia at the moment, Viv pulled up her big girl leggings, drank her soda, and waited for an opportunity to approach the woman. Not much time later, Evelyn and the loud, portly man called Frank rose and went outside. Viv didn't know what kind of shady doings were afoot, so she followed them at a careful distance. As it turned out, much to Viv's relief, the two simply went outside to smoke a cigarette. Viv didn't smoke, so she fiddled with her phone for a minute or two while she gathered up her nerve and approach her.

She got close enough to hear the man say, "Come home with me, baby. My wife is out of town with her girlfriends for the weekend. Do you think I deserve a girl's weekend of my own?"

"I gotta kid I need to go check on."

At least she remembers she has *a kid*, Viv thought.

"Your kid's old enough to entertain herself while we have some fun. She took care of herself last time, didn't she?"

"It's not attractive when you beg, Frank."

"You didn't say that last time either," he returned and then laughed off his rejection with a loud chortle that carried clearly across the whole parking lot as he walked away from Evelyn.

Viv took her time but eventually approached her with caution.

"Excuse me, but are you Evelyn?" she asked, just to make sure there wasn't some evil twin scenario going on.

Viv thought she might get a snappish "who's asking?" in return, maybe because she had been living in the northeast part of the United States for many years now, but instead, she got a very southern "Yes, ma'am" in response.

"Hi. I was having a soda inside and I saw you. I ran into your daughter at her school. I'm a researcher and I offered to help her look into a few things about her Uncle Kip. I think he was your brother, is that right? I'm so sorry for your loss."

Technically, it was all vague enough to be true. She had picked up Claire from school and she was a researcher of sorts, of the highly connected, electronic armchair warrior kind. However, if she had been expecting Evelyn to continue with the warm and friendly demeanor, she had been sadly mistaken. The emotional shutters came slamming down faster than if it were hurricane season.

"What do y'all want with me?" Evelyn asked, her voice dropping much lower, the previous syrupy customer service quality dissipating like the tide going out. She took a drag off her cigarette and the burning tip briefly illuminated her face. Under her shaggy jet-black dyed hair, she briefly looked like Claire playing dress up.

Join the club. I probably look about the same in this silly wig.

"You probably already know that Claire had to submit a lot of documents when she was signing up for public school when she first went to kindergarten all those years ago," Viv fudged again, but with facts she knew were more or less true for school districts everywhere. "In addition, a lot of those documents are public record, so anyone could get access to them, including Claire herself."

Frowning, Evelyn blew out a large breath of smoke and used two fingers to pluck a flake of tobacco off her tongue. "I'm sorry. What are you saying? I'm not following you at all."

She looked around for her male companion, and he abruptly revealed his location in the darkened parking lot with a burst of laughter at another friend. Viv effectively had a captive audience because of her need for a nicotine fix.

"Claire's birth certificate says that her Uncle Kip was her father."

A series of conflicting expressions traveled across Evelyn's face, from anger to defensiveness. She landed on a studied apathy that seemed like she was trying to be tough and streetwise. "So what?"

CHAPTER TWENTY-EIGHT

Viv thought Evelyn's bravado, her fake nonchalance, was a weird and unexpected reaction. Personally, Viv thought she should have tried anger or intimidation, especially at the accusation that she had done something illegal or morally reprehensible. Neither fraud nor incest were comfortable options.

"Was Kip in the hospital room when Claire was born?"

"No, I was alone."

"And you put his name on the birth certificate?"

"Yeah. No one said I couldn't."

Except having a child with your brother in North Carolina was a felony. Apparently, no one at the hospital or in vital records looked into who he was, fortunately for all of them. Otherwise, he could have had a stay in prison and a mountain of legal fees to fix it.

"If Kip was Claire's biological father, I'm guessing you're not really Kip's sister like everyone thinks. Were you ever planning to tell your daughter that the man she thought was her uncle, *for her entire life*, was actually her dad, according to her birth certificate? Is that record even correct?"

Viv watched the woman's face carefully for signs of regret or even shame—she still wasn't sure what Evelyn's relationship was with Kip. At last, the woman sighed and stubbed out her cigarette on the heel of her black work shoe. She shivered in the night sea breeze and pulled her sweater together closer.

"I don't want to do this out here. Not outside. I'm freezing. Come sit in my car with me, and I'll tell you more."

All too aware of her dead phone and no means to call for help, Viv followed her to a beat-up Toyota and sat in the passenger's side with a great deal of trepidation. The car smelled like cigarettes and dust. A sneeze tickled Viv's sinuses, threatening to detonate, but she pinched her nose until it went away. She grabbed the rusted old door and had to use most of her strength to pull it shut. It creaked like a haunted house and then slammed closed.

North Carolina was one of those states where people loved their guns, and Evelyn's frame of mind was none too stable, from what Viv had gathered so far. To her relief, however, Claire's mom seemed to want just to sit somewhere out of the chilly air. However, she didn't turn on the engine, whether she was environmentally conscientious or her gas tank was running on Empty.

"Are you from CPS?" she asked Viv. "My neighbors sent them to check on me once so far. I told them that I was one hundred percent sober."

Apparently one hundred percent didn't mean the same thing to both of them. Not unless that fishbowl back inside was full of frickin' Kool Aid instead of whatever gross swill Viv suspected it really was.

"No, I'm not from Child Protective Services."

"You're not here to report back to them or any kind of agency like that?"

Viv frowned, wondering where this was going. She was hoping and praying that this wouldn't be a confession of incest, consensual or otherwise. "No, I'm here only for Claire. To find out the truth."

"Then, go ahead," Evelyn said in the darkened front seat of the beat-up car, which smelled like cold French fries and stale smoke. "Ask me whatever you want. I'm done keeping secrets. Even from Claire. I'll tell her whatever she wants to know. I'm just…tired of all of this—of fighting to make ends meet, of trying to keep everything together all by myself, of fighting to stay sober, of being alone. Just, all of it. I've been putting on these clothes and trying to pretend I'm doing okay, but I gotta tell you, my mask is about to slip and there's nothing I can do about it."

"Was Kip Claire's biological father?"

Evelyn hesitated before she answered, as if trying to overcome the long habit of keeping the secret, but then she admitted it. "Yes."

"And you're her mom?"

"*Yes.*" Now the woman frowned in defense. Viv moved ahead quickly.

"What was your relationship with Kip?"

Another pause, and then, "I thought we were going to be a family."

"Why does everyone think you're Kip's sister? Why do you go by his last name?"

"I just wanted to be a family." Evelyn shrugged. "And it was something Kip allowed to happen. He wanted to keep us close by. He wanted us to be his, and he didn't care what people assumed. I just never bothered to try to change people's minds, but..."

"Was it because of his wife?"

Evelyn nodded. "He wanted to stay married to Felicia, but he also wanted Claire in his life. I changed my last name to Baldwin when I found out I was pregnant. I thought we were going to get married. We were practically living together. I believed him when he said he was going to divorce Felicia—he told me he was going to. He promised he would, but he never did. Instead, he set Claire and me up in an apartment and told his wife I was his sister. I was from Charlotte. No one knew me here."

"How did you and Kip meet?"

Evelyn took out her pack of Pall Malls and turned it over and over in her hand without removing a cigarette. "Back in Charlotte at an airport bar. I was working there. I was just plain old Evelyn Carter back then. He was in town a lot for work. He was always trying to learn more about the restaurant business, making connections. He went to Nashville a lot, too. I swear I didn't know he was married—at least, I didn't realize it at first. Maybe there were signs I was ignoring or something, but then it didn't matter. I'd already fallen for him, and honestly, I just wanted to be with him. I was totally in love. I'd never been with someone like him who was just such a nice guy, so romantic, and so caring. After I found out that he was married, of course, I felt sick about it. But...I just couldn't make myself leave him. I was stupid, but I had this vision of us together and it was my one chance at a decent man. Guys like him don't come along more than once for someone like me."

Viv began to wonder if Kip had been the player that Evelyn made him out to be. She imagined what it would be like if he had so-called starter families in every one of his business stops—women who had been charmed into thinking that what they had with him was unique and would last forever—but she kept that to herself. No sense in further upsetting the already skittish Evelyn. As it was, the woman's anxiety was pushing Viv's own issues to the background, but she didn't want to examine too closely the idea that hanging around with a person more messed up than herself could make her feel almost normal.

"Please don't judge me," Evelyn said. "I had this vision of what the perfect life could be. He gave me the dream, the fantasy that I knew I didn't deserve. I mean, looking at you, I can tell you're the type of woman who can go into a bar and get any type of guy she wants. You have self-confidence. I can tell you stayed in school, so you're smart. I don't have any of that. I dropped out of high school. He offered me something I never in a million years thought I would end up with. A nice guy, a pretty home, and a baby girl. And it turned out I was right. None of that was real. It was just a dream all along and I was too dumb to realize it."

Viv did feel a little sorry for her, but it still didn't excuse her from going home to take care of Claire on a weekday night during a time, her teenage years, when the girl was most vulnerable. It was one thing if Claire was safely at home in a gated community, and speaking of which...

"Did Kip have a will?"

"Yes, a lawyer sent me a letter. Kip split everything three ways between me, Felicia, and Claire, but Felicia is contesting it. She wants everything, including his townhouse and the restaurant. I called the lawyer and took Claire in to do a DNA test, but I haven't heard back yet."

"You mean Claire, the one person who doesn't know anything about this? How did you explain the cheek swab to her?"

"I told her we were getting the test as part of a university study for money. I bought her a hamburger and a milkshake afterward." At Viv's exaggerated grimace, she added as she played with her cigarettes with a shaky hand, "I was planning to tell her everything. I *swear* I was. I was just waiting for the right time."

"Look," Viv finally said after an awkward silence, hugging her shoulder bag to her chest for comfort. "I'm not a parent and I can't tell you how to live your life. But I've been a kid in a situation similar to Claire's and I know how things can turn out when parents aren't around."

She knew she was straying off her script—the rough agenda she had in her mind she had rehearsed before tracking down Evelyn—but she *had* to say something. She really liked the kid, and someone needed to look out for her. Even though Viv didn't have any experience being a parent and definitely less world-weary, she had to speak up.

Evelyn held up her hand. "I already know what you're going to say."

Viv gritted her teeth, her patience with the woman growing thin. Yes, alcoholism was a disease, but Viv was out of her literal and figurative comfort zones in this smelly car on Claire's behalf, so she was a bit irritable. "Then why aren't you changing your behavior? Get an AA sponsor. Go to some meetings. For God's sake, don't work at a bar. Do whatever you have to do to fight your addiction. Treat it like a disease and seek professional help. You're not expected to overcome it by yourself, but you are expected *to do something* when a young, vulnerable person is depending on you."

Evelyn stared straight ahead for a good long moment of silence, and Viv thought, *This is when she shoves me out of her car.*

"You're right. I know this. All of it is true," Evelyn said, flipping her cigarette pack over and over. "I'm trying to get myself together. I know I have to. Not just for Claire, but for me."

That seemed like some backward logic to Viv, but whatever. As long as Evelyn got her butt home at night. And tried to get sober.

"I'd like to give you my number," Viv said, acutely aware that she might be making a mistake as Evelyn begrudgingly handed over her older iPhone, which was the same model Claire had and just as beat up with a cracked body as well as a screen with wonky lines across it. "Please call me if there's anything you need, even if it's just someone to talk to. I know you don't know me at all, but sometimes that might be better when you're having a bad day."

Evelyn took her phone back. Her silence signaled that it was time for Viv to get out of the car and leave the woman alone.

Although Viv didn't say it, she wished her nothing but the best of luck. For Claire.

CHAPTER TWENTY-NINE

Viv was ready to drop from exhaustion by the time she arrived back her parents' house. However, her mind was buzzing from everything she had learned during the day, and she wasn't sure how she was going to shut down her thoughts so she could sleep. Her go-to method was to crawl back into her onesie, drink some warm milk, and maybe take a melatonin tablet.

She parked in a space underneath the house, gathered up her phone and bag, and slid out of the car with shoulders that ached from the tension of having been out among actual real, live people the entire day. She walked up the wooden steps on aching feet, pushed her house key into the lock, and almost screamed her head off when a figure moved out of the shadows on the front porch.

Her screech echoed down the street as it was. If not for the sound of waves coming over the dunes, people on the west coast of Africa might have heard her.

"Hey, hey, hey. Take it easy. It's just me," Benjy said with his hands up. He moved under the porch lamp and the light shined off his blond hair. The relief she felt almost buckled her knees.

"Holy heck," was all she could manage to say as she clutched her chest and tried to get her erratic heart rate under control.

Her crazy mind had thought he was Christopher Kahoe looming in the shadows waiting to attack her like some restaurant debt enforcer boogeyman. It wasn't until after Benjy took the key from her, picked up her bag, which she had dropped after preparing to slug him with it, and led her inside that she had the wherewithal to ask, "What are you doing here?"

Although Benjy's job was flexible—he dabbled in a lot of things, but his most recent business venture meant he owned and managed a collection of mall kiosks, thanks to some seed money from his father—he was the last person she had expected to find on her doorstep.

He handed her a glass of water. "I traveled down to check on you, but instead I think I almost killed you from heart failure. Oopsies? I left you a couple messages. Is your phone dead?"

She held it up to show him its darkened screen just before she attached it into the charger that she had accidentally left plugged in the kitchen outlet that morning. "Basically, you're saying it's my fault that you scared the crap out of me?"

He shrugged and smiled that trademark irresistible Benjy smile. "Maybe a little bit?"

"Have you been waiting for me all day?"

She tugged at her wig, which had started to itch. Oddly, after a whole day of wearing it, *only now* it was bugging her. She didn't want to take it off in front of him though. Even though they had known each other forever, undressing in front of him would have been way too intimate.

"I got here a few hours ago, but when you weren't answering your phone, I went down to that crazy bar with all the cats and hung out for a while."

"Sassy Ann's. Not a bad way to kill a few hours."

When, at last, Viv couldn't take it anymore, she began to peel off her fake eyelashes. He trailed behind her as she walked upstairs. She paused on a step and lifted one foot at a time, removing her shoes on the way up.

"What have you been up to all day?" he asked, flopping down on her bed while she went into the bathroom where a familiar terrycloth comfort hung on the back of the door, waiting for her.

Taking off the wig and netting that had smashed her natural sandy blond hair to her head was such a sweet, sweet release, she almost moaned with pleasure. Removing all the makeup on her face was a close second.

"Hey, *there* you are. That's the person we know and love," he said when she emerged with a clean face and flopped down on the bed next to him.

Without hesitation, she began to go through the events of the past couple days. She started with how she had read Claire's story on the internet. To Benjy's credit, he didn't blink an eye when Viv mentioned her various possibly illegal delving into bank, credit, and phone records that the average citizen didn't have access or skills to obtain.

Whether it was the pleasure of seeing him or the deliverance of having survived a full day away from familiar surroundings, she completely unloaded all of her thoughts and fears about Claire and the death of her uncle, including her talk with Sandy Sommers and the DNA lead about Delroy Bennett, whoever that was. Poor, lost, alcoholic Evelyn who was not a good mother to her child. Claire's birth certificate—which lay at the bottom of Viv's shoulder bag—which the girl herself had never seen. Arletta and the confrontation with the intimidating and explosive Christopher Kahoe.

As she was falling asleep on top of the bed covers next to Benjy, she said, "And I don't think that boy Terrance is gay at all. Maybe bi or non-binary, but I'm pretty sure he's in love with that girl and she just doesn't know it."

Just as she drifted off, she thought she heard him say, "Hm. Sounds familiar," which was weird.

CHAPTER THIRTY

Viv slept soundly and awoke to the vision of an angel in the bed next to her. The sunlight was shining on Benjy's hair as he breathed evenly. He smelled good, like warm laundry and just him, and she decided she needed to get up before she started to have inappropriate thoughts about her longtime friend. Who was in love with Josie. The man didn't even snore. He never had, even during drunken college sleepovers on each other's couches. Who ever heard of such a thing?

She got up, showered, donned her Olivia uniform and makeup. Today was orange leggings with a purple spandex mini shirt and contrasting swirl-patterned tunic top. Then, she went down to the kitchen to check her phone messages. She had a couple from Benjy asking where she was, but nothing from Sandy Sommers or Claire. She also had a few things she needed to research before she got going for the day, including who in the ever-loving-heck Delroy Bennett was.

And who could have sent Sandy that anonymous note?

After Viv powered up her laptop, the first thing she looked into after ripping open a bag of M&Ms trail mix, was who Delroy, the mystery man, might be. Unfortunately, Facebook alone listed a couple hundred people by that name. She would have to postpone that research for now. She had to get more information from Sandy Sommers so she could narrow down the search. Until then, Viv felt like a whale shark, a passive feeder swimming around with her mouth open, just taking in tons of plankton.

Next, she moved onto looking into Evelyn's background. Viv already knew to look in the Charlotte area for traces of her, including her birth name, Evelyn Carter.

In less than five minutes, Viv found an article in the *Charlotte Witness* about seven-year-old "Evie" Carter singing with her church choir at the Lakewood Living Faith Baptist Church, complete with a grainy black-and-white photo of towheaded and pigtailed Evelyn who looked pretty much as if Claire had gone back in time to the 1980s.

Viv calculated Evelyn's age. She was thirty-three now, so she had been nineteen when she had had Claire, and almost a full decade younger than Kip.

"No… Waitaminute." With an M&M in her cheek, Viv's mind tripped over itself. In Kip's desk drawer, he had had photos of himself when he was young, with a little blond baby on his lap. Viv had assumed that was baby Evelyn because the child had resembled baby Claire. However, if he and Evelyn were not siblings, who was the baby in the photo with young Kip?

"Talking to yourself?" Benjy asked from behind her. He'd stumbled down the stairs and sat on the second to last one, looking rumbled and kind of adorable as he yawned and tried unsuccessfully to tame his hair by running a hand through it.

"Now I'm not, since you're here. But I am confused about something, and my brain doesn't know what to do."

He held up a finger. "Lemme make some coffee and I'll be right with you."

When he came back with two mugs, one of which he set next to her, which she peered into and discovered it was deliciously dark and unpolluted by cream or sugar, both of which she knew he liked in his, she sighed in appreciation. She took a fortifying sip and then explained the situation.

Then he summed it up, saying it back to her. "So, the baby that Kip was holding when he was a kid couldn't possibly be Evelyn because she isn't actually his sister. However, she looks like she could have been his sister? Is that your stumbling block?"

"Precisely. If she's not his sister, he's oddly attracted to people who look like they could be related to him. And what happened to his actual sister?"

Benjy swallowed a swig from his own cup. "Josie once told me this weird statistic about how many people look for partners that look like themselves. For some people, it's a predisposed urge to find a mate genetically similar to themselves. There's an actual website called siblingsordating.com where you can guess whether people are dating or related. Because so many people look like their partners, it's hard to tell."

"For real?" She stared up at him, trying to keep herself from wondering whether his golden summery features resembled her own.

Would we make a good couple?

"Absolutely. There's no research about whether it makes couples stay together longer or not, but it's a thing. With Kip Baldwin, however, maybe you should find out what happened to his real sister. Is she still around?"

Maybe her brain was mush in his presence, and she chastised herself for not thinking of searching for another sibling sooner. She noted, with interest, that he didn't have the least bit of doubt that she could find out, which she could...and did within a few more minutes in the Atlanta birth and death public records.

After gaining access to the Fulton County Vital Records Office, she let out a sigh. "Ahhh. Looks like he had a sibling named Lisa Lynn Baldwin." She did another search of the local news archives for Atlanta and found a small obituary and funeral home notice. "Aww. She passed away at age four. Looks like from a drowning incident, possibly in a backyard pool based on the comments people left on the memorial notebook. That's super sad. Look at her cute little face in the picture."

Benjy leaned over her shoulder for a closer look, brushing a stray strand of her wig off his chin where it had caught on his beard stubble. "So is that also what the girl—Claire—looks like?"

"Pretty much."

Viv peered at Kip's real baby sister in the photo. She was definitely the same one who had sat on young Kip's lap in the picture from his desk drawer. Her death must have made a great impact on him at such a young age. Maybe it had sparked his protective instincts early on.

Benjy stepped back and gave Viv an assessing look. "Huh. I'm not making you nervous, am I, being here and all, and getting up close and personal in your space."

And actually, he wasn't all at, which should have been weird, but it was Benjy after all.

"No. Why do you ask?"

"Because you aren't interrupting to tell me about Johnny Cash's world-famous concert at Fulton County Prison or whatever trivia your brain comes up with when you're anxious."

Well, now that you mention it, you are standing close enough for me to smell your soap and the sugary delicious coffee that you just drank.

She told him, "The live album that Johnny Cash released in 1968 was recorded at Folsom State Prison in California, not Georgia."

He smiled. "See, now you're a little nervous since I pointed it out."

"After he recorded the song, 'Folsom Prison Blues' in the mid-1950s because—*I am not.*"

But Benjy wasn't an arguer and he never had been. That was one of the things she liked about him, that unlike some of her past boyfriends, he didn't always have to be right. Not that he was a boyfriend, past or present, she quickly amended.

"What's on the docket for today? I see you're all armored up and ready to go," he said with a nod to her Olivia clothes, and she was grateful for the change of subject.

"I want to find Felicia Tofana, Kip's ex-wife, and see what she has to say about the townhouse. I think she's been staying there. Also, maybe she'll have some insight about Evelyn or even some new leads to track down."

"What, like Aqua Tofana the seventeenth-century poison?"

"I don't know what that is." She squinted at him. "Are you making up trivia to mock me?"

"No! Are you serious? Do you mean to tell me I know some trivia that you don't? We need to mark this day down on the calendar."

She rolled her eyes. "Whatever I don't know, I can always Google. For instance, I'll tell you what I know about Felicia."

Earlier, Viv had discovered that Kip's ex-wife was now a licensed Realtor in Wilmington. She specialized in beachfront properties not unlike the one Viv's parents owned and had apparently made a new name for herself, literally, because she had adopted the professional name Felicia Tofana. Her smiling face with fuchsia lipstick and bright white teeth popped up all over the internet in ad banners and open house announcements.

While Viv had the financial means to pose as a potential client of Felicia's, what she lacked was the nerve. It was one thing to play pretend sleuth for a kid and a small-town gossip columnist, but for a multi-million-dollar saleswoman who most likely had her scam radar turned up high, a woman who was probably as concerned for her own personal safety as Viv was? Viv didn't know if she could do it. She felt a little faint just thinking about it.

Ted Kohlhepp was an American serial killer and Realtor who murdered at least seven people in South Carolina in the early 2000s, including one poor woman whom he chained to the inside of a metal storage container on his private property.

A real estate agent was just about the very worst career Viv could imagine. If she had to sell homes, she would always think the very worst, that every meeting she set up was with someone who was potentially going to harm her. Never mind trying to avoid being maimed, scammed, or lost trying to find the right property, there was all that *peopling* involved.

Viv shivered. Maybe she could do a phone interview. Maybe Felicia was quick to email back. Or text. What if they could do the whole thing by text and Viv wouldn't even have to leave the house. She could just crawl back into bed for a little bit.

Benjy was looking at her as if he had asked a question, so she said, "Sorry. What?"

"I asked if you want me to go with you today."

Do I ever.

She gave a slow and thoughtful nod and tried to hide her deep, gasping inhale of relief, since she realized her spike of anxiety had been preventing her from breathing properly. "Yes. I think that might be a good idea."

CHAPTER THIRTY-ONE

Although Viv wasn't sure if it was wise, Benjy dropped his full name in order to get them a same-day appointment with Felicia. Viv did not want to be handed off to an underling at Felicia's company. As he had once explained to Viv after he knew he could trust her, his family wasn't exactly the Kennedys, but they had been neighbors at one time. In this day and age, Viv could completely understand a woman's desire to protect herself from grifters, murderers, and other general scum of the earth, but still...it felt really wrong to have Benjy expose himself and his credit all in the name of Viv's investigation, even if it was for a good cause.

Benjy was a trust-fund kid even though he and his father often didn't get along and he was frequently shut off from his family accounts, for example, when he picked Business as his college major instead of Pre-Law or Pre-Med. Then again after they graduated and Benjy refused to register for the exams to get into graduate schools. And again when he refused to date a nice Jewish girl that Arthur Goldsmith had set him up with. The girl's name was Rachael, and Viv had instantly disliked her even though she had never met her and knew *less than* nothing about her.

"Maybe I should have changed into more conservative clothes," Viv said, smoothing down her Olivia wig as Benjy drove them to their appointment in his Range Rover that signaled he was currently on speaking terms with his father. She rolled the vintage ring she had put on her wedding ring finger to help them pose as an engaged couple.

"You look fine," he said, without glancing at her.

"She probably ran a credit report on you. That's how we got this instant meeting with her. She can probably smell money from here."

"It's okay. My credit can take it, and if we don't find a house that we want to immediately buy today—impulse buy with my old-world gold bullion that I've dug out from under my mattress—so be it. Perhaps it's not nice to use a ruse like this, but what if you end up solving a murder because I used my bank account to get us an appointment? I think my bank account won't mind. Might as well use it to open a couple of doors while Arthur still allows me to have access to it."

It probably could do just that. Viv had always thought of her own parents as well-off, but Benjy's dad was way up in the stratosphere by comparison. Definitely a one-percenter. Like, high-rise apartments in multiple cities, a yacht, and possibly a chateau somewhere with seasonal but genteel wintering.

Benjy was an only child, which could have explained his father's laser-like focus on him as well as the Atlas-like weight of his vicarious hopes and dreams. However, the fact that Benjy had access to his funds at the moment suggested that his father was also happy, which usually meant there was a woman in the picture, possibly a third future ex-wife.

Speaking of which, Felicia Tofana would have been just his type. She gave Viv's hand a squeeze after Benjy's as she led them through her richly appointed offices that smelled like citrus and something spicier, like sandalwood or possibly bergamot. Viv was just guessing—she had no earthly clue what bergamot actually smelled like.

Physically, Felicia was not what Viv expected. Yes, the real estate agent's face and her Extreme Dream Team logo was all over her website as well as every one of her property listings, but Viv had not been prepared for her impressive height or her well-muscled physique. She looked like an Instagram influencer who could have sold protein powder or a sure-fire weight loss solution. Because of the warm weather, Felicia was able to display the bronzed, lean muscle of her shoulders to full effect with her sleeveless bright lemon business blouse and coordinating straight skirt.

Good gravy, just look at those deltoids! And those biceps. She could be a fitness model.

Viv was not a short woman by any standard except perhaps the

WNBA. She was 5' 7", which was a good three inches above the average American woman. However, Felicia was a bronzed goddess, an ultra-tanned, dark-haired Amazon—no, a *Glamazon*—who towered over her in Louboutin Galativi bi-material ballerina flats, if Viv wasn't mistaken. After all, she *knew* shoes, and if she was wrong, she would box up her prized Judith Leiber Couture Pepperoni Pizza Clutch Bag and toss it into a charity collection bin.

"Y'all please have a seat. So nice to meet you. I'm absolutely tickled to death y'all called me and we could fit you in today during your visit here. I've been busier than a moth in a mitten, but I just knew I had to make time for y'all," Felicia told them with an accent thick enough to fry hush puppies, and then she leaned over her glossy mahogany desk and whispered at Viv. "I hope you don't mind be being a nosy ninja, but—"

Uh oh. Here it comes.

"Is your blouse a Betsey Johnson?"

Viv glanced down at her bright top that she had chosen mostly to draw some of the attention away from the fakeness of her hair.

"As a matter of fact, it is. It's marketed and sold as a mini dress, but I like to pair it with leggings after the summer is over."

"I love how you did that. Some of those dresses are so short, you could see Christmas if you know what I'm talkin' about, but you look prettier than a peach. I adore that and I *love* the colors. It's how I dress away from the office. Colors are life," Felicia said with a tanned and manicured hand on her chest. "Y'all might like some muted coastal decor for your living spaces, but there's nothing like a pop of bright color here or there to do a heart good."

"The Betsey Johnson website has some amazing clearance."

"No?! Really? I need to take a look this evening when I get some downtime. Just me, a glass of cab, and my best friend. And by that, I mean my credit card." She flashed Viv her bright white teeth.

"Oh, definitely same for me." Although lately, she was more of a kid's juice box and PayPal kind of girl.

Viv was unexpectedly and helplessly delighted by the woman's candid rapport. When she glanced at Benjy in apology, certain he was uninterested and excluded by their fashion chatter, he simply gave an amused shrug. She'd definitely not expected she would bond with the woman within the first few minutes of meeting her.

Then again, she is a pro at her job, just as Kip had been a charmer and a schmoozer. Maybe they had been a match made in heaven.

"What kind of properties are y'all interested in?" Felicia asked, and Viv realized that having established a connection between them, the Southern saleswoman was now ready to get down to business. "And just so you know, I'm a full-service Realtor. I'm a buyer or seller's agent, so if you also have a property to sell, I can do everything from staging your old home to selling it—even after you've moved out, I keep a warehouse of items that I can bring to make it look appealing and irresistible to potential buyers— to listing it, to scheduling open houses. Anything you need, basically." She got out a yellow legal pad. "Now, let's hear what you're looking for."

"I'd like something close to the beach, not just as a seasonal place but a year-round home. Something with enough rooms that could accommodate a family, eventually," Benjy said without missing a beat, and Viv had to stop herself from boggling at him.

He wants kids someday? I never knew. I don't think I've ever seen him around kids to be honest.

She tried to imagine what he had looked like as a baby, and it was fairly easy. He had probably been one of those white-blond babies with the curls all over his head. Dimpled cheeks and a big smile not unlike how he looked now.

When she glanced at him, he beamed fondly at her in a way that was all too familiar, and which also may have been similar to an actual dream or two of hers. She had to avert her eyes before she totally lost it— whether that meant giggling like a third grader or cackling like a drunken barmaid, she wasn't quite sure, but it was a risk she wasn't willing to take all the same.

"Are y'all familiar with the Windfall area?" Felicia asked. "It's very nicely laid out, with eighteen holes of a PGA-designed golf course and not too far from the beach, protected from storms, which is something to think about in this area—but if you're looking to wake up in the morning, open your back door, and stick your toes in the sand, we can absolutely find something suitable as well. We just want our clients to be happier than pigs in mud. Of course, not literal mud, more like the lap of luxury, if you hear me." Felicia smiled broadly but was clearly classier than to laugh at her own joke.

"Neither of us golfs, but access to a pool is important. We both love to swim," he said, which was true. During their college years, he had swum competitively on their school's team, and she had sometimes met him at the indoor pool to swim laps. She'd almost forgotten about that.

"I think you'd love Windfall, but I should tell you that I'm biased toward the place myself," Felicia said. "I don't want to get too personal but—"

Viv knew this tone. The woman was totally about to spill the tea.

Do it, sweetheart. Bless us with the gossip!

"—I'm about to move into Windfall myself. A relative of mine recently passed away and left me a beautiful townhouse property. I'm sure I could make a tidy profit if I wanted to sell it. I'm not so poor I can't afford to pay attention, but this is something special. The property values are just going up and up in that area, so it's a wonderful investment. But this is a true *windfall*, no pun intended, and I'd be crazy not to keep it for myself."

What?!

Viv felt a little ill. Felicia was clearly referring to Kip's townhouse, and although Viv had been well on her way to being charmed by the fast-talking agent, she was ready throw hands and to go over the top of the pretentious shiny desk after her on Claire's behalf.

"Do you have any kids?" she asked Felicia feeling more than a little hot under the collar of her Betsey Johnson shirt that she had felt cute in not ten minutes ago, thanks to this Dixieland turncoat. "I hope that's not too personal of a question. I'm just thinking about schools in the area."

"Oh, no kids for me. I don't mean to delve into a TMI moment—you know, *too much information?*—but my ex wasn't able to have any children due to his nonviable swimmers, and I'm not the single mom type of gal. Not that there's anything wrong with adopting on your own if the right person doesn't come along. Or sometimes things just don't work out with the baby daddy, like my ex's little sister. She's a single mom, bless her heart. I'm totally in support of people who get themselves stuck in a situation that is out of their control. And some people can afford to do the single parent thing all on their own, like those rich and famous Hollywood types, but you literally need a whole army of people to support you if you do. Nannies and sitters and daycare. That's not for me. If I'm going to stay home with some precious little bundles of joy, I need a fella who's in it to support me like the queen bee I am. The royal lifestyle ain't just for Beyoncé, if you know what I'm sayin'."

Benjy said, "No judgment here. It's good to know your own mind about things like that, especially when you're talking about a child, a whole new life."

Viv shot him a look, but he was impervious to her glare.

"As for schools, the public schools here is solid, but there's also a private K through 12 academy that has an amazing ranking. Its graduates go to Duke, Chapel Hill, Harvard, Yale, and all the big-name colleges." She gave a wave of her tanned and manicured hand.

Benjy chuckled. "That's thinking pretty far ahead. Junior isn't even here yet."

Wait, what did he just do? He did not just say what I think he said, did he?

"Oh my goodness! Are you two expecting?" Felicia exclaimed.

Benjy reached across the space between their two chairs and grabbed Viv's hand, which he held gently. She nearly snatched it back but forced herself to relax and return his tender gaze—harder than it sounded when she wanted to bap him on his curly blond head with one of Felicia's thick real estate brochures.

Expecting? I'm expecting him to buy me lunch as soon as we're out of here. I deserve a pepperoni pizza after this torture. He shouldn't toy with me like this.

"Well, congratulations!" the woman barreled ahead after Viv's awkward silence. She was a true professional. "If there's anything you need, like doctor or birthing center recommendations, y'all just let me know. I even know a doula, if that's your preference. And don't you worry. A lot of people don't like to mention it early on, especially when you're just beginning to show. I'll keep it to myself."

Felicia patted the desk as if she were trying to soothe Viv, whose face must have revealed her irritation. She was starting to feel self-conscious about her belly and sucked it in.

Give me a break. It's just a food baby! Four months in baggy loungewear will do that to a person. I used to go to the gym six days a week. Now I'm a desk chair warrior. Fine. I'm doing some crunches as soon as we get back to the house.

"Tell us about the crime rate. Is it safe in that Windfall neighborhood?" Viv said, irritated and ready to be more aggressive in her line of questioning.

"Super safe! I wouldn't want to live there otherwise," Felicia assured them.

"But what about that man, Kip Baldwin, who was just murdered?" Viv pressed.

Felicia stuttered, but like a true salesperson, attempted to recover quickly. However, her body language had changed as she avoided eye-contact and straightened some papers and the pen holder on her desk. "Oh, did you read about that in the news? He wasn't at home when it happened. He was at his place of business way on the other side of town."

By Viv's calculations, it had been less than a ten-minute drive.

"I'm sorry," Viv said, with an apologetic frown. "You didn't know him, did you?"

To her credit, Felicia didn't lie. "Yes, actually I did. I was out of town visiting some friends in Asheville when it happened. Such a horrible and shocking thing to come back to find out."

"Forgive me," Viv said. "I didn't mean to be nosy. Deepest condolences."

"Thank you so much. Anyway, tell me what your schedule is like, and we'll get around to see some places lickety-split before you leave town. Just remember I am here for you, and I will do whatever it takes to help you find the perfect home for you and your family."

CHAPTER THIRTY-TWO

D o you think she was telling the truth?" Benjy asked when they were back in his car.

"About which part?"

"My mind is blowing up. I'm totally confused," Benjy said making finger explosions next to his temples. "I thought Felicia divorced Kip because he got Evelyn pregnant. But didn't she just say that Kip wasn't able to have children? And also, it sounded like she still thinks that Evelyn is Kip's sister."

"She *did* say that," Viv agreed, fussing with the air conditioner vents on her side. She was, as Felicia with all her Southernisms might have said, *sweating like a whore in church* from the effort of keeping up her fake Olivia identity. "She could be lying because she wants to publicly plant the idea that Claire isn't directly related to Kip and, therefore, doesn't deserve any of the inheritance from him, namely the townhouse and the restaurant. On the other hand, maybe it was Felicia who was unable to have kids and she was simply blaming Kip. Or, on the third hand, maybe she was just shooting the breeze with us, laying on the Southern charm thick just to make a sale."

"That's a lot of hands."

"Did her accent seem fake to you? I thought it was thick enough to slice with a knife."

"I don't know," he said. "I'm terrible at identifying accents. I thought I had a Connecticut one, but you said I don't have an accent at all."

"You don't. You sound like a generic American to me. In any case, it definitely seems like Felicia is making a play for the townhouse, which is unfortunate. Based on her appearance alone and her business's success, she probably doesn't need it as desperately as Claire and her mom do. I don't know how close they are to being homeless, but I imagine it's one paycheck or less."

Viv took a second to send a text to Claire to check in and say hi. She didn't have much progress to report that she felt comfortable sharing yet. She'd started looking at Kip's laptop earlier and hadn't found much other than bookmarks to his favorite adult entertainment sites—which was in keeping with his credit card history—and some fantasy football stuff. He didn't even do personal banking or keep his photos on his laptop. However, she wanted the kid to know that someone was making an effort.

"Where to next? I'm hungry, are you?" Benjy asked.

"Speaking of which...do I look pregnant to you?!" she exclaimed, recalling Felicia's comments. Viv put her hands on her belly, which she thought was only *slightly* more rounded than it was in their college days.

He glanced at her. "This is a trap, isn't it? There's no way I can answer that without sounding like a jerk."

"I won't get mad. I promise. Say whatever you want to say."

He took one hand off the wheel to gesture while he listed his options. "Okay, hypothetically, these are my possible responses.

"One: I like you any way you are. But that implies that you're not currently perfect because if I thought you were perfect, then I would just flat out say so.

"Two: You're perfect just the way you are. But that implies that you weren't perfect before and if you change—and all people change—then you won't still be perfect. Kind of like saying, 'Don't change a thing,' which is impossible.

"Three: You're perfect because your whole being is perfect. But that implies that there's something wrong with your physical appearance, which there isn't, but why am I focusing so much on what's inside? It's like saying, 'Oh, but you have a *great personality*.'

"Four: You can change if you want to, but don't change for me. But that implies that even though I want you to be happy with yourself, I don't care how you look, which wouldn't be true exactly—"

"I'm flabbergasted at the amount of thought you've put into this." She felt like boggling at him in the classical sense of cartoon boggling where the character's eyes bulge.

And did he just say he likes me? Or is this about a hypothetical woman in a hypothetical relationship? Color me confused.

"I admit that I *have* given it some thought," he said, running a hand through his hair, which he did when he was nervous.

See, he has a tell, too.

"It also kind of makes me wonder *who hurt you* that you don't have a single and honest gut reaction without all this anxiety. Was it that Kelsey person you dated a few years ago? She struck me as being an over-thinker."

"Well, she certainly was one, but I don't think she can take the blame for this. I've always been this way."

"In all these years we've known each other, I had no clue you were so messed up on the inside." He shot her a concerned look, but she was smiling. "I'm laughing *with* you, not at you," she clarified, just in case he was really worried. She absolutely didn't think he was very messed up at all. In fact, he was one of the more well-adjusted people she knew.

"All I really wanted to know was if you're hungry," he said.

"Sure. There's a restaurant called It Smells Fishy in Here that—"

She caught a glimpse of his appalled grimace at the restaurant's name —who wouldn't cringe at it?—but her phone's text alert tone cut off his answer. She thought it was Claire responding, but instead, the message was from Sandy Sommers, and it said:

U in the neighborhood? Wanna show u DNA info that came up. Easier to show than text.

"Change of plans," Viv told him, directing him not to It Smells Fishy in Here but to the Beachin' Beans Café. "But I *promise* I'll buy you lunch right afterward."

He groaned, but of course he was amenable. He was always up for a plot twist, an interesting change of plans, a fork in the road, or a chance to improvise. After all, he was Benjy, and she made a mental reminder never to take advantage of his kindness for the rest of their lives, if at all possible…at least, to the best of her ability.

When Sandy saw them, she gave a little shriek of happiness. "Oh my lord," she said. "As I live and breathe, it's like looking at Bradley Cooper's identical twin in the flesh. And then there's you with your orange hair, you two look like the stars of that spy show on TV I just started watching obsessively."

Viv knew exactly what show she was talking about but decided not to mention that—*spoiler alert!*—the cute Bradley Cooper character died in a bathtub in one episode. Although, like any TV drama worth the pixels it used, he—*spoiler alert again!*—wasn't dead for real.

"Uh, thanks?" Benjy said, right before offering to buy them each a coffee. Viv opted for an iced green tea. Sandy declined because she had already gotten an Americano, and they watched him shuffle off to the counter to order in that unhurried, slightly slouchy but endearing way of his.

"He seems like a keeper," Sandy said, tilting her head sideways to better appreciate his retreating backside. "Apologies about objectifying your boyfriend and his cute buns. Interesting ring, by the way. It's not a usual kind of engagement bling. I didn't notice it yesterday."

"It's temporary," Viv said, for some reason feeling defensive on Benjy's behalf that he was being accused of being cheap and giving her an unworthy fake engagement ring for their also fake engagement...which was completely ridiculous.

"Try before you buy?" Sandy asked.

"Something like that."

No, not like that at all, to be honest. Not anything. Just a bit of unreciprocated crushing.

"Well, let me know if you throw him back into the sea. I may be too old, but I have a niece who'd appreciate him."

"I'll...keep that in mind."

At least, I would if any of this was real.

"Haha! Made you re-appreciate what you've got, didn't I?"

When Benjy came back, he had the good manners not to ask why the columnist was cackling like a banshee. He did give Viv a sideways glance, but he didn't follow it up with a spoken question, which was probably for the better.

"So, what did you find out about the DNA? Do you have information about Delroy Bennet?" Viv asked. As much as this conversation was both amusing to her and at the same time making her squirm with discomfort, she was dying to hear Sandy's news.

The older woman pushed aside her cup and scooted her chair closer.

"Are you ready for this? Now, I got this information from a friend of mine at the police department, but I had to promise not to use any of it in a story until I get the okay from them. Do I have your word that none of this will be public knowledge? I mean, if you spread any of it around, I'll have to deny that you got it from me."

Viv swore vehemently that she would abide by Sandy's rules, even though she knew full well that she could be recording their conversation secretly. Sandy should have realized this as well. After all, she had seen Viv record their previous chat. Interestingly, Sandy didn't make Benjy also swear not to talk, too. Maybe she had judged him trustworthy based on his looks. Viv eyed him.

I mean, he does look trustworthy. Like a priest.

She imagined him with a clerical collar.

A hot priest... This is a fantasy I didn't know I had until now.

Thankfully, Sandy interrupted her thoughts. "As a journalism student, you might think that success in this career means being as cut-throat as possible and trying to get the scoop on other reporters to be the first one to publish a story, but that's simply not true anymore. This isn't Hollywood. This isn't the movies. This is a very connected industry, which means if you get a reputation for stabbing other people in the back or sabotaging another person's work, that stink will follow you around for the rest of your days like dog crap on the bottom of your shoe."

Duly noted. Instead of a gentlemen's agreement, this is a gentle-journalist's agreement, so to speak. Sandy is counting on me to be honest, and this is her final warning.

Viv nodded her agreement. "I hear you."

"The police department found a vial with traces of arsenic in it in the garbage bin outside the restaurant. Now, the vial itself didn't have any fingerprints or DNA on it, but some rubber gloves were also found in a separate bin. The gloves not only had traces of arsenic but also DNA of the person they suspect put the poison in Kip's sweet tea."

"Are you serious?!" Viv exclaimed. "They found this right outside the Time & Tidewater?"

"That's just one of the bombshells. Here's the second bombshell. The vial wasn't found outside Kip's restaurant but *outside the Kahoes' restaurant.*"

Alarm bells rang in Viv's head. "Does this mean he was poisoned at It Smells Fishy in Here?"

"I don't think he could have been with the amount of arsenic in him. I'm trying to get access to the autopsy report—I'll let you know when I do. All I know is, from the amount he ingested, he died really fast. That means he had to have drunk the sweet tea at his own restaurant, and then the container was dumped over at the Kahoes' place."

"And the DNA on the gloves?"

"It was from this Delroy Bennett man, whoever he is. My contact at the police department says this fellow has a record. That's why they got a match so quickly, but he lives out in California."

"That's the entire opposite side of the country. What was he doing here in North Carolina?" Viv frowned. "What are you thinking?"

"Girl, I *know* I'm thinking what you're thinking. You're just not saying it out loud—this guy Bennett has to be a hired killer and he was trying to frame the Kahoe family for it."

PART IV
MERMAIDS, UNICORNS, AND CHIMERAS—OH, MY!

"It's not magic, it's science!" —unknown meme guy

CHAPTER THIRTY-THREE

The first thing Viv wanted to do when she got back to the beach house after a quick drive-thru lunch, even more than taking off her Olivia wig, was to log into her laptop to find out everything she could about Delroy Bennett. Now she had a home state to narrow down the hundreds of hits her earlier search had gotten. Presumably, Delroy had a connection to North Carolina that might further assist her in finding him in a haystack of other Delroy Bennetts.

Cracking her knuckles, she got to work at her keyboard.

As it turned out, with all of these extra factors to filter the data, there were only three Delroys left, which was worlds better than the hundreds she had found on social media.

Benjy had made himself another mug of coffee. She declined because she couldn't drink it after noon or her insomnia brain would throw a nocturnal dance party, complete with a disco ball in her head and a deejay that played only earworms. He pulled up a chair next to her as if he were in the passenger seat of a car she was driving.

"I have to admit, I really misjudged you in the beginning," he said as she typed and clicked her way around California public records.

"In the beginning of what?" she asked, dividing her attention. She was excellent at multitasking although she suspected that every time she did it, parts of her brain were probably crumbling away and turning into dust. Brain cell dust bunnies inside her skull. One day when she was old and in a nursing home, she would probably have to be reminded how to blink *and* breathe at the same time. Grim, yes, but it felt like the truth.

"In the beginning, you know, when we first met. That initial week before school started during freshman orientation at college."

That made her pause to look at him. This was too important for multitasking. She needed more information, more context before she knew how to take his words…and whether she was supposed to internally freak out or not.

"Don't get me wrong," he said quickly but not quite backpedaling. "I still liked you and wanted to hang with you, but I didn't know there was all this underneath that icy cool exterior."

When he said *this*, he gestured with his non-coffee-mug-holding hand at her, sweeping from head to toe and back again. However, she got hung up on the words *I still liked you* and could easily have gone into over-analysis mode, except his overall point confused her.

"I'm still the same person I was then," she said carefully.

She'd heard words like this before, usually when someone discovered she had a full *Star Trek* TOS costume hanging in her closet, complete with a tricorder. Or, usually right before a man broke up with her. She trusted herself less and less often to understand people's motivations and meanings these days. Everything about her judgement and perception of the world—and even her good friends—seemed slightly off kilter.

I mean, I was ready to marry James, and he turned out to be involved in a murder. If it hadn't been for Josie and that fateful trip to San Francisco, who knows what would have happened to me?

Bless his heart, Benjy tried again to explain what he was saying. "I didn't know you were a hacker! I thought you were a fashion influencer or Instagram star or something."

She snorted. "Arguably, a unicorn onesie is on the cutting edge of fashion right now. I'm still ahead of the curve, but just so you know, I'm not actually a hacker. I have some pretty good connections and decent research skills. I know people who know things. That's about it."

He dropped his feet from where he had rested them on the chair. "I beg to differ. I've been watching you for the last few minutes and I have no idea how you even got to this site or wherever it is you are. That's definitely not Google right there." He tipped his chin toward her laptop's screen. "Is that even legal what you're doing?"

She gave him a sideways look.

"Right. Don't answer that. I don't want to know. Plausible deniability. I've seen all the Jack Ryan movies."

She rolled her eyes. "I'm not a spy. I'm not even an agent of some no-name department that would definitely have a TV show made about it."

"But I bet you could be."

"To be honest, hot TV actors notwithstanding, it sounds like a terrible way to live your life," she said, thinking about her parents, who had spent at least a quarter of her childhood on a different continent than she. "And a lousy way to raise kids. No golden retriever in the yard. No house with a white picket fence. No relentless parade of mortgage payments and a fascist homeowners' association."

"Is that what you want out of life?" he asked, suddenly seeming to find the inside of his coffee cup fascinating.

She wasn't sure what he was getting at, but she shrugged. "Kids and a shabby chic decorating scheme? I don't know. I'm just saying, if you're going to have kids, you should go all in. You know what I mean?"

He, with his similarly hands-off father, would know.

Whatever he had been about to answer, she cut him off as a hit on her database search of California public records appeared on her screen.

"Well, well, well. Look at what the search criteria dragged in."

"I don't know what that means, but it looks like you found *our* Mr. Delroy Bennett."

She opened another window on her screen, typed and clicked, and opened a driver's license photo of a middle-aged, clean-cut African American man in a plaid, button up shirt.

"Bingo." Then, she read aloud, "Delroy Ferguson Bennett, aged 52. Born in Riverside, California. Never married. One adult daughter, who is married with two kids, which makes Delroy a grandpa. He has an arrest record with a couple of charges, including a shoplifting conviction in 1998 of an item under $950 in value. In the court records, Delroy's lawyer stated that the store owner falsely accused him of shoplifting, and when his pockets were searched and nothing was found, the store owner allegedly planted a stolen Timex watch on him."

"That case sounds ludicrous. Maybe a personal vendetta or blatant racism?"

"Could be. It says he received a fine of $250 but no jail time."

"So, they probably didn't have his DNA on file for that trumped-up misdemeanor. How did the police find a match to connect him to Kip Baldwin's poisoning?"

She traveled down a couple more internet rabbit holes through the minutiae of Delroy Bennett's daily life from his driver's license and last known address, to his participation in a volunteer city park clean-up day.

"Here's another hit on him at paternity.com. He and his biological daughter did DNA tests to prove their relationship. Maybe that's how the South Pier PD connected him to the arsenic container and gloves. His daughter is Cara Jones, and *aww*, she legally changed her name to Cara Bennett Jones not long after she and Delroy matched their DNA about four years ago. I'm picturing a heart-warming reunion."

"Despite the alleged arsenic murder-for-hire connection?" Benjy asked.

"The method of Kip's death doesn't match with the vibe I'm getting from what I've found out about Delroy. In fact, it contradicts everything about the man, the more I read. It just seems like life handed him one rotten lemon after the next. Here's another subpoena for his DNA just last year in a sexual assault case—yikes."

Delroy had been mixed up in bad things more than once in his life it seemed, but Viv couldn't tell if it was his fault or if he's just been in the wrong place at the wrong time—*multiple* times in his life.

"In the more recent case, the DNA sample was collected from him and stored, but no charges were pressed when the match turned out to be from another suspect. So, definitely lives life under somewhat of a black cloud, and—ooh! I just found some collection agency notices posted against him." She leaned forward in her chair as if it would get her closer to finding out the truth.

"Maybe he did a murder-for-hire poisoning to pay off some debts?"

"Hmm. Looks like some of the bills were never paid off and they were to..." Her heart sank. "A cancer treatment center in Riverside, California."

The poor man, falsely accused of more than one crime, has cancer, too?

"Shoot. More reasons to feel sorry for Delroy. Don't tell me he's sick, too. This just gets worse and worse." Benjy leaned forward in his chair so they were shoulder to shoulder at the keyboard. He peered at her screen.

"What is this? It says, 'acute myeloid'...I don't know what that is, but it sounds terrifying." She opened another browser tab to look it up. "Oh no. That's not good. It's leukemia."

She didn't even know the man, yet she felt every bit as crushed by the diagnosis as if she had been sitting there with him when he heard the news.

And the bills had been astronomical. The final tally of the ones that

Viv could find amounted to well over $120,000.00, which was a stunning sum to have to pay when you were fighting for your life. When someone was first diagnosed with a terrible ailment, it seemed that too often their first concern wasn't how they were going to fight it but how they were going to pay for it.

"How much does chemotherapy cost anyway?" Benjy asked.

"Depends on your health insurance, I guess. If he had stem cell or some other newer kind of treatment, it would have been more."

Screw you, American healthcare system. Murder is terrible, but this is straight-up criminal.

The hospital had mailed final notices to Delroy several times before turning the whole thing over to a collections agency. Viv clicked through a couple more links trying to discover if he had made any attempt to pay the medical bills or to at least renegotiate them, which she knew was possible in many cases. If he made money off the arson poisoning, his bank account would reveal it. She was eventually shuttled back to the California website of Vital Records.

"Oh," was all she managed to say. The wind was sucked out of her sails and her stomach sank as another official certificate opened on her computer screen.

Whatever treatment he had received hadn't worked. Good thing he hadn't paid for it because he certainly would not have gotten a money-back guarantee.

The document was Delroy Bennett's death certificate. He had died ten months ago after losing his battle against cancer.

CHAPTER THIRTY-FOUR

Benjy said, "I don't mean to be insensitive, but am I missing something? You can't pin a murder on a man who was dead long before the crime happened. That's a rock-solid alibi as far as alibis go." His empty coffee cup banged down on the kitchen table. She could tell that, like her, he was angry on Delroy Bennett's behalf.

Viv had to agree. She'd pushed away from her keyboard and now paced around the kitchen, feeling irritable and helpless that nothing could be done for the man now that he was dead. Delroy could not have possibly been involved in Kip's death—he was dead himself—yet now someone was dragging the poor man's name through the mud.

"It doesn't make any sense to me. Who was this man and why would anyone want to frame him if he was sick and dying all the way on the opposite coast? Did he live under such a dark cloud that he was harassed by the system endlessly and then had to fight cancer on top of everything else? We must be missing something here."

"DNA doesn't lie—it's absolute. This is why we rely on science now. Why would someone go to all the trouble of planting Delroy Bennett's DNA on some gloves thousands of miles away?"

Benjy got up to refill his cup, which seemed like a bad idea to Viv. They were both already agitated. As if reading her thoughts, he changed his mind at the last minute and put his mug in the sink. When he came back, he said, "Let's back up for a minute. Go back to the beginning.

Before you knew anything about Delroy Bennett and his DNA, who was the number one suspect in your mind?"

"Christopher Kahoe, hands down," she said, feeling almost as if she had to suppress a shiver just thinking about that menacing douche-bro and his explosive temper...which didn't add up either. "Now that I examine it, it's not a logical reaction. From every psychological study of poisoners, he doesn't match the temperament."

"How so?"

"Well, even Agatha Christie speculated that poison was a so-called woman's tool, meaning it's a calculated, long-game kind of weapon. The killer has to plan the murder out. They have to obtain the substance. Scheme about how to administer it, including the way the victim ingests it, how much to give, and how to do it without detection. Add in the fact that the killer most likely wouldn't be present to witness the death, so there's no visceral connection, no observation of the crime, it's usually not a crime of violent passion. It's more like revenge, which as the saying goes, is a 'dish best served cold.' The poisoner has had time to cool off, to think about what they want to do, and to deliberately choose to commit the act anyway."

"And Christopher Kahoe doesn't fit this description?"

"Not in the least bit. From what I witnessed first-hand, he has an explosive temper. He's big, with a mean scowl, and he uses his size to intimidate his opponents."

However, Viv was filled with misgiving as she knew why she, personally, would have an instant and negative reaction to someone like the Kahoes' son. Viv had dated more than one man just like him. Parts of her dating history read like a personal rap sheet of bad judgement. She was definitely guilty of poor taste in boyfriends.

Accused: William Coldwall the Third: dated for five months freshman year of college.
Physical and character traits: Charming, blond, ultra-wealthy from upstate New York, and the first in a long line of horrible boyfriends.
Charges: Consistently treated waiters poorly. Once "forgot" to pay a restaurant tab and claimed it was an oversight that happened "all the time." Did not return to pay the bill until threatened with breakup. Regularly called her disparaging terms like "dummy" and "stupid," passing them off with smiles and a baby talk voice.

Accused: Blaine Temple: dated for four months during third year of college.

Physical and character traits: Tall, dark, and handsome. Physically aggressive and handsy at inappropriate moments, such as grabbing her chest in a restaurant while she read a menu.

Charge: Potentially stalker-like behavior, such as showing up at her job interview for an internship in a suburb fifty miles from where they attended school. Rang her doorbell three times in the middle of the night highly intoxicated and demanded to be let in for sex. He also attempted to choke her once in the bedroom without her consent.

Accused: Layton Morganstern: dated for four weeks after graduation.

Physical and character traits: Wiry, intense, and an avid runner. Controlling and jealous.

Charge: Wanted to check her phone for messages from other men after three weeks of casual dates. Numerous other red flags, such as disparaging comments about her food choices and her close friends.

This list was by no means comprehensive, and the mistakes had continued for a while longer. She was not proud of this tally and had not held onto any of the gifts from these particular horrible boyfriends, however much they had insisted she keep them. Just thinking about them made her shiver, so she certainly didn't need any items to remind her of her bad judgement. At least she had been smart enough to remove them from her life, even if she had failed to notice how terrible they were from the start.

Benjy cleared his throat, signaling that he, too, was aware of Christopher Kahoe's resemblance to some of her past dating failures.

"Yeah," was all he said.

Viv felt the awkward moment acutely, but somehow Benjy managed not to make it any worse, and she was able to move on from it. She said, "Okay, so let's set him aside for a minute. Let's go strictly based on motive. The next choice on my list of suspects is Felicia Tofana."

CHAPTER THIRTY-FIVE

Hold that thought. Just give me two minutes," Benjy said and left the kitchen. When he returned, he was carrying the chalkboard with the cutesy beach messages that Viv's mother had hung by the door. "I saw a piece of chalk in a drawer this morning when I was looking for a spoon."

With a damp paper towel, he wiped the board clean and then wrote Felicia's name at the top in block letters. "Okay. Ready. List your reasons for suspecting her. We'll do this just like they do on a detective show on TV."

"Make wild leaps of logic based on flimsy evidence?"

"Exactly. Let's get to it, *Baby Girl*."

She gave him a look that would have cowed a lesser man, or at least a less blithe and foolhardy man, but then she cracked her knuckles, pushed the loose bright orange strands of her wig behind her ears, and got to work at her keyboard.

"Felicia Tofana. Realtor, extraordinaire. Originally Felicia Rodriguez. Born in Miami, Florida. Age 45—ah, she's older than Kip by four years, so I guess they didn't meet in school. She attended the University of Florida in Gainesville with a major in Marketing, which is not much of a surprise. Married once, to Kip. Engaged, wow, *seven* times, according to this marriage announcement column when she and Kip finally tied the knot.

Maybe she had chronic cold feet and was waiting for the right man, but, as we know, her marriage to Kip didn't last long."

"Can you find proof she was out of town on the evening Kip was poisoned?"

"Sure. Let's just dig into her bank charges, shall we? I just need to go all the way back to the days before Kip died—Wow! She wasn't lying when she suggested she has an unnatural relationship with her credit cards. Look at all of these accounts. Amazon. Belk. Ann Taylor. Charges are shoes, clothes, nutritional shake delivery service, lots of online shopping—"

"I don't really want to know how you find all that out, do I?"

"—no plane tickets, which would probably be really cheap from here, but Asheville is only five and a half hours from here by car. Maybe she's a road-tripper by choice."

Viv could hardly fault her for that after having driven all the way down from Boston this week herself.

"Looks like she stopped for gas outside of Charlotte. Then a wine shop. Maybe to pick up a gift for friends—or for herself. This is a no-judgement zone for wine. Her charges are consistently in the Asheville area for the next two weeks after that, including the days leading up to and after his death. Looks like she was absolutely telling the truth about being out of town at that time."

"What's her past look like? Any arrests or anything like that?" Benjy asked.

"Good thinking. We'll see if she has any previous charges relating to crimes, violence, or revenge kinds of things. She still may have hired someone to kill her ex."

Viv clicked around and searched public arrest records.

"Bingo. Here's vandalism, destruction of private property, and a Protection Order."

"I knew she was a brawler just looking at her. I mean, did you see those biceps? I'm pretty sure she was flexing at us the whole time. Who took out the restraining order against her?"

"Hm. Not Kip or Evelyn, if that's what you were guessing. It was a rival real estate agent. I guess Felicia took her dream of being a real estate queen to the *extreme*."

Benjy snorted. "I see what you did there."

"If the woman didn't want her logo stuck in my mind, she wouldn't have plastered it all over everything. Personally, I would have gone with something a little milder, maybe like *She sells by the sea shore.*"

"Cute. And fair enough point."

On the chalkboard, he wrote:

FELICIA

Motive: Money

Alibi: Out of town, proven

Viv said, "Like Chris Kahoe, she seems to have a more explosive personality than the scheming and poisoning type of sneaky underhandedness it requires. I feel like she would sooner have dropped a Buick on her ex's head than had someone sneak some arsenic into his sweet tea."

"Agreed. She doesn't seem like one for subtlety. Who do you want to consider next?"

"Let's do Arletta Malone, Kip's business partner and co-owner of the restaurant."

Viv watched Benjy scrawl Arletta's name under Felicia's and realized she shouldn't be having this much fun—well, maybe *fun* wasn't the right word when dealing with someone's murder. However, she was enjoying spending time with Benjy on this joint effort.

There. Did I sufficiently cover my butt for the forces of karma?

Their friend Josie was a strong believer in the idea that the evil deeds a person did would come back to haunt them one way or another, that nature had a way of balancing out. Viv wasn't sure if she felt the same way. Various religions had the Golden Rule, the idea that you should do unto others as you would have done to yourself. Witches often cited the Rule of Three or the Law of Return, that whatever good or evil a person put out in the world, it would return to them threefold. Viv also wasn't sure what to think of that even though she had lived in Massachusetts long enough now to have absorbed some appreciation for All Things Salem, whether it be historical or tourist-based.

Scientifically speaking, those three concepts, each from vastly different schools of thought and different sections of the globe resembled each other just enough to give Viv pause, as a scientist of sorts, a compiler of facts and data from various sources. It made her wonder if there might be something to it. It made more sense to leave the option open rather than dismiss it outright.

Wouldn't it be better to be safe than sorry?

"I just thought of something. We'll talk about Arletta Malone in a second, but first I want to see if I can find Kip's medical records," Viv said.

"Wait. What?" Benjy, who had been standing at the ready next to the DIY decor chalkboard, rubbed his nose and got a smear of chalk on his cheek. "First of all, *you can do that...?* But why am I even asking? Of course you can. And second of all, how do you jump from one thing to the other and back again without losing your mind? You're giving me brain whiplash as it is."

"This will just take two minutes. I swear," Viv said.

The truth was, if she didn't do something immediately when she thought of it, she was more in danger of forgetting it than if she attacked it quickly. She messaged a friend quickly for tips about getting access to the data she was looking for. Within minutes, that person had contacted another in their circle of conspirators and sent her an administrator login and password to the system she wanted.

"Doesn't that violate some kind of privacy law...? Again, *why am I even asking this?*"

"The HIPAA privacy laws apply for fifty years after a person dies," Viv said absent-mindedly as she found a way into the local medical system's network. "Incidentally, accessing a person's medical records has become so much easier for me since everyone instated these online patient portals. It's really helpful. This used to take me a couple hours, and now— presto!" She gestured to her screen where she had brought up Kip's medical information.

Benjy shook his head. "Even if *you* have security clearance of some kind, *I don't.* Should I even be here right now? I don't even know how many rules I'm breaking just sitting next to you! I mean, does it strike you as weird that you're doing illegal things all in the name of catching someone who broke the law?"

Viv paused in mid-keystroke. "Do you want me to stop?"

To be honest, she wasn't sure if she could restrain herself even if he asked. This was the first time in a long time—maybe even in her entire life—that she felt like she had a purpose, maybe even a true calling. Could she give this up if he wanted her to stop? He meant more to her than probably anyone else, if she were being starkly honest with herself. Josie and Drew rounded out their foursome of best friends, but Benjy had always held a special status for her, along with the knowledge that he was unattainable because he loved Josie best.

But he was here now, and his opinion meant the world to her. One day, she might even admit it to him.

"Give up and stop your search now?" he asked. "Hell, no. This is amazing. I'm in awe of you and what you can do."

Whew.

"That's good to hear because I just found out something interesting. Kip Baldwin had a vasectomy at age twenty-four. According to his follow-up lab tests, it was a successful procedure. The year he had it done was about three years before Claire was conceived."

CHAPTER THIRTY-SIX

Benjy's shout of confusion rang in Viv's ears. "What is wrong with these people?! Can't any of them tell the truth?!"

"I'm wondering the same thing myself. But you know, you kind of expect people to lie when they're guilty of something."

"Fair point."

Viv felt like she needed a dark room and a quiet two-hour lie-down to untangle everything they had learned so far. She'd put on her Olivia armor earlier, but she really craved her onesie at the moment. Instead, she forced herself to talk things out since she had Benjy there to help her.

"Let's separate the facts from fiction. Do you have room on that chalkboard for another list?"

He made a separate column on the far side. "Go ahead. I'll write smaller this time."

She began to talk and when she was finished, his list read:

FACTS:

- Kip had a vasectomy before Claire was born.
- He's listed on Claire's birth certificate as her father.
- Evelyn is so confident in Claire's DNA makeup, she voluntarily gave the lawyer a sample.

Viv quickly went down the list. "We have the write-up of Kip's vasectomy and the results of the follow-up appointments proving that the procedure was successful. I mean, I just read that to you. Unless there's an elaborate plot with frozen embryos, which to be frank, seems well outside of Evelyn's budget and know-how. She was nineteen when she had Claire."

"Agreed," Benjy said.

"Next. When I interviewed Evelyn, she told me herself that Kip was Claire's father, but she did hesitate just slightly before she confirmed it. At the time, I thought she was hesitating for some other reason. However, when I asked if she was really Claire's mother, she was emphatic about saying yes. No hesitation at all. I also noticed that when I asked her what she had thought might happen between her and Kip, she said she thought they had become a family—not that they would be married or that they would be a couple. Just that they would be a *family* unit."

"Okaaay, but I'm not sure where you're going with this yet," Benjy said. He still had the smudge of chalk on his cheek and Viv thought it was kind of adorable.

"Combine point number two with the next one. Evelyn was so sure that Claire's DNA would come back to match Kip's that she sent a sample to the lawyer to prove paternity. However, what if Evelyn has an incomplete understanding of how DNA testing and genes work? I might be stereotyping, but she's a high-school dropout who doesn't seem like much of a reader. What if, yes, Claire has DNA in common with Kip, but it's because Evelyn *really is* Kip's sister?"

"We need to see the results of that DNA test. Is that something you can track down?"

"Possibly. I'd have to find out what firm did the testing. I'd be more likely to get access to their database than crack a lawyer's encrypted emails. But there's something else I'd like to look into. Remember Kip's little sister, Lisa Lynn Baldwin, the one who died when she was four years old? Evelyn is too young to have been mistaken for that sister, but what if she was another sister, born much later after that?"

"So you need to find Evelyn's birth certificate?"

"*Exactamundo.* You're getting the hang of this."

"How long do you think this is going to take you?" Benjy rubbed his flat midsection, which she knew was usually tanned and muscled from swimming—*Dear self, could you please stop picturing your best friend's abs?*—

and Viv realized a few hours had passed since they had eaten their fast-food burgers.

"I'm not sure. It could be a while, maybe hours."

"In that case, I'll go out and get us some takeout for dinner."

Viv didn't quite know what to do with all the emotions she was feeling. She'd never been part of a team like this before. Yes, her group of friends was wonderfully close, but to have someone this invested in what she was working on and whether she was hungry. Sure, his stomach was also empty, and in fact, she heard it rumble, but he was looking after her.

"Come here a sec." She gestured for him to approach, which he did silently. Her face must have displayed her trepidation because he wore a concerned expression.

"What's wrong?"

"Nothing is wrong."

He leaned in, squinting slightly, which deepened the crinkle lines at the corners of his eyes. Incidentally, they were a really nice tawny green color. She was staring so intently into his eyes, she didn't realize he was doing the same to her.

"Were your eyes always green or am I losing my mind?" he asked.

She had to laugh, and the moment—whatever it was between them—was over.

"Color contacts. It's part of my Olivia look."

While he was so close, she reached out. Surprise flashed across his face, when she rubbed his cheek with the tip of her finger.

"You have some, uh, chalk right here."

"Oh. Thanks."

Could I be any more awkward?

CHAPTER THIRTY-SEVEN

Benjy went out to hunt-and-gather some dinner for them, and Viv dove headfirst back into her search for information. It was better than thinking about ways to communicate better with the almost-decade-long object of her affection.

Because avoidance is my go-to MO. I mean, I even avoid going outside my house.

Viv had three things on her research to-do list. First, explore Arletta Malone's motives and alibi. Second, find Evelyn's birth record to see exactly how she fit into this Hydra of a mess and figure out exactly which parts of her story were true. Third, track down Claire's DNA test results. Essentially, what Viv needed was some science to help her cut through the snarl of B.S. and lies that people had been piling knee-deep all around Claire.

Viv figured Benjy would be back before she got through more than one of those things. However, she wanted to impress him, so she stepped on the proverbial digital gas. Evelyn's biological parents was the easiest thing to discover, so she tackled that first.

Kip was born in Atlanta to parents Lawrence and Mary Ellen, so she delved into that data first. She knew Evelyn's name mentioned in the old newspaper article was Evelyn Carter and that she had been born thirty-three years ago, probably in the Charlotte area.

"Hmm. *There* you are."

She read the certificate of birth out loud:

State of North Carolina
Bureau of Vital Statistics
Certificate of Birth
Child's Name: Evelyn Carter Baldwin
Place of Birth: Charlotte Medical Center
Mother's Name: Lydia Carter
Father's Name: Lawrence Baldwin

Aha. So it seemed Evelyn and Kip shared the same father, which made her his half-sister. When she put his name on her daughter's birth certificate, she had probably done so out of ignorance and the misguided attempt to make him financially responsible for her daughter. He had Claire's birth certificate in his safe, so he had obviously known about it. Viv still couldn't accept the idea that brother and sister were biological parents—*this was the South and all, but let's get real, please.* Unless someone explicitly said that was the case, she wasn't going down that morally repugnant, stomach-churning road. In any case, she wasn't going to tell Claire about any of this until she had more proof.

"Okay, next, I need to confirm this through Claire's DNA test results."

For this challenge, she hit up one of her contacts online to ask if they —non-gendered pronoun because that's how they identified and also, she honestly didn't know if it was more than one person—could help her get access to the correct genetics lab for the test based on Claire's full name, date of birth, and Social Security number.

Twenty minutes later, just as Benjy walked through the door, the full report arrived in Viv's message inbox. The screen door banged shut just as she was about to open the file.

"Hi there," he said, plunking down three boxes of fried clams and fish 'n chips on the kitchen counter next to her.

She frowned at the mountain of food. "I didn't know you were that hungry."

When she looked up at him, she found he had a split lip and an eyelid that was swelling shut.

"What happened to you?!" she exclaimed and scraped back her chair so quickly that she knocked it over. It crashed to the floor in her haste to get closer and examine his cuts and bruises. Nothing seemed to be bleeding too badly, but his eye was going to need some help.

She headed to the freezer to look for some frozen vegetables, which she didn't find. However, a first aid kit in the pantry had a cold pack that she could activate by kneading it. She held it up to his wounded eye until he took it from her.

"I may have gotten into a slight kerfuffle," he said. "But I got a free meal and dessert out of it."

He brought over the last takeout bag and pulled out a container, which he opened to reveal a mound of rich dark brown cake with liquid fudge spilling out of the center. "It's a chocolate volcano."

"Where did you go?"

Satisfied that he wasn't mortally wounded, she took a fry out of one of the boxes and jammed it into her mouth. Not only was she upset but hangry.

"Funny story..." he started as he handed her a fork from the kitchen drawer. "I went to It Smells Fishy in Here and met Christopher Kahoe."

"*You didn't!*" She already had a mouthful of food, but for some reason, it didn't taste any less delicious even knowing the son of the restaurant owners had punched it out with Benjy.

"I did! Now, before you make any assumptions, I didn't go there to pick a fight."

She believed him. It made sense. She'd never known Benjy to get in anyone's face or intentionally provoke another person in all the years she had known him. He was more likely to encourage someone to talk out their feelings than to have a dust up.

"I admit I drove to the restaurant to see what the fuss was all about, and at first glance, it looked like a normal kind of tourist town institution. It was totally fine. I didn't get a mob storefront feeling about it or whatever those laundering places are. It just seemed normal. But then I saw Chris Kahoe pull up in this fully tricked out DoucheBro Jeep with all the lights, attachments, big jack, and whatever added to it. The thing might as well have been rigged like one of those pickup trucks with twelve wheels, you know? And he's harassing this cute little waitress in her Fishy t-shirt and her apron who's arrived for her shift. He's honking at her and making comments out his window. Then he hops out of his Jeep and leaves it running in the middle of the parking lot so he can chase after her. He put his arm around her. I mean, she was pushing his beefy ham-fists off her shoulders and saying, 'Cut it out, Chris. Knock it off, Chris. Leave me alone, Chris,' which was a pretty clear *no* to me."

"What did you do?" Viv's heart was pounding thinking about it. Maybe

Chris Kahoe wasn't a full-blown sexual predator, but he was at least an entitled prick who was used to physically bullying people to get his way.

"I may have rear-ended his Jeep."

Was a fist pump appropriate at this moment? Viv wasn't sure, but she had a hard time refraining from doing one.

"And that got you punched in the face?"

"Yeah. One punch and then an elbow, and I hate to admit it, but I didn't land any of my own."

"Aw, Benjy. What were you thinking?"

"I know, right? Maybe I should take the same boxing class Josie does at home. Next time something like this happens, I need more skills."

"That's not what I meant. I don't care that you didn't hit him. I'm sorry you got hurt!"

"That's not even the weird part," he said. "Two seconds after he pulled me out of my car and used my face as a punching bag, an older guy comes barreling out of the restaurant and starts yelling at Kahoe to back off. He's totally groveling and apologetic to me. He offers me a free meal—which I tried to decline, but he insists. I mean, I was going to order anyway. Meanwhile, Chris stomps back to his Jeep and drives off, and this other guy, who I figure out is his father, is still apologizing and offering me comps like he does this every day."

"As he should have!" Viv said, still flummoxed that Benjy, of all people, had gotten into a fistfight. "I'm so sorry you were punched. I feel like it's my fault."

"That's the thing—the fender bender was *my fault*. I did it on purpose because Chris was being an ass to that poor waitress. I *deserved* to be punched, not to get a free meal."

"What does this tell us about the Kahoes? That they're used to cleaning up Chris's problems, I think. But did he *kill* Kip or is he simply the muscle who enforced repayment on the loans they gave to Kip, which he's now demanding from Arletta? Frankly, it doesn't make sense to kill the person who owes you money. You'll never get repayment that way—and poison still doesn't seem like a Kahoe thing at all, judging from that shiner coming up on your eye. It's a beaut, by the way."

Benjy sighed and adjusted his ice pack.

Viv sat down heavily on her kitchen chair. While she stuffed fried seafood in her mouth and tried to absorb what Benjy had just told her, she absent-mindedly clicked on Claire's DNA report and read through it. She wasn't sure how many more times the rug could be pulled out from under her theories in one afternoon, but this, at least wasn't the worst of them.

"Claire *is* Kip's niece, not his daughter, which is very good news, because Evelyn is Kip's half-sister—a result of what sounds like their mutual father's extramarital relationship. The bad news for Claire is, she might not be next of kin and may not be entitled to his townhouse now, even though she could really use a little good fortune in her life."

"Ugh. It's a Greek tragedy up in here. Back to square one," Benjy said shoving a huge spoonful of chocolate fudge cake into his mouth and grimacing at his split lip. *"These people."*

CHAPTER THIRTY-EIGHT

Across town, Claire sat at her kitchen table after school, fiddling with the snake tail on her art project when the text from Viv popped up on her phone. She didn't feel like answering it just then, so she read it but didn't respond. Terrance FaceTimed her after that anyway.

"What's the word from the bird, classy chassis Claire?"

He was wearing a fedora. For his sake, she hoped he didn't bring it to school. Although knowing him, if he did, he would start a trend. No one had bullied him since he grew a foot and a half last summer.

"I have no idea what that means, but I'm just working on my art project."

She'd used tiny broken bits of shell she had collected at the beach for scales on her creature's tail. She'd molded the center of it out of sculpting clay and had run a wire through the middle so she could stick it onto the body.

So far, so good.

"You got it made in the shade? That thing is due, so you better beat feet and burn rubber, if you're picking up what I'm throwing down."

"Yeah, I'm almost done," she said, hazarding a guess at his meaning. She wondered how long this phase of his was going to continue. His goth vampire stage had lasted two years. "I just got a text from Viv."

"Anything new?" he asked, his ridiculous old-time mannerisms thankfully falling off.

"Nothing yet." Claire honestly didn't mind if Viv didn't have any new information yet. It was just really nice to hear from her. At the moment, she felt like she was part of a team, even though she wasn't expecting much to come of it.

"What are you going to do now, just chill and see what happens next?"

She was about to adjust the snake tail on her project for the millionth time, but she took her hand back. *Leave it alone. Don't touch it.* Some things were better when you left them alone. With any luck, it would dry properly over the weekend so she could carry it to school on Monday without it cracking off.

She heard the mailbox lid clang shut outside the front door where their landlord had mounted the box on the outside of the house, so she went out to get the bills. Most of their mail was just people demanding money. Why did living have to cost so much anyway?

To try to help her mom, Claire usually opened the envelopes, got rid of the double notices, and stacked the rest on the kitchen counter in order of when they were due first. The electricity bill was usually the worst, especially in the summer or winter. Spring and fall weren't as scary. The first time Claire had opened one of those bills, she had freaked out at how much money they owed. She'd had no idea it cost that much just to not sweat or shiver inside their own house.

The rest of the mail was a bunch of flyers for grocery stores and fast-food coupons. The Shop Now store ad reminded her that she wanted to look at their online job application. Maybe it would list the minimum work age for the store.

"Do you know how old you have to be to get a real job?" she asked Terrance, still FaceTiming her as he tried on different hats in a mirror.

"Do you think Viv wears a wig?" he asked instead of answering her question, which she was kind of glad about in hindsight. She didn't want him to think she was desperate for money. She and her mom weren't homeless. As far as she knew, they were paid up on their rent.

"It's definitely a wig. One hundred percent. I don't think that color occurs naturally in the world, but I think it looks really good on her."

"Definitely," he agreed.

"Maybe she screwed up her real hair by dyeing it too much. My mom did that. It's still growing out, but then she went dark black."

"Maybe she has alopecia or that mental disorder that makes you pull

179

your own hair out obsessively."

"Maybe we should all try wigs, just for variety."

"Definitely something to consider in the future when we have jobs and income to spend on frivolous things."

After all, Mr. Fedora over there was the last person on earth who could judge Viv for her wig. Being a theatre kid was all about experimenting with how you present yourself. Putting on costumes wasn't for Claire personally. She didn't want to be anyone else—she was struggling with just being a human from day to day—but she fully supported Terrance on his journey of self-discovery, wherever it took him.

Outside the house, the mailbox clanged again, which was weird because she had already collected today's stack of bills.

"I think we just got a package or something. The mail lady came back," she told Terrance.

"Maybe it's special delivery papers from your lawyer telling you the townhouse is ready for you to live there," he said. He had a feather boa on now, which actually looked cool with the fedora, and he was digging through his makeup drawer.

"I'll be right back. I'm going to go check," she told him and set her phone down on the table. Probably, all he could see was the kitchen ceiling, but she was coming right back.

Nothing was on the porch, and no delivery truck was parked at the curb. She turned to peek into the mailbox, but it was just as empty as she had left it. It wasn't a windy evening, so it wasn't the lid blowing open, not that she had ever seen that happen before, not even during Hurricane Florence.

She pressed the lid down firmly just in case she had left it open before and it had fallen shut. It would be creepy to hear that in the middle of the night if she was alone in the house. Or if her mom was passed out and dead to the world after she eventually came home from work.

Claire took one last look at the street to make sure it was empty. But then, something covered her face. A strong arm snaked around her midsection and jerked her backward off the porch. She tried to shout but found her mouth wasn't just blocked but taped shut. A hood went over her head and blocked out the light. Big hands yanked her down the sidewalk and shoved her into the trunk of a car. She tried to wriggle herself into a seated position, but the trunk swung shut and banged her head. She saw stars for one extremely pissed-off second. She felt the fight drain from her body as she went limp. Then, everything went dark.

CHAPTER THIRTY-NINE

T alk to me about Arletta Malone," Benjy said, cleaning up their dinner containers. Half the chocolate volcano was left, but if Viv ate anything more, she would slip into a food coma and wouldn't be able to access the reason and logic centers in her brain for the rest of the night.

"From what I observed, she was going down on a sinking ship with the Time & Tidewater Grill. Without Kip there, she's totally lost, and unless she wanted to go bankrupt paying off his loans from the Kahoes, she's much worse off without him around."

"How long have she and Kip been partners?"

"Sandy, the reporter lady, said about a year or so. Let me see what else I can find out about Arletta and her husband. I think his name is Brad—he sounds like a stand-up kind of guy."

Viv began typing, doing her special variety of digital digging to see what she could come up with. Her phone pinged with a text notification, but she didn't look at it immediately. She assumed it was Claire messaging her back.

"Arletta has an Accounting degree from UCSD—that's San Diego," Viv clarified. "She and her husband, Brad, lived there until last year. They've both done a lot of charity work, including voter registry and work with the American Red Cross. It looks like Brad organized a rummage sale and two separate blood mobile donation days at their church."

"They totally did it—if this were a TV show, they would be the murderers," Benjy said. "Way too squeaky clean. I mean, do they also save whales and feed orphan children?"

Viv rolled her eyes. When her phone made another texting sound, she reached for it but didn't recognize the number.

"Thanks for your input. I'll be sure to keep them high on the suspicious persons list, just as soon as we can find a motive for her wanting to sabotage her main source of income."

This time, Viv's phone rang instead of chiming with a text message. She reached for it again, frowning, and answered instead of ignoring it. The caller turned out to be a very upset Terrance. She began to apologize for not answering earlier, but he interrupted.

"Someone took Claire," he said and his voice cracked with fear. "I heard it. I was on a video call with her and she heard someone walk up to her porch. She thought it was the mailman or someone delivering a package. She put the phone down to look. She left me on the call to go check, I heard voices, and then she didn't come back. I think someone kidnapped her!"

A sick feeling squeezed Viv's stomach.

"When did this happen?"

"About ten minutes ago. I'm *freaking* out. I didn't know what was going on. I wasn't sure at first. I was hoping it was someone she knew. Like, did she just forget about her phone? But she wouldn't do that. I hung up and tried to call back, but she didn't pick back up. What if she's lying on the ground? Should I go over there?"

"Did you call the police?" Viv asked, even though it sounded like Terrance had called her first.

"No, I'm too scared to talk to the police. I'm brown and I'm gender fluid, and this is the South."

"Okay, Terrance. It's okay. We'll figure out what happened. Stay where you are. Tell your parents that Claire is missing. Can they help you talk to the police while I go over to check her house? You just stay where you are, do you hear me?" She knew she was repeating herself, but he was panicking and she had to make sure he understood. He was not to put himself in danger in any way.

"Right. Yeah. My mom can help me, but what should I do after that? I can't just sit here." He sounded like he was going to cry.

Join the club, she thought.

"After your parents report Claire missing, see if they can try to call

Claire's mom. They may be able to contact Evelyn before I can. Also, be sure to keep your phone charged up in case Claire tries to contact you."

"All right. I can do that. Just hurry, please."

When Viv hung up soon after that, Benjy had already put on his shoes, grabbed her bag, and stood by the door waiting for her. His face looked about as grim as she felt. They jogged downstairs to the car. She put her laptop in the back.

"I'll drive," she said since she had been there before, and he tossed her the keys.

"The one good thing about getting my face punched," Benjy said, clutching the overhead bar as Viv took a corner sharply, "is that we know where Chris Kahoe was just now. He couldn't have gone from a fistfight directly over to Claire's house to abduct her. My black eye is his alibi."

"This is a mess," Viv said.

People have done countless studies on the relationship between humor and stress, that a sense of humor is a natural reaction to traumatic events.

While she appreciated his attempt at levity and trying to find a small positive, anything good at the moment—and he was probably right about Chris Kahoe—she was attempting to keep her food down against the natural, gravity-defying inclination of her knotted stomach.

"Claire *has* to be all right," Benjy said, the tone of his voice more hopeful. "She's been gone less than a half hour."

According to national statistics about child abduction in America, in more than three quarters of the missing children murder cases, the child, meaning a person under the age of 18—is dead within three hours of the abduction. In almost 90 percent of those situations, the child is dead within 24 hours.

Viv didn't bother saying that out loud. It was bad enough that one of them was already suffering under the burden of that knowledge. A person didn't have to share everything all the time with the people they loved, and this was one of those situations.

Within fifteen minutes, Viv pulled up to the curb outside of Claire's house. The front door stood open although no one, including the police, were there yet. Viv didn't go inside—even she knew not to disturb the scene. From where she stood on the front walk, however, she had a straight view into the kitchen where she could see Claire's homework project she had mentioned and her phone on the kitchen table. Nothing had been disturbed, but the girl was gone.

CHAPTER FORTY

laire woke up in the dark, her mouth still taped, and a hood making her face sweaty. Her scalp hurt pretty bad in one spot on the top, and she thought it might be bleeding because her hair was damp, although it could have been the sweat from her own trapped breath. Otherwise, she was more confused than anything else. She remembered some creep had pushed her into the trunk of a car and when she felt around her, she was certain she was still inside of it. However, this stupid trunk was the cleanest one she had ever seen. Well, not actually *seen*. She couldn't see anything.

This definitely wasn't her mom's car, which had like a pound of beach sand in the back. The trunk of that crusty old Corolla actually had a rusted spot Claire could see daylight through it. Mostly, it was filled with garbage and old clothes from when Claire was a baby. *Borderline hoarder much?* Her mom's car wouldn't have room for a body, dead or alive, not even a ninety-pound string bean like Claire.

She wriggled around to get her hands free because they were bound at the wrists with rope or something. Another good thing about being underweight was that she could hold her hands together and still have a ton of wiggle room between her wrists—so she got the binding off after just a few minutes of wrestling with it. Who knew bony wrists would come in handy? With her hands free, she could take the hood off her head. Then, with a fingernail—thank goodness she hadn't bitten them all off—she found the corner of the tape that covered her mouth and peeled it off.

The trunk she was trapped in smelled like…vanilla? One of her mom's infrequent old boyfriends had worked at a carwash and he sometimes smelled like chemicals and vanilla. Maybe it was car soap or maybe it was new car smell? That was something Claire had read about in books, but she didn't know what it smelled like. This scent was more like the candle her kindly history teacher sometimes burned in class when they were all super stressed out during state testing days. Or when the principal was sent to observe her when she kept losing control of the class. That was after Eric Rawlins went off his ADHD meds and threw the globe out of the window.

Another perk of being small was that no one really noticed Claire at school.

This was a nice new car. She knew her mom's old clunker one hundred percent didn't have a trunk release latch on the inside like this one did. She didn't know how long she had been inside, but the handle was still visible because it was made of glow-in-the-dark plastic—hopefully not radioactive or whatever. Since her hands were free, she pulled the handle and the trunk popped open, almost silently.

She looked at her surroundings in confusion. Inside the trunk, she had assumed she was still near home, maybe in a parking lot or in someone's driveway, but she had no idea where this was. Just exactly how long had she been knocked out? Her captor had taped her up and abandoned her here, parked inside a huge storage building. Cement floor. Metal beams. Windows high up. Not a lot of noises from outside, but a little echo-y inside.

If Terrance were here, he would describe this place as *cavernous*. It was large, mostly empty, and echoed like a…well, a cave. The person who'd nabbed her had been able to park their car inside, but in truth, there was room for about thirty more cars. Speaking of which, she felt vulnerable out in the open standing in the center of the building, so she closed the trunk as softly as she could and walked quickly to the side of the place where there were some weird, pointy tent-like things. She didn't know what they were, but she figured she could hide behind them.

What would Charlotte from *Grovemire Girls* do? Probably scream and cry for help until some burly off-duty fireman who happened to be walking by could come and rescue her. Although there was that one episode where Charlotte hit her head and turned into Opposite Charlotte, who was loud and brave. She'd confronted a bully and asked a guy out on a date, which had been super satisfying after all those seasons of whining.

She paused, waiting for someone to notice she'd escaped. But no one shouted or ran at her. No guard. No bad guys. Nothing. Had they left her for dead? Had they dropped her off and forgotten her just like all the other adults in her life tended to do?

Right about now, Claire really regretted leaving her phone on the kitchen table when she had gone out to check the porch—she wished she had a way to call for help. Never mind the fact that Terrance was probably annoyed when she didn't come back to say goodbye and hang up their call. Not that she had ever done it before—although he had, several times, wandered off in the middle of a conversation with her to practice piano, eat dinner, or watch a movie with his family. One time, she listened to the entire old Cary Grant movie, *Arsenic and Old Lace*, that way— second-hand through Terrance's phone because he had forgotten they were on a call. It was pretty much her first family movie night. Before that, she had figured it was just something TV families did.

She made it to the far side of the huge room, which wasn't a room because cars drove in here and the floor was dirty. *Wait a minute*, she thought. *Is this a warehouse?* In answer to her question, a nearby boat on the Cape Fear River honked its boat horn, or whatever they were called. She knew that warehouses were where they stored stuff from boats, trains, and trucks. Then she realized that the tent-like structures were piles of furniture with old sheets covering them, probably to keep them clean. The tallest ones were couches, stood on their sides. Thinner points were stacked tables and weird artsy vases. She also found bags of designer throw pillows and rolled up carpets. None of it was brand new, but it was all in pretty good shape—definitely better than the stuff in her mom's house.

She carefully let each sheet fall back into place so as not to disturb anything. At the end of the row of furniture, she found a large stack of signs, like those political signs that people stuck in their front yards during election time, leaning against the rest of the things. When she separated the stack to read one, it said, "Dream Team Extreme!" with a woman's big fake-tanned smiling face with blue-white teeth and a phone number.

"Now, I *really* wish I had my phone. I'd crank call the heck out of you, lady."

Claire recognized Felicia Tofana from her billboards all over town, but she had no idea why some bigwig saleslady would want to have her thrown into the back of a car and then keep her in a warehouse.

Since she had heard the river noises outside, Claire had a pretty good idea where in the city she was. When she looked around, she saw a red exit sign in the corner of the warehouse. All she had to do was follow along the same wall near her and she would reach it. As far as she knew, exit doors had to stay unlocked from the inside, thanks to a fire safety day she had attended in elementary school—*what do you know, school actually taught me something.* When she made it to the door and pushed the bar to open it, she was shocked to find it pitch black outside.

How long was I in that car anyway?

For a split second on the sidewalk outside of the warehouse, she had one of those weird *Did the apocalypse happen while I was unconscious?* moments that she had seen in movies. Liminal space. Everything was dark and quiet with only the silent blinking of a traffic light on the corner a block away. Then a car drove by and she heard a siren in the distance and the eerie feeling dissipated.

The question was, she didn't particularly want to go home, so where was she supposed to go? She had been grabbed there once before. Who was to say someone wouldn't come and get Claire again as soon as she found out she had escaped? Yeah, returning to the house didn't seem like a very good option.

If she could find someone to let her borrow their phone, she might be able to call Terrance. Like, if she found a restaurant that was still open or maybe a gas station. She didn't want to knock on someone's door even though some of these buildings looked like they could be apartments. They'd probably yell at her for bothering them.

Maybe she could use the phone at a fast-food place that was open late. Some of those places didn't want to help you out if you didn't buy anything, like you couldn't use the bathrooms unless you were a paying customer. She didn't have any money with her or even have her wallet. Honestly, she was lucky that she had been wearing her flip-flops when the lady had grabbed her, and that they hadn't fallen off her feet along the way. To tell the truth, they were a little small and tight, so they had stayed on really well.

But none of that mattered because she had no idea what his number was—or Viv's either—because they were in her phone contacts and she didn't know any of them off the top of her head.

Guess I better start walking.

CHAPTER FORTY-ONE

H as anyone located Evelyn yet?" Viv asked. She'd set up a command center of sorts at Evelyn and Claire's house since the police had finished taking statements and asking neighbors if they'd seen anything or had video doorbells. Most of the cops had left, but one patrol car was still parked in front of the house. In this neighborhood, the answers to both of those questions had been firmly in the "no and are you kidding?" range.

Benjy gingerly moved the clay sculpture—clearly a work in progress since it sat on a piece of newspaper drying—to the counter so Viv could work on her laptop at the table. The kitchen counter didn't have any stools to sit at. In fact, as Viv looked around, the place didn't have much by way of furnishings. Just an old plaid couch with wooden arms and a rocker that looked just this side of ancient.

To be honest, Viv couldn't tell them anything about who might have taken Claire. She had no clue, and honestly, spent more time trying to explain her role there than share a theory. An "adult friend the teenager met on the internet" was a terrible definition of who she was, which she tried to avoid at all costs. Could that sound any shadier? She settled on telling them she and Benjy were family friends who had volunteered to help Claire find out more about her uncle.

"Oh, damn," the cop, whose badge said his name was Brunswick, said to his young partner, Cage. "That's the guy who was murdered over at the Time & Tidewater a couple months ago."

"We haven't caught the person who did it yet," Cage said and shook his head.

"Do you know what progress they've made on that case?" Viv asked, not expecting them to be forthcoming. "I know there were some hard feelings between him and the other fish restaurant owners across the street."

Brunswick frowned. "I hadn't heard anything like that."

"I'm friends with the son, Chris Kahoe," the younger officer said. "His whole family is in the dark, just like the rest of us. It's a shame that there was evidence found outside their place. It drags them into it when they didn't have anything to do with it at all."

"Yeah, that's too bad," Viv said with a sympathetic expression, although she made a mental note that the younger officer might also be a DudeBro outside of the uniform. DudeBros tended to attract their own kind—they ran in packs.

Behind the officers, she could see Benjy's eyebrows shoot up. Since one of them had a personal connection to the Kahoes, she didn't think they could offer her any objective details about who killed Kip or who might have taken Claire. If it was Chris Kahoe, would they protect him?

Viv had been worried that they would write Claire off as a runaway because she was a teen who didn't have a great home life, especially in light of Kip's recent death. However, they dutifully took down her information and started the process for initiating a missing child Amber Alert.

Cops didn't make her nervous—unlike her friend Josie who avoided them like the plague as a result of her misspent youth—but Viv didn't want them prying too deeply into who she was or what she did. She *really* didn't want to have to cover up her presence here, or make a hasty retreat back to Boston. Either of those missteps would result in her failing Claire.

So far, so good.

The boys in blue had taken their names and statements and had left to see if they could find Evelyn. Apparently, they had stopped by the bowling alley and she wasn't at work as she should have been. The bowling alley manager had told them that she had been scheduled for a three to midnight shift, but she hadn't shown up at all, not even called in sick, which although wasn't exactly normal for her, was something she had done once before. Her manager was forgiving enough to have given her only a warning both then and now. He said without irony that it was a "three strikes and you're out" kind of place—no pun intended.

But seriously though? Evelyn had immediately fallen off the wagon without even getting on it. And this is right *after I talked with her about acting more responsible and being there for her kid. Maybe rehab would be an option if someone could come and stay with Claire.*

Viv refused to believe anything other than the absolute certainty that Claire would be back home within a few hours—a day at the most. One way or another, they would find her. Unfortunately, without her cell phone to track her, it was going to be a challenge.

It was mild for an autumn night, so they left the front door open hoping that they would hear news soon. Maybe the police would find Claire and drive up to the house with her riding safely in a patrol car. Maybe she would be scared and grateful for rescue. Maybe she would be sullen and withdrawn. Hopefully, she would be unharmed and back to her normal self within a day or two. Viv didn't care, as long as she was back.

"She wouldn't have left on her own, would she?" Benjy asked when they were alone.

Although she had parked herself at the table, he paced the small front room with nervous energy. Viv appreciated that he had waited for the cops to leave before he speculated about what might have happened. No need to include anyone else if they were going to think about worst-case scenarios.

"I honestly didn't get that vibe from her, but she's a kid who doesn't like to show her cards. I think she's independent and scrappier than she first seems. She might have had a plan or some scheme she wanted to look into on her own. I just wish she would have trusted me enough to tell me, if she did."

Benjy paused in the kitchen to listen, but then resumed his metered track across the front of the house. The old floorboards under the carpet creaked with his weight. Viv, sitting at the table, felt the vibration of his steps through the old bones of the house and into her chair. The place had weathered a lot over the decades and had probably stood witness to many a sleepless night. Fights. Tears. Reunions. Joy. Hope. Maybe another anxious parent had sat in this same spot waiting for a child to come home.

On the kitchen counter, a chunk of Claire's drying art project fell onto the newspaper under it. Benjy went back to it and picked up the broken-off piece. He tried to reattach it, but the chunk fell again.

"What is this thing?"

"It's one of those three-headed mythological Greek monsters. Terrance said they have a mythological art project due on Monday."

Benjy frowned and set the tail on paper, unable to stick the broken appendage back on the body. "It's going to need a little surgery to stay on. There's a wire in the center, but it's not holding. There's nothing to splice it with. Do you think they have any glue here?"

The unspoken urge to stay busy and keep their minds distracted hit them both.

"Let me look in Claire's room."

She felt like a terrible snoop, but while she peeked in the girl's room for craft supplies, she also looked for clues about where Claire was. The door was a hollow-core door with a brown faux wood pattern that swung inward unevenly because the upper hinge was loose. The bottom of it had been scratched up by an animal, probably owned by a previous resident because Claire and her mother didn't have any pets. The green shag carpet was also a relic of a bygone era—or century, even. As Viv stood in the doorway, the marked contrast between this worn-down room of second-hand furniture and scuffed paint and the stylish and shiny new room for a teenaged girl at Kip's townhouse sent a spike of sadness and vicarious regret through Viv.

"Are you okay?" Benjy asked, coming up behind her.

"I honestly could cry," she said, and he gave her shoulder a squeeze.

"Don't give up hope."

"Her *mom* should be here, worrying about her, holding back tears for her."

Voices came through the house from the sidewalk outside, and Viv hurried back to the kitchen hoping it was Claire.

CHAPTER FORTY-TWO

V iv's heart sank. Unfortunately, it wasn't Claire.
False alarm.
     "Sorry. I know it's late. My mom brought me over for a few minutes just to check," Terrance said, coming through the door. "Is she back? Have you found her yet?"

"No. Nothing yet. I was hoping she would call you."

He held up his iPhone. "I bring my phone with me everywhere. I'm never putting it down in case she calls."

Viv introduced herself to Terrance's mom, a tiny Asian woman who looked as upset as Viv felt. "We haven't been able to find Evelyn," Viv told her.

"Are you a relative?"

Viv should her head. "I'm just a friend of Claire's."

"That's too bad. I was hoping you were an auntie or someone who could take Claire to live with you. She needs a better mother than the one she has."

"Mom!" Terrance exclaimed. "You can't just say things like that out loud."

Mrs. Bonaventure scowled up at him. "Well, it's the truth. I hope the police find her, but I think this might not have happened if—"

"Mom!" Terrance shouted again. "Just stop, please! We should concen-

192

trate on finding her, not blaming people. You can't change that right now."

The kid had a point.

But so did his mother, who shrugged and allowed herself to be led out of the house. She waved at Viv and Benjy and asked for Viv to contact them if she heard any news.

"Call us no matter what the time is," she said, and Viv nodded.

The hours dragged by.

The same police officers stopped by later to check in.

Viv still sat at the kitchen table in front of her laptop and by her phone, which hadn't rung.

Earlier, Benjy had gone out for a pizza, more out of anxiety than hunger. She offered the policemen some pizza because neither of them felt much like eating. Just as the younger one of them, Cage, accepted a slice on a paper towel, the radio unit that was clipped to his shoulder squawked.

"Unit 14, we have a 10-54 over at Broadway and Luna."

Viv frowned at Benjy. She turned to her laptop and quickly searched the police code on the internet. She didn't want to say anything out loud to distract the cops, but the expression on her face must have given away her horror. Benjy crossed the kitchen and sat in the chair beside her. She pointed at the screen.

10-54 means a possible dead body.

The two streets sounded familiar. She pulled up a map to locate the intersection that the dispatcher had listed, Broadway and Luna. Then, she zoomed in to a street view to find out what was in the area. The camera angles were strange at first, but then the image cleared up. A big yellow sign in the shape of a fish came into view

It Smells Fishy in Here was at the intersection of Broadway and Luna.

The police officers beat a hasty retreat. The younger one didn't know what to do with his pizza slice, but then he took it with him. Viv wondered if he had a tough enough stomach to eat it on the way to the possible new crime scene.

With shaky fingers at her keyboard, Viv pulled up the live audio feed for the South Pier police department scanner on her computer so they could listen in real-time after the officers left. She didn't want to hear whose body they had found, but at the same time, she *needed to know*. If the person they found was Claire… The What ifs were already lining up in her mind, ready to pummel her with their swift and unrelenting gut punches.

I don't want to think about that.

"Stop. Don't even think it," Benjy said out loud, echoing her thoughts. "It's not going to be her. Don't even allow yourself to go down that path."

She was using her mobile phone as a hot spot, but the voices were still loud and clear.

"Unit 32, please respond."

"This is Unit 32. We're about five miles away from Broadway and Luna."

"Dispatch, this is Unit 14. We're just pulling up to the Fish place right now."

The dispatcher responded with, "Go around to the back. Should be in the dumpsters area."

"Who reported the body?"

"It was a dishwasher at the restaurant."

"Not anyone in the Kahoe family?"

"No. Not a relative or any of the owners."

"You know them?"

"Yeah, I was a waiter there for a couple summers while I was doing my associate's degree."

"Nice."

"Yeah. Really good tips."

"Okay, dispatch. We're getting out of the car now. Someone called an ambulance."

"Wasn't me," the dispatcher said. "Maybe they were in the neighborhood."

There were a couple minutes of silence punctuated by random squawks. Viv assumed the officers were questioning people or making their way over to the location of grim discovery.

"Okay. Body is an adult female. Dark hair. Not the missing girl from earlier this evening. We're clearing the scene now. Waiting for Homicide."

"Thank you."

Viv seconded the dispatcher's last message and sent a silent prayer of thanks to the Powers that Be that it wasn't Claire with her slight build and fair hair, who would look more like a child than a grown woman if they had found her instead. She and Benjy stared at each other in relief as the anxiety that had gripped them lessened just a little.

"We still don't know where she is—and the body could still be

Evelyn's. She has dyed black hair right now. Lord knows she leads a high-risk lifestyle in the grips of her substance abuse problem."

It was well after midnight now and neither Claire nor her mother had shown up, but then footsteps rang out on the front sidewalk as someone ran up to the front door.

"Hey, who's in my house?"

CHAPTER FORTY-THREE

Evelyn's words were slurred and her eyes bloodshot as she stood in the doorway of her own house looking at Viv and Benjy, the virtual strangers who'd made themselves at home in her kitchen. Her dyed black hair stuck up in the front and her makeup was smeared, smudged eyeliner darkening her eye hollows to make her look like an underfed street urchin—not unlike Claire, Viv realized. After seeming to reassure herself that she was at the correct address, Evelyn came fully inside and dropped her beat-up purse on the floor by the front door.

"What are you doing here?" She squinted first at Benjy and then at Viv. "I know you. You lied. Did you come to take Claire away from me?"

Benjy stepped outside to make a call, hopefully to let the police know that Claire's mom had finally turned up. For Claire's sake and to spare her the emotional damage, Viv was glad that at least Evelyn wasn't dead—but since that was the case, who was the dead woman at the Kahoes' restaurant?

"Evelyn, Claire isn't here. We don't know where she is. We've been looking for you so we could tell you she's gone."

"Well, where did you take her?" Evelyn demanded to know.

"*We* didn't take her. We're trying to *find* her. She's missing." Trying to explain things to an intoxicated person wasn't much easier than arguing with an overtired toddler.

Evelyn frowned. "Did she run away? She's never done that before. We should call her friend, that tall boy."

"We talked to Terrance. She was on the phone with him when someone took her. She's missing."

Evelyn sat down heavily on the old plaid couch in the living room and wrapped herself in the thin blanket with what looked like a circular coffee cup stain that had hung over the back. "Well, I'm going to wait right here until she comes home. I'll have to give her a curfew after this time if she can't follow the rules." Her voice became more and more slurred as her eyelids lowered.

"Did you tell her?" Benjy asked, coming back inside.

"Yeah, and she's still a shoe-in for the mother-of-the-year award, as you can see." Viv rolled her eyes. "She was exactly zero help in giving me any information that could help find Claire."

Benjy was in the kitchen opening up the cupboards and peering into each one. "She doesn't have any coffee, and I think we're going to need a lot. I'm going to go out and get some. There's a 24-hour grocery just down the street. Or maybe I can find an all-night fast-food place that has coffee."

"That sounds like a great idea. Coffee might help us wake Evelyn up, too." Viv also recognized that he was struggling with waiting and having nothing to do but twiddle his thumbs and pace. She, at least, had her laptop so she could search local social media posts and keep an eye on both the news outlets and police reports for anything about Claire.

Benjy left, but he was back in about three seconds, running a hand through his hair the way he did when he was frustrated. "Evelyn blocked me in with her car. It's a wonder she didn't hit mine."

Viv wanted to go shake the woman up immediately and yell at her for driving drunk. While her daughter was out there somewhere, missing, she was risking getting arrested for a DUI. Or worse, possibly harming herself or someone else.

"Let me see if I can find her keys," Viv said.

Evelyn's purse was still on the floor where she had dumped it, and her keys were easy enough to find. They were attached to a large keychain with a "One day at a time" motto in bold letters, as well as a second tiny acrylic photo keychain of Claire as a toddler. Viv wanted to slap her own forehead, to perform an actual facepalm in real life. The rest of Evelyn's purse was pretty normal. Viv took a quick look while she was there—

might as well do a full-on snoop since she had already gone down that path.

Makeup. Hygiene supplies. Two lighters. Crumpled napkin with food stains. Condoms. Driver's license but no actual wallet. A few loose dollar bills and change in the bottom of the bag.

"Got 'em," Viv told Benjy, holding up the keys while still gritting her teeth.

She followed him outside into the warm night, unlocked Evelyn's haphazardly parked Toyota and wrenched the rusted door open. The stale smell of cigarette smoke, alcohol, and dust assaulted her nose. The other woman was a bit shorter than Viv. She didn't bother to adjust the seat, but folded her legs in under the steering wheel. She backed into the empty street to let Benjy pull his SUV out and then drove Evelyn's car into what she assumed was its usual parking spot, based on the oil stains on the pavement.

Viv opened the door to slide back out of the seat but paused to look around. She opened the glove box but found only car papers. The backseat had one bunched up beach towel. The trunk was a mess—packed full of black garbage bags that gave her a moment of terror, but they were full of old clothes.

She didn't think Evelyn had anything to do with her missing daughter, but even Viv could tell the woman didn't enjoy being a mother. Viv had never met anyone less fit for the job. No doubt, her life would be a lot simpler without someone around who depended on her. Minus Claire, Evelyn would be free to drink and party all night without guilt. If she even felt remorse about that at all. What if she persuaded one of her bowling alley friends to steal Claire away, take her far out into the Atlantic, and leave her there?

Viv used her phone's flashlight to peer under the driver's seat where she found a red leather woman's wallet and a stray expired credit card, both Evelyn's. She picked them up and took them with her when she went back into the house.

Evelyn was asleep on the couch.

CHAPTER FORTY-FOUR

Two hours later, Benjy was back, and Viv wanted to hug him. He'd bought enough groceries to feed an army of teenagers. Everything from beef jerky to frozen lasagna to an actual coffee pot because he had noticed that Evelyn didn't have one. Maybe she wasn't a coffee drinker before now, but she would be, starting today. Viv appreciated the warm, rich smell, and even though she was on edge, she barely registered the sound of a car pulling up outside until footsteps sounded on the wooden porch steps.

"What are you people all doing here?" Claire asked.

Viv was a big fan of personal space and not touching people without obtaining their consent first, but she raced to the door and grabbed Claire in an enormous hug.

"Oh my goodness, you're safe. I can't believe it. I was so worried about you. Where have you been? Are you hurt at all?"

She said all of that without pausing for a breath. However, she couldn't help it. Her emotional floodgates had busted open and there was no holding back, including the tears of relief that leaked from her eyes. She sniffled as she held Claire at arm's length to give her a once-over.

"Wait, you were waiting for *me?*" Claire asked. "I didn't know if anyone would notice that I was gone!"

"Of course, we noticed," Viv said.

From the couch, Evelyn gave a small snore.

Well, some of us did.

Behind Claire, Viv's now-favorite two members of law enforcement came up the steps. "We found her walking along Freeman Avenue about ten minutes ago. Can't really take credit for rescuing her because it sounds like she rescued herself."

"Where's Freeman Avenue?" Viv asked the officers over Claire's head.

"It's only about ten minutes from here walking, but—"

"I was all the way downtown, down by the river. Someone shoved me into their trunk and locked me in a warehouse," Claire interrupted, sounding like she was running on pure adrenaline. "I was *legit* kidnapped. It was insane. I didn't know what to do at first, but then the person parked and just left me there, so I untied myself and got out of there."

"You're so smart," Viv said, pulling her in for another hug. "So resourceful. So brave."

Claire didn't even resist the embrace. Viv felt the girl's hand tentatively patting her back.

"It's all right. I'm okay." When Viv finally let her go, she looked around and asked, "Where's my phone? I really wished I'd had my phone with me. I need to tell Terrance about everything. What time is it? Whoa. It's almost morning! Oh, is my mom here?"

"I don't think I've ever heard you talk this much. Your mom is asleep on the couch, but I'll bet she'll be glad to know you are back, safe and sound," Viv said, hoping that Evelyn would remember that Claire had been missing when the girl went into the other room to rouse her.

"Is the girl's mother here?" Officer Brunswick asked. He stood in the kitchen in that cop stance, feet spread wide apart and hands tucked into the sides of his belt.

"Claire's mom is lying down," Viv explained to him, not wanting to disclose the fact that Evelyn, the girl's only parent and guardian, was currently drunk out of her mind. "You can tell me what you found and I'll pass along the message."

"We sent another unit over to investigate the warehouse where Claire said she was taken. It's a large storage unit rented out to Felicia Tofana, the real estate agent. We found her Lexus inside. Everything was just like Claire said it was. She's a smart girl. We found the pieces of duct tape the kidnapper used on her and a pillowcase they put over her head. We have a detective dusting the car for fingerprints to see if anyone other than Felicia might have driven the car."

Felicia's car? What does she have to do with any of this?

200

A sinking feeling weighed down Viv's stomach.

The second cop cleared his throat and stepped in closer with an eye to where Claire and her mother were. He spoke more softly so he wouldn't be overheard. "We don't know what's going on yet, but the body of the person discovered at the Fish restaurant is a tall, athletic woman with dark hair. It looks like it could be Felicia who got herself murdered."

PART V
ONE FISH, TWO FISH, DEAD FISH—GET A CLUE, FISH

"If the fish had not opened its big fat lying mouth, it would not have been caught."
—old proverb

CHAPTER FORTY-FIVE

Viv felt uneasy about leaving Claire unprotected in her mother's house after a night like that. The person who kidnapped her was still out there. However, the weathered little house was the girl's home and her mother was there. At least she had food to eat and it was daylight, after all.

"Lock the door and don't open it for anyone except the police, Terrance, and me," Viv cautioned her.

"Got it," Claire said with a huge yawn. The adrenaline that had been coursing through her before had no doubt worn off. It seemed likely that Claire would be safe and asleep in her bed for most of the day with any luck. She'd certainly earned it, freeing and saving herself like that. Viv was *so proud* of her and had told Claire so many times she was probably sick of hearing it.

As Viv walked down the front steps what felt like days since they had first arrived, Benjy offered to drive them back to the beach house. When she yawned so widely her jaw cracked, she handed him the keys without argument.

In Benjy's top-of-the-line car, the gentle warmth from the seat heaters seeped through Viv's back and legs. Instead of finding relaxation and comfort in it *like a normal person*, Viv's mind began to churn.

"How could Felicia be dead? We just saw her at our appointment!

Never mind that Claire said it was her car that had been used in her kidnapping and her warehouse where she had been taken!"

Benjy, bless his good nature, didn't protest Viv's outburst in the quiet of the morning with the hum of the luxury engine and the gentle rays of the morning sunrise brightening the seaside sky. He turned down the jazz that had been playing on the satellite radio station but said nothing. He waited for her to continue, clearly vying for some kind of sainthood. Or maybe he was just too tired from their all-nighter to make words travel from his brain to his mouth.

Viv held up a finger—she knew she sounded crazy, as if she were having a full-blown conversation with herself that had spilled out from her mind directly into the silence of the car without stopping for logic and reasoning. "Unless she was already dead by the time Claire was taken."

Viv went on, speculating, "Of all the people we've met so far, the two who seemed most capable of hurting others are Felicia Tofana and Chris Kahoe. Both of them are physically intimidating, strong, and aggressive in nature." Viv glanced at Benjy, who had his eyes on the road. "Correct me if I'm wrong, or feel free to add your opinion. Sometimes I'm not the best at peopling. I'm much more comfortable at my computer screen."

"You're fine," he said and then added, "Just do your thing. You were like this in school, too, you know."

"Like what?" she said, using one finger to rub at her poor scalp under the Olivia wig. She hadn't noticed it all night while she had been distracted with worry for Claire, but now she just wanted the darned thing off. In fact, she considered burning it when this whole South Pier escapade was over.

"Whenever we pulled an all-night study session, you always hit your stride right at dawn, like some kind of Gucci-clad maniac. While the rest of us were either crashing or guzzling down the coffee, you would hit a natural high and have some of your best ideas right about now."

"I have very little memory of that."

"That's because you'd stay up until the next night and then crash so hard, you'd sleep through the following day. So, we should really pay attention to your ideas this morning." He finally glanced away from the road at her. "Go ahead. See what you can come up with."

"First of all," she said, holding up a finger. "'Gucci-clad maniac?'"

Maybe it was more accurate than she wanted to hear, but it sounded like the old her. It seemed so shallow.

As Claire would say, "That's so cringe!!"

But the whole thing, the habit of adopting a persona or a facade to protect herself from the outside world, was a very familiar defense mechanism, a tried and true way for her to cope with what would be—and what had recently been—crippling anxiety.

Even with her silly costumes and wigs, she still felt like she was grafting on a branch or an extra limb, not all that different from Claire's chimera project with its lumpy but effective bits of clay and shells. She simply didn't have it in her DNA to—

"Hold on a minute!"

Benjy, who had been just about to proceed through an intersection, braked immediately and swiveling his head back and forth at the cross traffic. "What?!"

"I need my computer!"

Viv felt virtually naked without her laptop and a network connection. She needed her digital PIC line and she needed it *now*.

After ascertaining that they were not about to be creamed by a rogue semi-truck and proceeding through the intersection, Benjy said, "Ah, you had a brainstorm. Hang on, we're almost at the house. We'll have you back online in a flash."

However, she couldn't wait that long. She dug out her phone and began rapid-fire typing with both of her thumbs, just to get the letters of her web search in quicker.

"I knew it! Listen to this," she said. "According to this article in *Human Science* magazine from a couple years ago, which I knew I'd read before, there are several known instances of something called human chimerism—"

"What now?" Benjy asked, as he steered into the vacant parking spot at the beach house next to Viv's cute little hybrid car. "Humans that are like those chimera mythical creatures? Like a person with a snake tail and a lion's head?" He grimaced.

"No. Not like that literally, just *named* for the concept. It's a single person who has two separate and distinct sets of DNA in one body."

He wrinkled his nose as he tried to understand. "How is that possible? I thought DNA is unique, other than for identical twins—like, if Delroy Bennett has an identical twin out there committing crimes and framing him, making him take the blame. The evil twin scenario, right? Except poor Delroy passed away, so that's not going to work. There's no one left to take the fall."

"There are actually several types of twins, not just identical and fraternal. There's conjoined, where one or more parts of their bodies are physically attached. There's mirror-image twins, which are like mirror reflections of each other to some extent—sometimes a mirror twin can have their heart on the opposite side of the body than usual. Chimerism in one person could also mean they had a fraternal twin in utero that didn't survive, but the remaining twin somehow retained the second set of DNA."

Viv gathered up her things and slid out of the car. Benjy met her on the passenger side and took her heavy laptop shoulder bag from her. "Thank you—and you're right, identical twins share DNA. In fact, there was a case a while back in which a man in Detroit was accused of sexual assault, but they couldn't prosecute him because he had an identical twin. They were unable to definitively prove which twin had committed the crime, and therefore were stymied."

They climbed the stairs and entered the house. Viv went straight to her perch at the kitchen counter and plugged her computer and charger into the outlet.

"Sweet, sweet mother of science. Drink of thine nectar—of a strong Wi-Fi signal. Fiber network, I missed you so."

"You're so weird," he told her and went to the fridge. "Scrambled eggs?"

"Yes, please. Can we have toast, too? Ah, here's more about twins. Apparently, they *can* tell identical twin DNA apart now, thanks to mutation from factors like environmental influence and disease, like cancer."

"So if Delroy did have an evil crime-committing identical twin, he still wouldn't get away with it because of Delroy's horrible cancer. They'd be able to find that in the DNA?"

"Exactly," Viv said, clicking away on her keyboard, feeling her fourth or fifth adrenaline rush in the last twelve hours, which meant she was probably going to crash soon just as Benjy had foretold. "But again— chimeras aren't two people with the same DNA. It's one person with two people's DNA. It's like a cookie jar with two flavors of cookie. Or bacon and hash browns on one plate. Or coffee and milk in one mug."

He froze with a spatula in hand. "I think you're hungry."

"Starving, why do you ask? But the thing is, there are a different ways absorption can happen. One way for example," she paused and opened another website, "is a person might *ingest* their unborn fraternal twin in the womb before they're born—not actually eat them, but absorb the cells

—*shloop*! As the remaining twin develops and is born, they may retain both sets of DNA. The two sets would be related, just as siblings are, but different enough to tell them apart nonetheless."

"More twins and more eating," he said. The sizzle of butter in the pan on the stove momentarily distracted her—her stomach gave a hopeful howl—but then she was off and mentally running again.

"There are other causes of human chimerism, however, and they have to do with medical procedures, such as major organ transplants where one person donates an organ like a kidney to another person and the recipient, thanks to anti-rejection drugs and stuff like that, also receives the donor's DNA."

"Delroy didn't get a new kidney, did he?"

"No, but what he did get as part of his cancer treatment was a very expensive *bone marrow transplant.*"

"Back up a second. I'm confused," Benjy said, setting down a mountain of scrambled eggs and toast on the counter beside Viv's computer. She shoved away her laptop in favor of the plate. "How did Delroy's DNA end up here on the east coast on the vial of arsenic at a crime scene?"

"No, no. The transfer is the reverse of that—it goes the other way," she said with her mouth full. She realized it was rude, but she couldn't help it because she was ravenous. She swallowed her bite and explained, *"The murderer's DNA ended up in Delroy."*

"We're looking for a *kindly* murderer? A person who would be willing to donate their bone marrow to a cancer patient but still be furious enough to poison Kip, kidnap Claire, and now kill Felicia?" Benjy asked. He looked skeptical, as if he knew she needed a good twelve hours of sleep so she could put together a more reasonable theory.

Which was the truth, but she had really thought she might be on to something.

"Well, it sounds odd when you say it like that." She stopped eating and grew thoughtful. "I guess that doesn't make much sense. Now that the person has attacked three people, that might even classify them as a serial killer. Or, at least, a serial offender." Although, to be honest, she didn't know much about what defined a serial killer other than what she had seen on TV. "But this person appears to be more like a hitman than a person with psychological issues. There's no component of sexuality. I think this is about revenge, money, or both."

With her stomach full of delicious warm food, the exhaustion was beginning to hit hard and quickly. The heaviness in her eyelids blurred her vision. She pushed away from the table and her keyboard and stood up.

"I can't even think anymore. Everyone who seems like they could have done it has an alibi, like how your face ran into Chris Kahoe's fist while Claire was being kidnapped. Or, Felicia being dead as well. Do we not even bother with the DNA and Kip and just focus on Claire? Or maybe we start from the end and try to find out what happened to Felicia? Instead of investigating one crime, this turned into three."

She'd left the house closed up all night while they were away, and even though the curtains had been pulled shut, the full sun on the balcony had warmed up the inside. She felt like she was in a lovely cocoon despite having worked herself into some fairly circular arguments about who might have committed this sequence of terrible crimes.

"That's it," he said. "I recognize the signs. You're about to crash. You'd better get horizontal before it happens."

Benjy followed her up to the bedroom as she began removing the pieces of her costume-slash-armor. He picked up her orange Olivia wig off the stairs when she accidentally dropped it, trying to remove a shoe and move to the next step. By the time she reached the attached bathroom, she had a hand full of magnetic false eyelashes, oversized hoop earrings, and had already begun scraping the wig netting off her head.

In the bathroom, she used about a gallon of makeup remover and half a bag of cotton balls just to get at least the main layer of her Olivia warpaint off her face and pop the green contacts out of her eyes. She maneuvered her arms underneath her tunic top to modestly remove her bra for Benjy's sake without bothering to close the bathroom door. However, Benjy was already passed out on the bed. He still wore his blue jeans, which had to be uncomfortable, but at least he had kicked off his shoes before he had fallen fast asleep. She sank down heavily onto her pillow and was soon out as well.

CHAPTER FORTY-SIX

The trill of her phone's ringtone woke Viv up from a blank, dead, dreamless sleep at around one o'clock that afternoon. She ignored it and fell back asleep to a weird dream that was straight out of a Katy Perry video with beachballs and whipped cream, except also with Esther Williams and David Lee Roth for whatever reason. If her brain was a computer, the programs it was running seemed a bit buggy to her. It was nice Benjy thought she was able to work some kind of magic late at night while she was sleep-deprived, but she honestly didn't believe his theory had any truth to it.

Later her phone rang again, and she sat up, disoriented and slightly sweaty because the balcony doors had been shut tight the whole time they had been unconscious in slumber. Benjy was still asleep, but the hair around his face curled more than usual because he was too warm as well. She stared at him for a minute, rapt, because he looked like a gosh darned angel.

Of course, she knew he wasn't one. She'd seen him suffer the after-effects of drinking too much after a night out. She'd been right there with him for more than one of those times before they had learned to "adult" a little bit better. But just watching him sleep, seeing the gentle rise and fall of his chest as he breathed, made her feel like there were good things in the world.

On her way to retrieve her phone, which had stopped ringing and then began to ring again, Viv cracked open the doors to let in some of the cool Atlantic breeze. The curtains swayed as she padded down the stairs in bare feet, a sensation she had almost forgotten after spending months in onesies and slippers.

She found her phone still plugged into its charger in the kitchen.

"I have some late-breaking news for you," Sandy told Viv when she answered the call. "Are you sitting down? You're not going to believe this, but the one and only Mr. Christopher Kahoe has been taken in by the police for questioning, not only for the murder of Felicia, which I'm guessing you've heard about. It's all over the news today, but also for questioning in Kip Baldwin's case."

"What?" Viv couldn't stop the surprise from spilling out of her mouth. "They've got the wrong guy. There's no way he could have done it."

"What do you know that I don't know? You changed your mind about him! I thought you didn't like him. You said he gave you bad vibes. I thought you'd be glad hearing this news and happy that your gut instinct was right."

Viv debated with herself about how much she should tell Sandy. However, the woman had already met Benjy and openly declared herself a big fan—at least of his tush—she decided to go for broke and spill the beans about everything.

"I don't think Chris Kahoe could have kidnapped Claire and killed Felicia because Benjy saw him that same evening at the Kahoes' restaurant."

"Hon, are you sure it was Chris?" Sandy asked, and Viv could hear the shuffling of papers on the other end of the line. Maybe she was flipping through her white pages looking for people to call.

"It was definitely him. He pummeled Benjy's face after a slight fender-bender."

Sandy gave a sharp gasp. Viv wasn't sure if it was in horror that Benjy was no longer as pretty as when the reporter had first met him, or if her impression of Chris Kahoe as a stand-up, decent guy had been shaken. Personally, Viv didn't think Kahoe had that far to fall. Nevertheless, this line of argument still put Viv in the awkward position of having to defend the guy when it came to the latest murder.

How did I get to a point in my life when thinking the words "the latest murder" is normal? One day I was hunting lost fiber capsules and the next, a killer. The internet is absolutely a slippery slope to...more interneting.

Sandy said, "I'm heading over to the Kahoes' place in about an hour to see if I can get some more information about him being taken in and maybe to lend my support if that's the way it goes. Do you want to meet me there?"

First of all, I don't think that's how objective, unbiased journalism works. But second of all...

"Absolutely. I'll see you in the parking lot."

Viv hung up the call and jogged upstairs, suddenly energized. In the bedroom, she sat on the bed next to Benjy, who slept on his stomach, now in his t-shirt and boxers. When the mattress dipped down under her, he groaned but didn't open his eyes. She patted him gently on the back, feeling the warmth of his body through the soft cotton in a way that was more intimate than she was prepared for at the moment.

"Hey," she said. "Want to come with me to the Fishy restaurant? Sandy and I are going to see what the aftermath is like. Because—listen to this— they took Chris Kahoe in for questioning."

He grunted again but didn't move, his face still turned away and nestled in his pillow.

She patted him one more time. "I'm going to take a quick shower and put on my Olivia armor. It'll take me a bit to get ready. If you want to come along, I'm leaving in I'd guess about twenty minutes."

If he went back to sleep, she could hardly blame him, but she'd enjoyed feeling like they were a team, so she lingered just a minute longer before she gave up and went to start the water. Today's garb consisted of a royal purple with a bold white swirl patterned wrap dress that was a bit on the clingy side. Orange spandex leggings and a bright green head scarf over the Olivia wig would top off the outfit. Maybe a tad bright for a crime scene, but she didn't think anyone would be paying attention to her.

After she showered, got ready, and finished applying her makeup, she emerged from the bathroom to find an empty bed. She found him downstairs in the kitchen, chugging coffee. His face looked like he'd gone a couple rounds inside a washing machine...with a gorilla.

"I'm going to have to detox from caffeine when we get home," he said. She had a sudden pang of guilt because she was picturing him living with her in her apartment, standing in her kitchen drinking coffee from a jointly owned mug.

What am I doing?

Setting herself up for a fall, was what.

By the time they left here, she was going to be used to having him around. In fact, she already was. That realization didn't leave her with the best of feelings.

"You look pensive. You want me drive so you can keep brainstorming?" he offered.

She smiled. "Sure."

CHAPTER FORTY-SEVEN

In retrospect, going to the It Smells Fishy in Here restaurant was not a good idea. Neither was it an original thought either because half the town of South Pier had also showed up to lend their support to the Kahoe family. The other half had also shown up to scream at them on Felicia's behalf.

As Benjy rolled them to a stop on the street in front of the turn, they encountered a stream of cars in line for the parking lot, as well as people waving homemade signs and blasting airhorns. They shouted at passersby to "honk to free Chris." Viv clutched the arm rest as anxiety coursed through her, but there was no time to scramble for a lollipop now. This was a crowd scene with potential for violence, and it was best to stay as vigilant as she could.

On the opposite side of the street, people with "Justice for Felicia" signs had already begun to gather. Although Viv was a self-professed vigilante, she was one hundred percent sure that neither of these angry and extremely vocal options was how the American justice system worked.

A car traveling in the opposite direction slowed in the flow of traffic opposite their vehicle and the driver rolled down the window. Viv released her grip on the center console and pointed. "It's Sandy. What is she saying?"

When he rolled his window down, Sandy shouted at them. "It's a madhouse here. Meet you at the Time & Tidewater instead?"

Benjy gave her a thumbs up and eased back onto the gas pedal. They caught up to the traffic in their lane without angering the drivers behind them any more than they were to begin with. When Viv checked the mirror on the passenger side, she saw the occupants of the car that followed them honk, wave, and pull to the side of the road near the crowd of Kahoe supporters. She ducked down so she could watch them in the mirror as they began to fall out of sight, scared that violence was about to break out. Fortunately, the occupants of the car had joined into a crowd of Chris supporters and seemed to be like-minded. Mollified that they weren't leaving a riot behind them, she focused on the street ahead, still on edge. One air-bound beer can or rock was all it would take for a massive fight to erupt.

"Please let Claire and Terrance *not* be here," she said under her breath.

Benjy proceeded with caution down the street and turned into the parking lot of Kip's restaurant, in what felt to Viv like a return to the beginning—like coming full circle. Except this time everything seemed to be imploding for the Kahoe family.

Luckily and ironically, the public's negative opinion of the Time & Tidewater had carried over into today and the spaces were mostly empty. Sandy had parked far away from the door, close to the street, where presumably she still had a straight-line view at the action across the road at the Kahoes'.

"Can you believe this insanity?" she asked from her car after Viv slid out of theirs and approached Sandy's window.

Benjy had parked and now came around the front of their vehicle, his eyes on the growing and restless crowd across the street. He glanced at Viv, and Sandy gasped at the state of his face.

"Oh my goodness me. You poor thing! I can't hardly believe he did that to you."

"I think it makes me look kind of macho and hunky," he said with a half-smile, probably more because his lip was swollen than sarcasm.

"Honey, you didn't need any help in that department," she told him. "And I hope I'm not offending you—I swear I'm not harassing you. I'm just stating the objective truth like any journalist worth her salt."

Viv was ready to object on his behalf—to "throw hands" metaphorically—but Benjy said, "Thank you kindly. I'll take all the compliments I can get."

Across the street, someone started playing music from their car speakers. Viv expected country music or maybe some bubblegum pop. Instead, a classic rock song came on. Another person inflated a beach ball and they were tossing it up in the air. Don Henley and The Eagles started singing about a hotel in California, and Viv blinked.

Sandy got out of her car and walked away from them. She began to take some photos of the crowd.

"What's that look on your face?" Benjy asked in a low voice. "I recognize that expression. It means you just made a discovery, but what is it about?"

"It's the California connection. I was dreaming about Katy Perry, who released 'California Girls,' and David Lee Roth, who sang 'I Wish They All Could Be California Girls,' and now this." She gestured vaguely at music coming from across the street. "Delroy Bennett was from California, *but so were Arletta and Brad Malone*. I was trying to find Delroy's connection to North Carolina, but it goes the other way. She went to school in San Diego. They lived there, and I'll bet you a million dollars that Brad Malone, the good guy known for organizing blood drives, stepped up and donated his bone marrow to Delroy Bennett."

"Yeah, but why would he want to kill Kip or hurt anyone else? Why would he take Claire?"

"That's a good question, and I think all of our answers are right in there."

Then, she turned her back to the chaos across the road and stared at the Time & Tidewater.

CHAPTER FORTY-EIGHT

Another good reason existed, other than negative communal opinion, for why the parking lot at Kip's former restaurant was empty—its front doors were locked. A server in black pants and a white shirt had just finished trying the door and had begun to retreat to her car. Viv recognized the slender, dark-skinned girl from the night of the disastrous chicken sandwich, when she'd witnessed Chris shouting at Arletta.

"What's going on, Lindsay?" she asked.

"Oh, hey," the girl said with recognition dawning in her eyes. "Looks like I'm finally out of a job. I hope you weren't planning on eating lunch. To be real, I wouldn't eat over at It Smells Fishy in Here either. Looks like some scary mob mentality is about to happen. I'm getting myself back across the river as quick as my butt can go."

"Good advice," Viv agreed, although she probably wouldn't follow it herself.

Sandy came up behind them just as the server girl got in her car and, with a final wave, eased into the heavily crowded street. The reporter tried the front door to the Time & Tidewater, rattling it to discover on her own that it was locked. "What's going on here?"

"Looks like they might have finally given up and closed for good," Viv said.

"I'll go around and see if the side door is open," Benjy told them, and disappeared around the corner where the dumpsters sat.

Sandy leveled a look at Viv. "All right, girl, let me know your theory. You got something cooking in that head of yours."

"I think the person who killed Kip and Felicia is trying to frame Chris Kahoe—and I think the killer is Brad Malone, Arletta's husband. All the clues seem to point to him, but I just can't nail down *why* he did it."

Sandy brought her phone out of her pocket, but she didn't dial even though she was a self-professed fan of the Kahoe clan, and this would clear Chris. Instead, she crossed her arms and said, "Go on. Tell me your reasoning. If you can back up your story, I'll call my contact at the South Pier PD right now to come get Brad."

"Okay, hear me out," Viv said, and began to pace across the wooden planks of the restaurant's entryway. She nearly ran a hand through her hair before she remembered she still wore the Olivia wig and a head scarf. "Who wanted Kip dead? My first mistake was that I followed the money and tried to find a financial motive. I thought maybe Andrea wanted the restaurant all to herself. But what did she immediately do? She sped it along its course to failure, and herself to near bankruptcy. She tried paying off Kip's loan to the Kahoes, but she couldn't keep up with the payments." Viv dug in her shoulder bag and handed Sandy the crumpled up canceled check that Claire had found. "She had no reason to kill Kip."

She continued, "What about Evelyn? She might have wanted all of Kip's assets, including his townhouse. But she's not organized enough to poison him and plant evidence of it in an attempt to frame someone else. Never mind the fact that she was out drinking with her friends when Felicia's car was stolen and used to kidnap Claire, her own daughter. And is she even strong enough to overpower Felicia, beat her to death, and dump her body in the Kahoes' trash? I don't think that's possible, even with the help of her overweight bowling alley boyfriend."

"Oh my," Sandy said, but she gestured for Viv to continue.

"What about Chris Kahoe then, either acting by himself or on behalf of his parents? What motive did that family have for wanting Kip dead? He owed them money, and his death certainly wouldn't make extracting Kip's repayments from him any easier. Additionally, why would they poison him and then plant evidence of it *at their own restaurant*? Why would they take Claire? And again, why would they put Felicia's body at their *own* place? That makes less than zero sense. That's just dumb, and while Chris

has a temper and exhibits wildly inappropriate behavior toward women—
as Benjy witnessed—there's nothing to indicate he's particularly stupid.
Nor his family, who have continued to operate their restaurant without
any actual fishy business going on, despite their New Jersey connection
and my apparent biases and mental stereotypes about mobsters."

"Next, we have Felicia. Yes, she became a victim herself, but what if
she was responsible for at least the first one or two of these crimes? We
have her motive—she wanted the Windfall townhouse. In fact, she had
already been living there, as the kids and I found evidence of. Incidentally,
that gives her motive for kidnapping Claire. If she believed Claire was in
line to inherit either the townhouse or partial stake in his restaurant, she
might have been willing to take Claire out of the picture. There's also the
fact that Felicia's car was used to kidnap Claire and hold her in the warehouse where the girl might have died if she had not been able to escape,
thank goodness."

Viv paused in her pacing to sum up. "What if Felicia committed the
first two crimes and someone else killed her in the end?"

"Aha!" Sandy said, reminding her. "That's where the gloves and the
DNA come in. They didn't match Felicia."

"*Exactamente*! DNA doesn't lie, does it?"

Sandy frowned. "But it pointed to that Delroy Bennett man."

Viv held up a finger. "Who had a bone marrow transplant from
someone in California—and Arletta and Brad used to live there until just
recently. We need a new DNA test from Brad to confirm this because his
DNA is not on record, but I believe he is the source of the DNA on the
gloves."

Sandy frowned. "Who sent me the anonymous note about Delroy?"

"It would have to be someone who knew about the transplant. That
means, either Arletta or Brad. Brad might have sent it to throw everyone
off the scent by using Delroy as a scapegoat. But Arletta—"

A series of escalating shouts from the alley next to the restaurant
interrupted Viv.

CHAPTER FORTY-NINE

At the noise, Viv swiveled around to look, fear making her jumpy. She expected Benjy to come around the corner first, but in a worrisome turn of events, it was Brad with Arletta. To be more specific, it was Brad using a thick arm to clamp his wife to his chest. He had a hand on her throat, while the much smaller woman was pulled along, her feet barely able to reach the pavement. Behind Viv, Sandy had immediately assessed the situation, and began dialing for help on her phone.

"Where's Benjy? What did you do with my friend?!" Viv shouted, feeling the blood drain out of her head.

If anything had happened to him, I'll never forgive myself.

"He's back there," Brad said with a tip of his chin in the direction of the alley behind him. "Back where that idiot playboy Kip died. Couldn't keep his damn hands off my wife, and he got what he deserved."

Arletta wriggled in his grasp. "You're crazy, Brad," she choked. "Kip and I never had anything together."

He shook her by the neck. Behind the lenses of her thick glasses, her eyes looked panicked. She coughed and scraped at his hand with her fingers.

"You loved him!" he accused. At least, he loosened his hold on her slightly.

When she got her breath back, she said, "That wasn't his fault. He never reciprocated any of my feelings. Do you really think he would go for someone like me? I mean, look at me! I'm not his type. You didn't need to punish Kip!"

"He took advantage of your feelings. You can't deny that."

"Maybe he did, but it still wasn't his fault. You didn't have to hurt him —and what you did to his kid and the other woman. Why are you doing all of these horrible things? You killed two people, Brad, and you could have killed that child, too."

Sandy tilted the phone away from her ear and shouted at Viv, "They're already in the area! They're right across the street. Go find your man!" On cue, a police car's siren sounded close by.

That was all Viv needed to hear. Like a she'd been shot out of a cannon, she took off running, grateful she was in flat shoes, around the corner and down the alley. Benjy was slumped against the brick sidewall of the restaurant, not far from where Kip's body had been found. He looked dazed and his previously split lip bled again.

"Benjy? Are you okay?" She stroked his cheek.

His eyes moved behind their bruised lids and his forehead wrinkled in pain, she assumed. He groaned and brought a hand up to gingerly touch his jaw.

"He cold-cocked me. I think I still have all my teeth, but no caramel apples this Halloween."

"I can't believe Brad was the one who did this. He seemed so innocuous and he was such a community-minded volunteer, ready to help out a stranger. We all thought he had a generous soul. Outwardly, he seemed like a perfect husband—a mythical creature like a unicorn. Except when it came to his wife, I guess."

"It's always the quiet ones," Benjy said. He tried to scowl but ended up wincing instead.

She helped him into a standing position.

"Any dizziness?"

Cars squealed up to the front of the building.

"Not too much," he said, and allowed her to guide him slowly down the alley as he found his footing.

When they re-emerged around the front of the restaurant, she saw a police officer fold a handcuffed Brad into the back of a patrol car, doing that hand-on-top-of-skull thing so the big man wouldn't hit his head. When Brad was settled in his seat, he glowered at them all through the window. Then, he faced forward without another glance at his wife.

Sandy stood with a crouched-over Arletta, who was speaking with a female officer. When they saw the state Benjy was in, the policewoman unclipped the radio at her shoulder and called for a second ambulance.

"No, it's fine. I'm okay," he told them.

Even Arletta looked skeptical as she rubbed her own bruised throat. However, the first ambulance pulled up, EMTs emerged from the cab, and they led her to the back of the ambulance to evaluate her.

"I'm fine," Benjy insisted and began to walk toward his car, which was still at the far side of the lot at the street's edge. "I don't have a concussion. He stunned me for a second, nothing else. I really just want to go home. Let's get out of here."

On the other side of the road, the crowd had grown noisier. Now, their competing chants of "Free Chris" and "Justice for Felicia" sounded like a call and response at a sports match.

"This isn't good," Viv muttered, eyeing them. Her distrust of crowds and other people in general made the sweat drip down the center of her back, even with the cool autumn breeze coming in off the ocean. She picked up her pace, hurrying to catch up to Benjy who was nearly halfway to his car.

Sandy jogged along behind them and quickly caught up. "Arletta said that husband of hers has always been controlling. She didn't write me that anonymous message about Delroy and the DNA, so it must have been him, that arrogant, cocky son of a gun. He thought he could outsmart us and pin the crime on someone with no ties to this area."

"But *why*? Why did he go to all those lengths? Poor Felicia. And Claire, too. She could have been trapped in that car for days." Viv could hardly say the words.

Sandy stopped to look at Arletta, who was now seated on the gurney in the back of the ambulance. The EMTs had put a blood pressure cuff on her arm and had wrapped a blanket around her. They slammed the back of the doors shut and slowly maneuvered out of the lot and into the street.

"She told me when they moved out here, he cut her off from the rest of her family back in California. She hasn't talked to them in months. He was so paranoid and controlling, he thought Kip was trying to seduce her. After he eliminated Kip, he figured Felicia and Claire were the only ones who might be able to take part ownership of the restaurant, which he wanted to win for Arletta. As much as he abused her, he was—"

A strange *crack* cut off whatever Sandy had been about to say.

Viv couldn't follow what was happening it was all so fast.

What caused that sound?

The crack was like an unfathomably loud sharp tear of paper or the rip of cardboard. Maybe even thunder—it was frightening, loud, and she nearly shrieked even though she wasn't the type of person who screamed.

A blast of air hit her back, and they were all shoved off their feet by the unseen gust that sent the three of them sprawling on the pavement. Her palms and knees hit the ground hard, skin tearing open on the asphalt, and then her cheek landed on the white painted line of a parking space. Her eye was so close to the ground that her eyelashes brushed the parking lot's surface.

Viv's hearing became muffled, or maybe she just couldn't process the sounds for a minute. When her brain came back online, she heard distant screams and car alarms wailing. Glass and dirt showered the ground around them and *plinked* on the roof of Benjy's car, which was covered in dust—and soot.

Viv whipped her head around, catching a glimpse of Sandy who lay on the littered pavement a few feet from her. The woman's previously white blouse was grayish and a sleeve had a rip in it from which a large splinter of wood protruded. However, Sandy stirred. She began to push herself off the ground and slowly rise up, looking as stunned as Viv felt.

Behind them, the restaurant was nothing but smoke and burning ruins. Charred parts of the frame remained, as well as a sheered-off palm tree trunk and the front walkway. The entire side where the kitchen had been, as well as the brick wall where the alley had been—where Benjy had sat just a few minutes ago and where Kip had lived his last moments—was entirely gone.

The Time & Tidewater Grill was no more.

Viv sat in the rubble for who knew how long while she tried to wrap her big old computer-searching brain around what just happened.

Hands pulled her off the ground.

When she looked around for Benjy, she felt the sting of tens of tiny cuts on the back of her arms and neck, caused by flying debris. She didn't feel them as much when she found Benjy right behind her in better shape than Sandy and she were in.

She thought maybe he'd just reached his car when the restaurant exploded. In any case, he'd already gotten his fair share of bumps and bruises—he didn't need shards of glass and splinters as the cherry on top of his bad guy knuckle sundae. He had been the one to help her up, and she'd never been as glad to see him in her entire life.

When the second ambulance arrived, the three of them made use of its services. Sandy accepted a ride from it to the hospital to check out the nasty puncture wound she'd received from the flying piece of wood siding.

"Text me later," she told Viv, partly through hand gestures. "But don't call—I can't hear anything."

Viv gave her a thumbs up.

Benjy's car was filthy and dented but reasonably road-ready other than a broken back window. At least, it didn't have flat tires, no lights were broken, and it started up without a problem.

"I'm going to bleed on the upholstery," Viv said, chagrined, as she examined the tiny cuts on the backs of her arms. The EMTs had examined her skin for glass, removed the biggest pieces, and cleaned up the cuts they'd found. She'd refused offers of more care after that. She suspected she'd find a lot more as soon as she stepped under the water in the shower she so desperately wanted. Miraculously, her wig, although ruined beyond belief, was still in place, held on by her head scarf. She touched the back of her neck and came away with more blood.

"Not important," he said looking at her, not at the seat. Dust and soot had turned his hair gray. His face, too.

A good portion of the crowd that had gathered earlier across the street seemed to have had just enough self-preservation to flee in the face of disaster. Some foolhardy looky-loos remained, probably capturing video to post on their social media accounts, but the lessening of traffic made it easier for Benjy to navigate back onto the street.

Within twenty minutes, they were miles from the chaos. Just two soot-covered, bleeding, and slightly shell-shocked people traveling through everyday traffic.

CHAPTER FIFTY

A few days later, the aches and pains felt more like normal ones. Viv could tell her cuts and bruises were better because they irritated the heck out of her instead of actually incapacitating her in any way. The swelling on Benjy's face had gone down. He was almost back to normal other than his skin looking like a crayon box of colors, predominantly green and yellow around his eyes and on his jawline.

She crammed all of her Olivia outfits other than what she was wearing —minus the grimy wig, which she threw in the trash—back into her vintage suitcase. They hit the road in her little hybrid car since the broken window of his SUV was in a local shop being repaired. He said he'd either send for his car later or fly back down to drive it up. He shrugged while telling her he'd get it later, as if it didn't matter either way—typical Benjy.

"Do you want to visit Claire before we leave?" he'd asked her. The girl was temporarily staying at her friend Terrance's house until a relative could come stay with her.

Viv declined. She was much better at online relationships than at in-person interaction, especially when it came to goodbyes with her special mermaid of an adopted little sister. While he drove them toward the Virginia state line, she texted Claire that she was on her way home. Viv could practically hear the eye roll when the girl responded.

Claire: u told me that last night when we chatted for like the zillionth time

Viv: I just want to make sure you dont feel abandoned until your moms aunt arrives

Claire: im srsly fine

Viv: your mom promised she'd go to into a program

Claire: im helping her google rehabs

Viv: i just feel bad leaving u but ill be back soon

Claire, probably rolling her eyes again: i know and also ur friend Sandy already called me

Viv: perfect

Claire: like actually called me instead of texting smh old ppl

Viv: lol

Claire: really im fine

Viv: i know see u soon

In fact, Claire was going to be somewhat well off. From what Viv had found out during some late-night research, Claire would receive both the townhouse and the insurance payout from the restaurant when she turned eighteen, depending on any resulting legal fallout. A lawsuit was a big possibility, of course, but Claire wouldn't be on her own in that fight if it came to that.

Viv put down her phone feeling a little bit better. She glanced at Benjy as they followed the interstate signs toward Richmond and unwrapped a lollipop.

"Can I ask you a question?" When he cocked an eyebrow, she asked, "Why did you come down here on this wild goose chase with me?"

Wild geese? More like mythical beasts: unicorn onesies, mermaids, and chimeras. No need to go chasing after them. In truth, she was looking at the one true unicorn in the universe right now.

He laughed. "It's not complicated." Her heart sped up a little, but all he said was, "I didn't want you to be alone."

She half-expected him to drop the *that's what friends do* line and firmly place in her in the friend zone, but he didn't say anything after that, and she was too chicken to press further. Or actually, she wasn't quite ready to learn more, whether the truth be disappointing or...the other way.

After spending so much time in her apartment, she had only just ventured outside. If they had a future together, she wanted to make sure was prepared to live outside in the world with him.

"My turn to ask you a question," he said. "What's with the lollipops? I don't remember you being such a candy fiend before."

She brought the green apple flavored sucker out of her mouth with a *popping* sound. "I've been using them as a distraction and soothing technique when the Olivia outfit wasn't working for me. I probably need to consult a dentist when we get home."

There was that word again—*home*. She didn't like thinking about going back to her empty apartment and sitting in her onesie at her desk, going for days and days without seeing him.

"I'm sorry—I should have offered. Do you want one?" She held up an array of three more lollipops for him to choose from.

"Nah. No, thanks. I'm not really a fan," he said, and then smiled. "But it's kind of sexy the way you eat them."

CHAPTER FIFTY-ONE

A couple months later, Claire waited with Terrance outside the townhouse for his mom to pick him up. They sat together on the short retaining wall right outside the huge front door that made Claire feel extra safe every time she locked it at night.

As they waited there, she realized it was late and dark, but living at the townhouse was a trip. Every house, every street in this subdivision was well-lit and people walked around at night with their dogs, or just for exercise, like it was the middle of the day. These people lived in a bubble, and Claire was glad she'd been placed into it with them.

She and Viv still texted all the time—not every hour, but definitely every day. Claire kind of liked telling someone what she was doing and thinking. Viv told her ridiculous jokes and random trivia. *Like, how does one person even know all of that?*

Also, a man named Mr. Horowitz that Viv knew had called Claire. He seemed really chill. He promised he would teach her everything he knew about money, and she was really looking forward to getting started.

Even though Terrance's feet were pressed flat on the ground while they sat on the short wall, Claire could still swing her legs just a little.

"How come your mom won't let you just stay here overnight? We used to do that all the time in middle school, and tomorrow is Saturday," Claire asked him.

"Ever since she found out I have a crush on my best friend, I'm not allowed to stay over anymore."

It took Claire almost a full minute of frowning to work through the logic of his statement.

Duh.

Then, she smiled.

ACKNOWLEDGMENTS

Special thanks to John Hartness for chatting with me in a bar in Las Vegas, and to Rachel Carr for deflecting his attention by pointing at me.

ABOUT THE AUTHOR

EM Kaplan lives with her family in North Carolina near the beach. She spends too much time on the internet and communicates with friends mostly through memes.

ALSO BY EM KAPLAN

FRIENDS OF FALSTAFF

Thank You to All our Falstaff Books Patrons, who get extra digital content each month! To be featured here and see what other great rewards we offer, go to www.patreon.com/falstaffbooks.

PATRONS

Dino Hicks
John Hooks
John Kilgallon
Larissa Lichty
Travis & Casey Schilling
Staci-Leigh Santore
Sheryl R. Hayes
Scott Norris
Samuel Montgomery-Blinn
Junkle

Milton Keynes UK
Ingram Content Group UK Ltd.
UKHW010624080324
438959UK00001B/105